# of metal and wishes

ALSO BY SARAH FINE

Of Shadows and Obsession,
an e–short story prequel to *Of Metal and Wishes*

Of Dreams and Rust

# of metal and wishes

BY SARAH FINE

MARGARET K. MCELDERRY BOOKS
New York   London   Toronto   Sydney   New Delhi

MARGARET K. McELDERRY BOOKS

An imprint of Simon & Schuster Children's Publishing Division

1230 Avenue of the Americas, New York, New York 10020

MARGARET K. MCELDERRY BOOKS is a trademark of Simon & Schuster, Inc. For information about special discounts for bulk purchases, please contact Simon & Schuster Special Sales at 1-866-506-1949 or business@simonandschuster.com.

The Simon & Schuster Speakers Bureau can bring authors to your live event. For more information or to book an event, contact the Simon & Schuster Speakers Bureau at 1-866-248-3049 or visit our website at www.simonspeakers.com.

Also available in a Margaret K. McElderry Books hardcover edition

Book design by Debra Sfetsios-Conover

The text for this book is set in ITC Baskerville.

Manufactured in the United States of America

First Margaret K. McElderry Books paperback edition August 2015

10 9 8 7 6 5 4 3 2 1

The Library of Congress has cataloged the hardcover edition as follows:

Fine, Sarah.

Of metal and wishes / Sarah Fine. — First edition.

pages cm

Summary: In this loose retelling of The Phantom of the Opera, set in a reimagined industrial Asia, a ghost becomes obsessed with sixteen-year-old Wen, the daughter of a staff doctor in a slaughterhouse, who falls in love with one of the Noor, a despised group of men, racially different, hired as cheap factory labor.

ISBN 978-1-4424-8358-3 (hc)

ISBN 978-1-4424-8359-0 (pbk)

ISBN 978-1-4424-8360-6 (eBook)

[1. Love—Fiction. 2. Ghosts—Fiction 3. Social classes—Fiction. 4. Prejudices—Fiction. 5. Meat industry and trade—Fiction. 6. Asia—Fiction.] I. Title.

PZ7.F495678Of 2015

[Fic]—dc23

2014030266

For Asher, who would build.

of metal and wishes

Chapter One

IF I BELIEVED in the devil, I'd give him credit for the shift whistle at the Gochan One factory. Its shriek rips me from a dream of the wind whispering through flowering dogwood trees.

I fold my pillow over my ears, crush it down, and think of my mother singing me to sleep. She always used to, until her voice faded to a raspy croak and it hurt her to speak. Now there's no music in my life except in my memories, but that's okay, because I live there as much as I can.

The shrill of the whistle goes on and on, calling to the workers. It's as much a welcome as a warning; if any of them are still in their bunks, it's going to come out of their pay. But I don't have to worry about that. My father runs the factory's medical clinic, and it's always open. We live above it, and when people need the doctor, they ring a little bell outside the clinic door. When it's an emergency, they crash right in.

The awful sound ends as abruptly as it began, and I let the pillow fall away from my face. My father is standing a few feet from my sleeping pallet. He raises the window curtain and looks toward the front gate of the factory compound, then lifts his pocket watch to the light. It's a heavy old thing, too fancy to be clipped to his sagging trousers with patched knees, but my mother gave it to him when he graduated from medical school, and he's worn it every day since. He flips it shut with a soft click. "Five minutes earlier than yesterday. That's a rather dirty trick."

I pull my blanket over my head.

A month ago my life changed forever. Now, instead of living in a warm cottage with a lovely garden, I live on the factory compound. Instead of sitting in a kitchen and inhaling the earthy scent of stewing vegetables, I sit in a cafeteria and pick at starchy rice or thin soup shoveled from enormous vats. Instead of reading the classics, I read medical texts. Instead of the feather lightness of my mother's touch, I feel the dry, antiseptic rasp of my father's.

Instead of embroidering silk, I embroider skin.

I actually don't mind that part.

My father is looking down at me when I finally peek out from under the blanket. The lines of his round face are deeper in the shadows of almost dawn, and his brown eyes look as inky black as his hair. "You're going to have to get used to it, Wen."

"Don't remind me, please," I whisper.

He winces. "I'll make tea." He walks from the room.

I sit up and swing my feet to the floor. There's a chill in the air and I shiver. I pull my braid from the neck of my nightgown. It's a thick black rope, long enough to wrap around my throat in my sleep.

I get ready quickly, pulling on my forest green dress with the intricate embroidered vines coiling at the neckline and down the sleeves, which are thinning at the elbows. I need to patch them up before they become holey. I should go to the company store and buy myself some practical clothes, like the slacks and button-ups worn by the girls who work at the textile mill in Gochan Three. Here in Gochan One, the slaughterhouse, it's all men in overalls and rubber aprons. The only women in this factory are the secretaries and office girls, and they wear simple brown dresses, not ones that are embroidered and colorful like mine. I know I look pretentious and stupid and out of place, but my mother made this dress. She made all my clothes, actually. Her hands touched every stitch of this skirt, this bodice. She lined it with delicate pink buds and emerald leaves, gilded each of them with golden thread, made them too beautiful to be real. She pulled it tight at my waist and said I was getting a nice figure. She chose the color because it looked good on my toasted-almond skin. When I touch this dress, I touch her. When I wear this dress, she is with me.

I pull my thick apron on over it because I don't want to stain it with whatever's going to land on me today. Yesterday one of the slaughterhouse workers threw up in my lap.

My father and I eat a breakfast of bread and hard

cheese. We split the last apple from our small stash, the final gifts of the tree in our abandoned backyard behind the cottage on the Hill. We haven't been back since we locked the doors the day after my mother's funeral. It was her home, every inch of it, and it doesn't seem right to be there when she's not.

"The new workers are starting today," my father says.

"I heard people grumbling about it in the cafeteria yesterday. They wanted the extra hours during feasting season. Why didn't the bosses let them work more, if they wanted to?"

My father examines his apple. "It's been a hard year, and Underboss Mugo was looking for a new way to cut costs. The Noor are the cheapest labor available."

The Noor. They're not like us, the Itanyai. My mother taught me never to trust them. I've never seen one around here because most of them live in the Yilat Province, over the Western Hills, but Mother had warned me that if I ever did have the misfortune to encounter a Noor, I should run in the other direction. She said they were more like animals than men.

Now some of them are coming to work at Gochan One.

The apple is mealy and dry, and I choke it down. "Have you ever met one?"

"Not until last night." My father sips his tea.

"Isn't the company afraid they'll cause trouble?"

Father chuckles, but there's little humor in it. "I think the only thing they want to do is work and earn money to send to their families. When their train arrived, all they looked was . . . defeated."

And they'd had to stay on the train too, because they had lice. This morning they're being processed. My father is in charge of their decontamination and medical examinations. I don't get to assist because some of the processing involves their being naked, and he doesn't want me to see that.

I help him prep, counting the cartons of noxious delousing powder and germ-killing soap, making sure we have enough. The Noor are being issued company clothes, too, and their old ones are being burned. Father tells me all of this is coming out of their pay, even though they haven't started working yet.

A few workers come with handcarts to help Father with the supplies. As always, they give me funny, quizzical looks, like I'm some stray cat that wandered in off the streets of the Ring, the shops and neighborhoods that surround the three factory compounds of the Gochan complex. The Ring is almost a city, but not quite. It is as much a product of the Gochan industrial compounds as the meat of Gochan One, the war machines of Gochan Two, or the clothing of Gochan Three. It sprang up like a patch of clover around a pile of dung, fed by the money and jobs that trickle outward from the factories.

After my father leaves for his appointment with the lice-covered Noor, I focus on neatening already-neat things—lining up the gleaming plungers of the metal syringes, setting out clampers, and pulling the bowls and basins from our steam-powered cleaning machine. It makes a terrible racket but is much better than having to wash each of them by hand. Next I sweep the floor. I have to do this every day because there always seems to be metal shavings at the base of the walls, and some-times in little piles under chairs and tables. It must come through the vents from Gochan Two, which churns out monsters of steel to defend our country from enemies outside our borders . . . and within them. We probably all have metal shavings embedded in our lungs. If you cut us open, we'll sparkle in the light.

When I finish my chores, I go into my father's office. It's too far to walk to the school I've attended all my life, and too expensive anyway now that my mother's income is gone, so I am finishing my education here, under my father's instruction. He seems pleased that I have taken to his lessons. Today on his desk I find the cold, pink foreleg of a pig resting on a tray. Arranged beside it is a set of clampers, a curved stitching needle, some suturing thread, and a scalpel. Father left no note, but I know what he expects me to do.

I settle myself on his chair and catch my reflection in the scalpel's blade before I slice it along the leg, cutting to the bone, rending flesh from hoof to joint. Enough to keep me occupied with precise angles and tidy knots, to allow me to forget everything beyond the boundaries of the steel tray for a little while. Years of living up to my mother's rigid standards, of pulling and repeating delicate embroidery stitches until I got them just right, until my fingers blistered and then bled, are paying off now. Not really in the way I planned, but that's all right. I thread the suturing needle and grip it with the clampers. Eyeing the gash, I position the tip and poke it straight down into the flaccid tissue, then rotate my wrist, driving the point upward on the opposite edge of the wound. I will make these stitches perfect and do both my parents proud.

I am rewarding myself with a long stretch after completing the final knot when I notice the cloth pouch on the table next to the door. My father has forgotten his stethoscope. He needs it to listen to the Noor's lungs and make sure they are not bringing illness into our compound. And if I take it to him, I could perhaps catch a glimpse of a Noor. Despite my mother's warnings, or perhaps because of them, I cannot help but be curious about what these barbarian men look like.

I strip off my apron and hang the sign that says the clinic is closed for the lunch hour. The overhead lights buzz like bees as I tread the main hallway that leads to the cargo bays and pens in the southeast corner of the compound, where the factory connects to the rail line. This is how the cows arrive at Gochan to meet their fate, and it is how the Noor arrived too.

As I go through the heavy door that leads to the yard, a huge partitioned outdoor area with a corrugated metal overhang, I am greeted by the anxious lowing of cattle and the clatter of hooves. A train must have arrived, and the cows are being herded into the narrow, fenced lane that guides them to the killing floor. The air is thick with the stench of manure and urine-soaked hay, and I wrinkle my nose as I listen for my father's voice beyond the stained, rusted metal of the partitions.

A thickset young man in gray pants and a neatly pressed shirt strides out from an opening between the flimsy steel walls. He raises his head from his clipboard and pauses when he sees me. "You're not supposed to be here," he says, but not in a harsh way. He looks over his shoulder and frowns before turning back to me. Shuffling footsteps and mutterings I do not understand come from the makeshift chamber he just exited, as does the faintly astringent odor of delousing powder.

I hold up the pouch. "I need to give this stethoscope to my father."

"You're Dr. Guiren's daughter. Wen, right?" The young man smiles and stands a bit straighter, pushing out his chest. "I'm Lati. I'm in charge of making sure all the Noor are where they're supposed to be."

Lati looks only a few years older than I am, and the fact that he gets to wear slacks and carry a clipboard—instead of wearing a rubber apron and wielding a butcher's knife—means he is from a middle-class family like mine. He seems proud of himself, though it sounds like his job is to take roll and little more. Still, I return his smile, which feels stiff and unfamiliar after a month of stifled tears. "And where are they supposed to be?"

He tips his head toward the main hallway, allowing me to see the comb lines through his slightly oiled hair. "On their way to the cafeteria."

No sooner has he said it than two men trudge through the gap in the partitions. The smell of delousing powder makes my throat burn, and these men are covered in it, white patches and smears on their hands and faces, a dusting of it on their eyelashes. I squint at them with stinging eyes and know immediately that they are Noor. They're dressed like the rest of the workers, in brown overalls and white undershirts, but they don't look like *us*. They are bigger, for one. Not by much, but most of these men stand a few inches taller than the average Itanyai. Their skin is tanned, but there's a pinkish undertone that I've never seen in anyone around here. And their hair is so light, mostly muddy brown, not black and shiny like ours. Their eyes are also the color of street puddles, and they are red-rimmed and bloodshot and darting. I shrink back against the wall but continue to stare.

The Noor file out of the yard two by two and slowly walk toward the factory proper. Each of them has a paper tacked onto the shoulder of his shirt. Most of the papers are too high for me to read what's written there, but I see a few—Altan, Erdem, Savas, Zeki—and realize what they are, foreign names for strange, foreign men. Some of the yard workers accompany them, carrying electric prods, as if the Noor were cattle instead of factory employees. It hardly seems necessary, because what my father said this morning appears to be true. The Noor do not look rebellious or dangerous now; they look tired.

The ones at the front have deeply lined faces and hunched shoulders, but most of the Noor appear no older than twenty. Lati reaches my side as they begin to pass me. One, a boy with a mole on his cheek, sneezes loudly, then wipes his dripping nose on his work shirt, leaving a cloudy trail of mucus and delousing powder along his sleeve. Another, an impish-looking boy with sharp cheekbones and a scar that cuts through his left eyebrow, scratches his crotch. Then his muddy eyes find me, and he *winks*. I gasp, clutching my father's stethoscope to my chest, as if that will protect me.

"You must be very careful of them, Wen," says Lati, stepping in front of me to block their view. His gaze slides to the embroidery on my cuffs, and he follows a twisting vine of flowers until it entwines with others on my bodice. "It's likely they've never seen a girl who looks as fine as you do."

I bow my head, nearly as embarrassed by his overly familiar tone as I am about the rudeness of the Noor. I know he is trying to be kind, but it is too presumptuous, too intimate, and I have only just met him. "I'll be careful," I say, glancing at him and then at the horde of Noor. The line seems endless. "How many of them are there?"

"Just short of two hundred," he replies, checking his clipboard. "All from one village. They must breed like pigs. They look like them too." He says it loud, and when he sees my shocked expression, he laughs. "Don't worry—they can't understand us."

As he reassures me, two more Noor emerge from the yard, and I am completely distracted by them. Both are young—one looks Lati's age, maybe eighteen or nineteen, and the other can't be older than fourteen, which means he must have lied to get his work permit. Both boys are taller than the others, though the younger one looks like a weed, while the older one looks more like a birch, lean but solid. But what astounds me is that their hair is the color of the rust spots on the metal walls. I had no idea hair could actually be that color. They don't have much of it, though. Like the rest of the Noor, they look like sheared sheep. I wonder if they had to pay for these haircuts, or if the company gave them those for free.

"I have to escort these pigs to their troughs," says Lati, "but perhaps you should take the side hallway? So you don't have to be near them."

The older rust-head glances at me over Lati's

shoulder. He has eerie, jade-colored eyes, and before he turns away, I note a spark of cleverness and comprehension in their pale depths that makes my stomach tighten. Lati clears his throat, catching my attention again. "Give me the stethoscope," he says. "Your father is still examining the final few, and I'm sure he'll be happy to use something other than a tube of greased paper to listen to their lungs."

I hand him the pouch just as one of the passing Noor spits on the floor at my feet. I step back quickly as Lati grabs the Noor by the shoulder. "That's worthy of a fine," snaps Lati, checking the paper on the young man's shoulder, then conspicuously placing a check on one of the rows on his clipboard. He shoves the stunned-looking fellow, who bounces off one of his friends. The other Noor in line give us wary looks while the yard workers brandish their cattle prods. Suddenly feeling nauseated, I decide to follow Lati's instructions to take the side hallway. Before I reach the door, Lati calls out in a cheerful voice, "It was nice to meet you, Wen!"

I give him a tight smile and a small curtsy, then slip through the door and find myself in a dark corridor. My hand slides along the wall, seeking a light switch and finding none. For a moment I consider going back into the yard, but the memory of the rude Noor and of Lati's eager familiarity keep me where I am. A murky hallway cannot harm me, but being seen as too friendly certainly could. "I'm not afraid," I say, though I don't know why.

There's no one here to listen.

At least, I thought so. Somewhere, deep in the inky

darkness, there is a scuttling, clicking noise that makes my toes curl. Rats, maybe, though the sounds are a bit more rhythmic than rodents usually manage. "Hello?"

My voice is still echoing when the bulbs snap to life, first the ones above me, then the ones ahead, lighting my path. Though I should be relieved, my heart thumps like a rabbit in a snare. "Is someone here?" I call out.

The only answer is the low buzz of electricity, and again, perhaps I should find that soothing, but all I want to do is get out of this hallway. I hurry along, holding my skirt above my ankles so I don't trip myself up, jogging past little piles of metal shavings and closed doors leading to unknown rooms. As the administrative hallway comes into view ahead, one of the doors opens and out steps old Hazzi, who scrubs the floors and fixes the leaky toilets of Gochan One. His gnarled fingers curl over the handle of his mop, which is resting in a wheeled bucket he pushes along the floor. Blinking, he peers up at the lights, and then his eyes widen as he sees me coming.

"Thank you for turning them on," I say as I approach. Hazzi has been to see my father a few times for the pain in his joints, and though he cannot pay, my father does whatever he can to make the old man more comfortable—and able to keep his job here at the factory.

Hazzi shakes his head. "I didn't turn them on, Miss Wen." He smiles, showing a gap where his bottom front teeth used to be. "The Ghost must have thought you needed a little light."

I laugh. "I told you last week that I don't believe in ghosts." Which makes me different from nearly everyone else in this factory. They give up their hard-earned money and food to make offerings to the Ghost of Gochan One. They write their silly prayers and leave them at his altar at the front of the factory. They truly believe that he responds. I think he is nothing more than the bundling together of the useless wishes of people who must spend their days in a terrible place like this. "But it was a fine trick all the same, Hazzi." Fine enough to make my heart speed.

"No trick," he says with a raspy chuckle. "And you must be respectful of our Ghost. He is not all about the light. He brings darkness, too."

"That's certainly a useful myth to scare the workers into behaving." I nod at his cart and bucket. "Can I help you carry something to the front?"

"We can't splash wastewater on your fine dress," he says kindly as he rolls his bucket away from my skirts. "And it's not a myth, you know. A few years ago there was a young worker who proclaimed he was going to find out who takes the offerings from the Ghost's altar every night. His many prayers had not been answered, see, and he had decided the Ghost didn't exist. He was determined to prove it too. Right up until the day he disappeared. Atanyo was his name. I remember him well."

I arch an eyebrow. "Are you sure Atanyo didn't simply run away?"

Hazzi purses his lips. "Suppose he might've, though I'm not sure why he would, since he had a good enough life here and a family out in the Ring. If you ask me, he challenged the wrong specter and it devoured him. You shouldn't anger our Ghost, Miss Wen. He hears everything and can do anything. You should be grateful he favors you."

"Please, Hazzi. Forgive me, but I'm not superstitious." I try not to laugh again as I gesture at a set of light switches on the wall not two feet from his broom cupboard. "And I think you're playing with me."

The corner of his mouth twitches as he shuffles over to the switches and flips all of them down at once. The lights stay on. He flicks one switch up and down repeatedly, the sharp clicks echoing in the empty corridor. "These haven't worked for months, and this hallway has been dark that whole time." He grins at me. "Until you decided to walk this way."

Chapter Two

THE CEMENT FLOOR suddenly feels cold and hard beneath the soft soles of my woolen shoes. I thank Hazzi for his wisdom and leave him in the side hallway to wheel his rickety bucket to whatever place needs a good scrub. My skirt swishes with my steps as I enter the administrative corridor, hoping I've arrived in time to walk to the cafeteria with Vie, my best friend from school who came to work here a year ago. But when I reach the bookkeeping office, I see that she's already left for her lunch. I tiptoe past the office of the factory underboss, Mugo, whom my father warned me about as soon as I arrived at the factory compound. The whispered rumor is that Mugo has a thing for underage girls. Having just turned sixteen, I apparently fit the bill perfectly. I've kept a low profile since I've been here, but I can feel his eyes on me sometimes, prying and weaselly.

I enter the front section of the factory and pass the entrance to the killing floor. On the other side of the wall are hundreds of men, armed with their long knives, hacking away with merciless precision. The noise is deafening: the zing of the hooks, the wet slap and slash of blade against bone and muscle, the crash of metal on metal as the belts churn in their forever circles. Engines roar as the spinner machines rotate-twist-jerk-tear-dump the wheezing, lowing cattle onto the stained concrete. Their hooves clack and scrape, splashing their own blood on their dirty faces as they try to get up and run. This is how they spend the last few moments of their lives. If I turned my head, I could see it all through the tiny, round window set into the metal door.

I keep my eyes straight ahead and hold my breath until I get to the cafeteria. Even though I don't consider myself squeamish, I still can't understand how the men wolf down stew and soup and casserole after cutting out beef tongues and carving out hearts for hours on end.

The secretaries and office girls are already seated at their regular table in the far corner of the room, and among them I see Vie. The men are coming off the killing floor, through the antiseptic spray and the plastic sheeting. They strip off their rubber hoods, gloves, boots, and aprons and leave them lying in piles in the cavernous chamber that separates the killing floor from the cafeteria. They stride in, wearing matching imprints around their eyes from the goggles. And also matching tired, glazed expressions. It always takes a few minutes for that to wear off, for them to start talking and laughing again. But there's a strange intensity to them today, a layer of anger smeared over their usual fatigue as they notice that most of the tables are already occupied.

The Noor are here. All two hundred of them, by the looks of it. And I have to squeeze past them if I want to sit with my friends. The barbarian men lean forward as they eagerly shovel rice and beans into their mouths, moving their hands over their almost-bald heads, laughing and talking in their strange language. It's straight from the back of their throat, like something got caught there and they're trying to get it out. Now that no one's threatening them with cattle prods, their gestures are sharp and quick. Untrustworthy. I imagine them trying to pick my pockets, or worse, and press myself to the wall to edge by them.

A few of them turn their head to watch me, their darting eyes sparking with recognition, and suddenly the swishing of my skirt and petticoat sounds like an avalanche, a bulky crashing noise that I can't leave behind no matter how fast I move. As I pass the table closest to the wall, the impish Noor boy with the scar on his eyebrow says something to me, but I put my head down and ignore him. My heartbeat thuds against my temples. I wish I were invisible.

When the foot shoots out in front of me, I don't stand a chance. The toe of my shoe snags on his boot, and I fall forward like a sack of grain. As I push up to my hands and knees, I feel air on the back of my legs.

The impish boy has lifted my skirt.

My cheeks burning, I twist my hips in an effort to yank myself away, but he's got a thick handful of embroidered cotton in his grimy fist. If I pull any harder, my skirt will rip. If I don't, the Noor will have the chance to see parts of me no boy ever has. Somewhere in the cafeteria I hear an angry shout from one of the Itanyai workers, but it doesn't seem to register with this horrible imp with muddy hair and muddy eyes. He grins at me and makes a show of licking his lips as I try to scramble to my feet while preserving my modesty. Tears sting my eyes and all of them laugh.

Well, not all of them.

A wide, long-fingered hand cuffs my tormentor hard on the side of the head. The older rust-haired Noor is standing up and leaning over the table. He hisses at the impish skirt-lifter in that throaty language of theirs. The imp blanches at whatever he's said and drops my skirt like it's burned him.

I jump to my feet. In the moment before I turn away, the rust-haired boy turns his pale eyes to me. I should say "thank you," but I am so humiliated right now that I hate him as much as the rest of them. I whirl around and try to find my escape, and nearly burst into tears when Vie appears at my side, her round cheeks flushed with fury.

She makes a gesture of contempt at the Noor, sliding her hand over her shoulder in a way that tells them she thinks they're scum. She puts her arm around my waist and leads me to our table. Behind me I hear some of the Itanyai workers in strident argument, and I flick my gaze over to see the rust-haired boy speaking to them—*in our language.* Lati was wrong; perhaps most of the Noor don't understand us, but this one does. He's got his hands up and is making conciliatory movements, like he just wants everyone to calm down. Maybe to make a point, he smacks the imp on the back of the head, and the guy doesn't object as he stumbles forward with the force of the blow. I guess the rust-haired boy scared him a little. Against my will I feel a twinge of gratitude toward this strange-looking Noor.

I turn away as his head swivels around, like he knew I was looking at him. I put my back to all of them and sit down at the table with Vie. Jima, Underboss Mugo's personal secretary, sweeps her shining curtain of black hair over one shoulder and gives me a sympathetic look. She slides me her untouched tray of rice and beans. "So you don't have to walk past them again."

I bite my lip. My skin is hot with shame and I can't quite catch my breath. "Did they do that to all of you?"

Onya, who has been at Gochan for at least fifteen seasons, shakes her head. She is the oldest of us and tries to act like a mother. I don't mind. I know she wishes she had babies of her own, but her husband was badly injured in an accident on the killing floor a few years ago and died soon after. She gives me a pitying look. "Only you."

I look at them, and I look down at myself, and I know why. All of the other women are wearing simple brown dresses with straight skirts and plain sleeves. I look like a peacock in this embroidered dress of mine. I bury my face in my hands.

Vie rubs my shoulders, her plump fingers sliding over flowers and vines lovingly stitched onto the fabric. "Ignore the Noor. They're good for nothing. They'll be gone at the end of the feasting season, and good riddance."

"I wish they'd never come here at all. They don't belong here," I say in a choked voice. The men are still arguing with the Noor a few tables away, and I think I hear Lati's voice, though I am too ashamed to turn my head and look. I hope he fines them harshly. I hope he teaches those barbarians a lesson.

Jima pats my arm. "Until feasting season is over, Gochan One will run twenty-four hours a day nearly every day, and Underboss Mugo is under pressure to increase profits. He's been very . . . stressed."

I peek through my fingers to see her somber brown eyes, too widely set in what is otherwise a pretty face. She looks a bit like a hunted animal.

"*I'll* tell you why the Noor are here," says Onya, clucking her tongue. "Look how hollow their cheeks are. They're too incompetent to feed themselves, so they've come here looking for handouts. I suppose it's better than an all-out rebellion."

"I think rebellion *would* be better," says Vie, leaning forward. "Iyzu's father commanded one of the units that put them down the last time they tried to carve out a piece of Yilat for themselves. Iyzu told me that the Noor are so primitive that it wasn't much of a fight once our war machines arrived. Maybe they could be driven from the country for good this time."

Onya rolls her eyes. "You're a silly girl, Vie, and Iyzu is exaggerating to impress you. Good men died trying to keep the Noor from cracking the Yilat Province like an egg. No, much better to keep them in their place so they don't try to fight at all."

Vie gives Onya a pinched, petulant look. "If they know their place so well, why did one of them just expose Wen's delicates to the entire cafeteria?"

My stomach turns, and I push Jima's tray away. "I'm going to go back to the clinic," I mumble as tears burn my eyes.

Jima slides her arm through mine. "I'll go with you," she says.

I keep my head down as she leads me out of the cafeteria, and grip her hand tightly as we pass by the Noor. I mark each step, waiting for one of them to bar my way, but they are quiet and still until we reach the exit. It does nothing to cool my anger toward them, though. It's sitting in my chest like a burning coal, fueled by hot humiliation. In this moment I share Vie's desire to see them crushed and broken. No matter that the rust-haired one intervened to stop his imp friend from ruining my reputation—it was probably to save his own skin, not to help me.

When I turn to enter the administrative hall, Jima tugs me in the opposite direction. "Come," she says. "I promise you won't regret it."

I groan as she pulls me into the alcove where the Ghost's altar is set up. I've never ventured back here before, but I've seen many a worker and office girl duck in, carrying their gifts for the Ghost. Someone has lovingly carved a low table out of elm, and the wood alone must have cost a week's wages. Atop it sits a row of tallow candles, thirteen in all. Their tiny flames flicker and weigh down the air with a faint, greasy haze. Around the candles are prayers, scratched carefully onto scraps of paper or fabric, and on top of each prayer is an offering. A bronze coin from the Ring, a few plum cakes, a braided-thread bracelet.

Jima pulls an ink stick from her pocket, along with a piece of paper. "I was going to ask him for something. I could write your wish below mine—if you have an offering?"

"Jima, I appreciate this, but I don't believe in the Ghost. Or any ghosts, for that matter." If they were real, surely I'd feel my mother's presence. She wouldn't have abandoned me completely.

Jima's eyes shine with hope. "This one is real. Minny told me he cured her son of sickness after she left a prayer—"

"My father treated her little boy, and that's why he got better."

"Not everyone your father treats gets better, Wen."

My throat tightens as I remember how hard my father worked to cure my mother. "I know that. But still—"

"That's not the only thing the Ghost has done!" Jima says, clutching her ink stick. "He can bring feast or famine, frost or rain. He's powerful! He could avenge you. He could make the Noor pay."

"Lati can do that too."

She shakes her head. "Lati might fine them, but the Ghost can do more than that."

I put my hands on my hips. "Has anyone ever seen this terrifying apparition for themselves?"

"No one's lived to tell about it."

"Hazzi told me about that worker who disappeared— Atanyo. He could have run away, or someone else might have killed him. Seems like a good way to cover up a murder, if you ask me."

"I hadn't heard about that one, but I've heard of

others. Onya told me that the last few men who ventured down into the basement levels never returned. It's why no one goes down there anymore." She says it with such reverence, as if these rumors are proven fact. "But the Ghost protects the faithful. I know he does."

She scribbles something on her paper, cupping her hand around it so I don't see what she's writing. I glance over the wishes people have left on the altar today. Some of them are for good fortune and health. Some of them are very specific, like for the slurry machine on the killing floor to stop shorting out midshift. The Ghost is going to be very busy if he intends to reward all these true believers. I shove my fists into my pockets, willing myself to keep quiet. Something warm and metal brushes against my knuckles, and my fingers close around it. A tin factory coin, square with a hole in the middle, the currency of Gochan.

Jima finishes writing and looks up at me, her delicate face full of expectation. "He'll listen," she says. "He'll help. Tell him what you want."

I don't know what I'm supposed to say. I'm not religious. I've never been to the temple. I'm not used to asking anyone but my parents for what I need. And I know the Ghost isn't real. But as I think of that impish, muddy-haired boy, the way he licked his lips as he looked at my bare legs, the way he laughed at my shame, something inside me breaks.

I pull the coin from my pocket and toss it onto the table. People pray to the Ghost just to make themselves feel better about having to be here, but I shouldn't be here at all. I should be on the Hill, living with my mother, far from the stink of blood and cow, far from the imp boy and all the Noor. If I were there, if my mother were alive, I wouldn't have any reason to pray to a nonexistent ghost. But Gochan One is my home now, so: "Ghost, show me what you can do. Prove yourself to me. I want to be impressed."

Jima sits back on her knees and stares at my little coin lying among the lovingly placed offerings. "Be careful, Wen."

I scoff, too angry to do anything else. "Careful of whom, exactly?" I gesture at the bolt of purple cloth, the bottle of rice wine, the package of salted fish, the carved letter opener—all offerings left in exchange for wishes. "Who is this Ghost, that people think he is worthy of their best things?"

Jima folds her prayer. "He was once a worker here."

"Did you know him?"

She shakes her head. "I've only been here for two years. But Onya said he died on the factory floor. It was an ugly death."

"Any death on the killing floor is bound to be ugly, Jima, and my father told me there are at least three of them each year. Why would this one worker have the power to become a ghost?"

"I couldn't say," says Jima, "but he cares for us and has granted many wishes. He does not deserve your contempt." Jima touches her prayer and then sets her own offering—yet another molded tallow candle—between a small jar of curing salt and a thick roll of fine wire that was probably stolen from a maintenance closet. "He might even punish it."

"We'll see." And maybe I would deserve it. From the look on Jima's face, her wish means a lot to her, and she has been nothing but kind to me. It's not her fault that I can't bring myself to believe. "Thank you for trying to help," I offer, touching her sleeve. "I hope your prayer is answered."

She wraps her arm over her middle. "Me too," she whispers.

Chapter Three

"THANK YOU FOR bringing me my stethoscope," my father says when I enter the clinic. He finishes off a crust of bread and dusts the crumbs from his lap. "Lati said the Noor were rude to you when you came to drop it off. He was afraid you'd be distressed."

I will not tell him what happened in the cafeteria. My father seems like a fragile twig these days. Losing my mother almost snapped him in two. So I say, "Lati doesn't need to be concerned about me."

He gives me a gentle smile as he gets up from his chair to wash his hands. "The Noor endured a difficult and uncomfortable journey, and the decontamination process was unpleasant. I think they can be forgiven for not displaying their best manners. I knew you would understand."

I'm not so sure, but I will not argue with my father. "Do you have any appointments this afternoon?"

"Only Hazzi. He's having trouble with his hands again."

I think back to what my father has told me about how he treats arthritis. "Will you use ginger oil? Or maybe mustard leaves?"

"We're out of mustard leaves, so today it will be the ginger. I'm going to massage it into his fingers." He sighs. "It won't last long, though."

"Why does he continue to work here if he struggles so much?"

My father turns away from me to gaze at his shelf of medical texts. "If he could stop, he would," he says quietly. "Wen, you know that people who cannot work are not allowed to stay."

"Yes, but Hazzi has been here for many years—"

"Which has only given him more time to build up a debt to the company." He strokes his finger down the spine of a book. "It's easier than you might think. And once that happens . . ." His shoulders sag as he trails off.

I stare at his back, trying to translate the words he's not saying, but before I can, he draws himself up and looks over his shoulder. "You did an excellent job with your stitching this morning."

I bow my head to hide my proud smile. "I know some of the knots were not perfect."

Father chuckles. "Soon I'll have you doing all my suturing. I know she'd have preferred silk over pig's legs, but still, I believe your mother would be proud."

I look down at the delicate embroidery on my gown, a thousand stitches, all exquisite. This was made to suit the future Mother planned for me, a life of relative ease, dwelling in beauty and creating it. This is not the dress of a factory girl, and certainly not of a doctor's assistant, which is apparently my future now. And I need to accept that. Besides, my dresses are why I stand out like a cardinal among sparrows—the reason the Noor noticed me in the first place, the reason Lati looked at me the way he did.

"Can I buy a work dress?" I blurt out.

Father looks me up and down like he's noticing me for the first time. "I suppose your mother made your clothes a bit fancy for a factory life, even a sheltered one."

I smooth my hand over my skirt, running my fingers over a swirl of vine and thorn. "She didn't know I would end up here, obviously."

He blinks. "Obviously. And yes, I think we can manage it. Just one, though, all right?"

I nod eagerly, then slip on my heavy apron and help my father with afternoon tasks. I chop and stew a pot of ginger, create a paste of dried peppers and oil, and make sure all my father's instruments are clean and ready. Hazzi comes in midafternoon with his fingers curled against his chest. As my father helps him onto the examination table, the old man says, "So, Guiren, I believe the Ghost favors our Wen."

I expect my father to laugh, because he is a man of science who does not believe in things that cannot be proven. Instead his voice is sharper than usual as he asks, "Why do you say that?"

As Hazzi tells the story of what happened this morning with the lights, my father listens in silence. I don't understand it at all, but when Hazzi is finished, my father remains quiet for a few moments and then speaks slowly, as if he is choosing every word: "That is a very interesting story. Perhaps I will speak to someone about fixing the wiring in that hallway." His eyes meet mine. "Wen, why don't you go buy your dress now? The company store closes soon."

I remove my apron and excuse myself. Though I long to ask more questions, it would be disrespectful to stay now that I've been dismissed. I walk to the front of the factory, my soft shoes crunching over a few paper-thin metal shavings along the hallway. Before I exit the administrative hall, the awful shift whistle blows. I tense when I hear the scuff of boots and the throaty sound of the Noor language. They must be starting their shift, which runs late into the night. I edge along the wall and peek around the corner. Sure enough, in they shuffle, rubbing their eyes as if they've just awakened. The rust-haired Noor boy is at the front of the procession. He has dark circles under his eyes like the rest, but his shoulders are straight and his movements are anything but lethargic as he steps out of line and begins barking instructions to the others. As the Noor boys and men pass him, he shakes each one by the arm and slaps them on the back, as if he is trying to jolt them into alertness. A few Itanyai workers stride by, and one of them—whom I recognize as Iyzu, a friend of Lati's and the boy Vie has her eye on—slides his hand over his shoulder in contempt. Rust-Hair locks eyes with him and then turns away as if Iyzu's opinion of him doesn't matter at all. This Noor does not know his place, and when I see

Iyzu's sneering expression, I know that will make life at the factory harder for the rust-haired boy.

I am glad the Ghost doesn't exist. Maybe the Noor have enough enemies.

I stay out of sight until Rust-Hair joins his Noor friends on the killing floor and the metal door shuts behind him, then I walk to the squat building off the central square of the compound. The store makes it unnecessary to leave Gochan One, because technically everything we need is here. Out in the Ring, of course, are the things not allowed inside the factory gates. Like alcohol and cigarettes. There are also a bunch of hair salons that turn on a pink light at night, signaling they're open for another kind of business. The factory gates close promptly at midnight, though, right after the middle shift ends. All the workers live on the compound, and it's easy to get locked out. The gates don't open until thirty minutes after the day shift starts, and getting stuck outside is another way to lose pay.

At the company store they have no use for bronze coins from the Ring; it's either company coin or credit— which comes straight out of your pay, for your *convenience*. I show my father's work pass and my own identification papers, and the steel-and-silver-haired matron at the register waves me toward the garment section.

The clothes are made by the girls in Gochan Three. They make other things, of course, things that ship all over the country, and to wealthier countries that find it cheaper to buy from us than pay their own people to do the job. Here, One supplies Three with meat, and Three supplies One with brown things. The color of the puddles in the road after a rainstorm. The color of dead leaves. I wander around the store for a good long while, avoiding the inevitable, but then I try on a basic work dress, the same as Vie's and Onya's and Jima's, the same as every secretary and office girl who works here. It doesn't feel right at all. The size that fits in the chest is loose on my waist, and the size that fits my waist prevents me from drawing sufficient air into my lungs. I go for the size that permits me to breathe and almost cry as I stare at my new getup. No longer a peacock, I am a mud hen. No longer my mother's child.

"Get over yourself, Wen," I whisper to my reflection, swiping hot tears from my eyes. I fold my forest green dress and shove it into a paper sack, then sign the promissory note that makes me the owner of this ugly brown dress that would have made my mother gag.

My old dress feels like it weighs a thousand pounds as I carry it back to my home above the clinic. I don't spot the blood on the floor until after I've passed the administrative offices, but then I wonder how I missed it. I raise my head and see the clinic door is hanging open.

There's been an accident.

My heart picks up its pace, as do my feet. I glance down to see the droplets, then a bloody boot print, then a long smear leading straight through the clinic's entrance. I lift my skirt and jog, watching my steps so I don't slip in the blood. I haven't dealt with anything more than a deep cut or a throaty cough, and this looks worse than that. I'm glad this didn't happen this morning when I was here alone. But now my father is here and I can help him. I like to be useful, because it's in those moments of complete concentration that I feel best, most protected from the noise and strife and grief that has invaded my world.

A long, low moan is followed by a higher-pitched gasp, desperate enough for me to hear it echo down the hall. I swallow back dread and plow forward, tossing my sack into the corner as I come through the doorway.

And stop dead. The impish Noor boy is on my father's exam table, sweat dripping from his forehead as he stares down in horror at his foot. I can't tell how bad it is because my father is hunched over him, blocking my view. The imp's right boot is lying on its side in front of the table. Right next to it is another set of boots, and those happen to belong to the rust-haired boy, who is standing by his friend's head. His gaze darts over to me, and his already strained expression tightens.

The imp cries out, and Rust-Hair offers him his hand. Imp clutches it, his tanned knuckles turning white. It must be hurting the rust-haired boy, but he only whispers softly to his friend in their throat-catching language.

"I need to put him to sleep, Melik," my father says to Rust-Hair. "So I can set the bones and repair the lacerations."

Melik nods. "I'll tell him." He leans over and speaks to the imp, gently stroking the other boy's barely-there hair. The imp's eyes go wide as Melik translates. He shakes his head frantically, sending drops of sweat onto the cloth that covers the table.

I take a step to the side, unsure of whether to run upstairs or offer to help. My father must hear my tread, because he looks over his shoulder and makes my decision for me. "Ah. Wen. Perfect timing. Get a soporific sponge ready for me, will you?"

Melik's eyes are back on me. His gaze travels down my body to the sack on the floor, where the sleeve of my green dress has unfurled. With my head bowed, I tie on my apron and go to the basin to cleanse my hands. I scrub at my fingernails with a bristle brush and lather the antiseptic soap between my fingers, all the way up to my forearms. Then I dry my hands on a clean cloth and begin assembling supplies.

I try to ignore the metallic taste on the back of my tongue as I prepare the soporific sponge. I challenged the Ghost to prove himself to me, and now this boy is lying on my father's table. His blood is dripping between his broken toes and from the top of his foot, where two shards of bone have pierced his flesh and made it look like meat. He is shaking. His tan skin has paled to a sickly green. When he turns his head and sees me, his eyebrows come together and shoot upward. He recognizes me. And he looks terrified. Does he suspect what I've done? He couldn't possibly know about the Ghost, could he?

He squeezes his eyes shut as every muscle in his body tenses. My father is probing at his foot, wiping the exposed bones and torn flesh with purplish antiseptic. I swallow hard and step forward with my tray, which holds the sponge soaked in a solution of opium, mandrake, and henbane. The imp flinches as I come near.

"His name is Tercan," Melik says to me, watching my face.

I duck my head and focus on Tercan. When I open my mouth, I speak hesitantly. "Tercan." His name falls from my tongue all twisted and ruined, but the imp boy, despite his agony, actually tries to give me an encouraging smile. It's merely a twitch of his pale lips, but it makes me want to get his name exactly right. What he did to me earlier seems insignificant in this moment.

"Tercan, this won't hurt you. I won't hurt you," I promise him, but as I look at the wound, I know his time at Gochan is over before it has started. He can't work with a mangled foot like that. He may not even be able to walk again, which means possible starvation, both for him and for whomever he was planning to send money back to. He'll be turned out into the Ring, far from his home in the west, and who knows if he'll make it back there?

Did I cause this? No. No, I couldn't have. There is no Ghost, and this was an accident.

With steady fingers I grasp the sponge between the metal teeth of the clamper and lift it to eye level. As I explain the ingredients, and how it will put Tercan to sleep while we fix his foot, Melik translates smoothly . . . until he hears the word "fix."

"You cannot fix this," he says in a low voice, making one of those quick, sharp gestures at Tercan's foot. He leans over his friend, and it is all I can do not to step back. His eyes are so round, so pale, the jade irises striped with flecks of amber and blue. His mouth curls up at one corner and he adds, "Unless you have some magic we don't know about."

"I . . . I don't—," I stammer.

"She means we can put his foot back together and stitch it up," my father says, raising his head from his work to look at Melik, unflustered by this Noor boy who doesn't seem to know his place. "You are correct that he will never be the same."

My father's assessment is so blunt that Melik flinches like he's been slapped. I wonder how the words translate into his Noor language. I'm not sure, but I notice he doesn't translate what my father said for Tercan, whose head has sunk back onto the table. I turn my attention back to him, the reason all of us are hunched beneath my father's brightest lamp. My hand trembles only a little as I gently touch his arm. "Let us help you," I whisper.

His eyes lock on to mine, and they are full of hapless innocence, of pleading animal fear. He stares at my face, searching for some sign of malice, maybe, for any hint that I might want to harm him.

I do not look away. *I can forgive you for today,* I think.

He blinks a few times and nods. "Sleep," he says raggedly. "Yes."

I lower the sponge over his face, and he inhales while he looks hopefully up at me. It doesn't take long for his eyelids to flutter and for his breaths to stretch long and deep. The muscles of his arms and stomach relax. His face loses its strain, its worry.

"You should probably return to the floor," my father says to Melik. "You can pick him up when your shift is over."

I look up at Melik, who is watching Tercan's chest rise and fall. He left his shift to bring his friend here, and every minute he's away shaves a few coins off his daily wage. He needs to get back to work, and he knows it. He squeezes Tercan's hand and releases it. He squares his shoulders. "Please send someone if he wakes, or if something happens."

"We will," I say to him. I'm being rude; I should shut up and let my father do the talking. But Melik's mask of calm confidence has slipped as he looks at Tercan's foot again. He blinks away the shine of tears. "If he needs you, I'll come fetch you myself."

He rewards me with the faintest shadow of a smile. "Thank you . . . Wen."

With one last glance at his friend, Melik is out the door, and I can hear the clomp of his boots as he sprints up the hall. He's right to hurry; Mugo does not look kindly on workers who abandon their stations even for a minute, and Melik has been gone for at least half an hour.

As much as I mistrust the Noor and wish they'd never come to Gochan, I find myself hoping Melik does not get fired for this offense, this crime of helping his friend.

"He speaks our language very well," comments my father. "Only a few of them do. He's had some education."

I assist my father to reassemble Tercan's foot, knitting the boy's skin back together with tiny, perfect stitches my mother would have been proud of. All the while I wonder about the rust-haired boy. Why did he come here if he's educated? Working in a slaughterhouse, of all places?

Then I remember he is Noor and there aren't many paths open to him.

Tercan's crushed foot takes three hours to put back together. We drench it once again with antiseptic, splint it, and wrap it in a clean bandage. I hope we have done enough, and that he'll be able to keep his foot.

When we're finished, I scrub my hands, which are

aching and raw. My father says we'll let Tercan sleep off the opium and then give him a bit more by mouth to take the edge off as he wakes.

While my father tidies up, I climb the stairs to my room and pull a small white seashell from beneath my sleeping pallet. I turn it over in my hands. I need an offering and I hope this does the trick.

I tell my father I'm going to go to the cafeteria because I've missed my dinner. Minny, the cafeteria worker whose young son my father healed of a nasty infection a few weeks ago—using his own money to pay for the medicine—will surely give me some bread or rice to tide me over until morning. My father agrees readily, saying he thinks I'm getting too thin.

Nobody's thinner than he is, but I guess I should be happy that he's worried about me. I march up the hall. I'm not really coming down here to eat, though. After everything that's happened tonight, I wonder if I'll ever be hungry again. It's not that Tercan's wound was so terrible. I mean, it was, but I can handle that. What I can't handle: the nagging fear that I had something to do with it. Perhaps Hazzi's trick with the lights has gotten to me. Or maybe it was my father's unexpectedly serious expression as the old man told him the Ghost favored me. It could be the whispered stories, the fervent prayers, the hope in Jima's eyes as she scribbled her wish. I don't know, but I can't shed this feeling, this guilt, and I know only one thing that will help.

The administrative hall is dark. The workers may be toiling full steam ahead on the killing floor, but the bookkeepers, secretaries, and administrators are all safe in their beds, or maybe out in the Ring seeking other kinds of entertainment. My footsteps make hardly any noise as I sweep past the entrance to the killing floor and head straight for the altar. I can already see the candles glowing in the gloom up ahead.

I will talk to the Ghost of Gochan. With all my heart, I hope he doesn't answer.

Chapter Four

I KNEEL NEXT to the altar. The tallow candles are burning low. One has gone out, and I lift Jima's offering candle and tilt it to light the wick, then set it in the small pot that holds the old, spent candle. Now there are thirteen again.

It takes me only a moment to realize that the rest of the offerings are gone. The cakes, the bracelet, my coin. The prayers, too.

I pull one of my most treasured possessions from my pocket. I plucked this seashell off the white sand at the edge of the southern sea. My parents took me there for a vacation when I was a little girl, before the markets crashed and wiped out my mother's inheritance, before she had to go to work as a tailor and seamstress for women she'd gone to school with, before my father lost his position at the regional hospital and had to take the job at the factory. I still remember the roar of the waves, the crash against the rocks, the salty taste of the water on my lips, the burn of it in my nose.

This tiny, swirled shell holds all those memories. It's a good offering. Nicer than a lot of the trinkets and tokens left for the Ghost. Few people around here have even seen the ocean. I don't know if that matters to a dead person, though.

I set the shell on the table, right at the center. "This shell is a happy memory, from a long time ago. I'm going to give it to you."

I look around, hoping no one will overhear. I can't believe I'm actually doing this, talking to the air as if it will hear me. But I am thinking about Tercan, lying in my father's clinic, his foot swollen and misshapen, and I need to know it isn't because of me.

"Tell me something, Ghost," I say to the darkness.

I sit and wait—for what, I don't know, but every passing moment of stillness calms me.

The only sounds that come to me are from the killing floor. Muted by the thick metal door that separates this corridor from all that death, but still distinguishable. Lowing. Squealing. Grinding. Whirring. I'm sure this factory is much quieter than Gochan Two, with its crashing metal monsters, but it's as loud as any place I'd ever want to be. I keep listening, though, trying to hear beyond this noise to whatever lies beneath it, just in case.

After a few minutes I cover the shell with my hand. "This is your last chance, Ghost. I'm thinking you don't want my offering."

Immediately there's a faint metallic scraping, a pause, and then tapping. One . . . two . . . three . . . four . . . I look around, trying to locate it. Am I imagining it? Could it have come from the killing floor, or—

It stops.

I lift the shell from the table and stand up. "It's factory noise," I mutter. "And I was stupid to come here."

I am answered by a faint metallic ping.

"Ghost?" I whisper, dread rising in me like floodwater.

This time it's louder. A single, pinging tap. I put my hand against one of the many pipes that line this place. They're like intestines, tubes and coils everywhere, running along the ceilings and walls. A factory like this, which has been repurposed at least three times in its existence, has a lot of unused bits and pieces. I don't know exactly what these pipes are for, but I do know that one of them just pinged. I tap a pipe with the blunt tip of my fingernail, and it makes a hollow, mournful thunk.

I am rewarded with another ping. I shiver and pull my hand away from the pipe, noticing for the first time how fast my heart is beating. "Let's try this," I say. "Tap once for no, twice for yes. Will you?"

I absorb the distant sounds of killing while I wait. Finally—*ping . . . ping.* I have my answer. "Do you want this shell?"

Ping . . . ping.

I wiggle my tongue, trying to pry it loose from the roof of my mouth. "Are you real?" I can barely hear myself, but the Ghost doesn't seem to have trouble. His answer is two distinct pings, louder than before.

For all the world, it sounds like someone is tapping

41

the pipes. How would the Ghost do that? Shouldn't he be just an apparition or something? Then again, somehow he takes the offerings and prayers . . . but still, this could very well be someone playing a cruel joke on me. Not a ghost, but someone with flesh on his bones and an evil sense of humor. I circle the thick column that partially hides the altar from the rest of the open area outside the cafeteria. There doesn't seem to be anyone here. I pad across the floor and peek into the cafeteria, where a few bedraggled-looking Noor are sipping hot tea on their ten-minute break, which they get once each ten-hour shift, in addition to a twenty-minute lunch. They don't see me peering through the window. Their heads are low and their brows are furrowed. I wonder how well they know Tercan, and how Melik is faring. He's right at the edge of manhood, rawboned but obviously strong. I'm betting they put him at one of the carving stations, where his muscles could be put to good use, where fingers and the tips of noses can be sliced off in an instant of distraction. I rub my sweaty palms against my skirt. I don't want to have to try to reattach Melik's nose to his face. I hope he's good with a knife.

No one seems to know or care that I'm here. I sneak back over to the alcove and become aware of the nonstop pinging. It sounds almost . . . frantic?

"I'm sorry," I say. "I needed to see if anyone else was around." I try to get over the fact that I am attempting to talk to a ghost. "I didn't mean to walk away in the middle of our conversation."

The urgent pinging stops immediately. I hope that means he's forgiven me.

"Thanks," I say. "Now . . . you told me you were real."

Two sharp pings.

"And you haunt this slaughterhouse of ours."

Two sharp pings.

"I . . . I'm sorry, but wouldn't you like to be somewhere else? This is not a good place, and I would think there might be some other, nicer place for you." I recall someone at the funeral saying my mother was in a better place. I certainly hope this isn't as good as it gets.

Only one ping this time.

"You like it here?"

There are several moments of silence, then two pings.

"To each his own," I murmur, placing my hand against the pipe. My tight, dry skin is soothed by the cold metal, and after a few moments I lean my forehead against it. "I have questions for you that go beyond a simple yes or no."

I really say that to myself, but through the pipes I feel more than hear two pings.

"Are you alone here? I mean, you don't have any . . . ghosty friends?"

One ping, a small, forlorn sound.

"Are you lonely?"

Two pings, and I can almost feel their sadness vibrating through the pipes and up my arms. "I'm lonely too," I whisper.

Silence. In the distance a man shouts in Noor. I draw in a deep breath. "But now I have to ask you an important question." I am nearly choking on my own heart, which seems to have risen into my throat. "Tonight there was an accident. A boy got hurt."

Two pings. The Ghost already knows this.

A trickle of cold sweat slips down the neck of my dress, making me shudder. "This boy, his name is Tercan. He . . . embarrassed me in the cafeteria today." My cheeks are burning just thinking of it. Did the Ghost see this, too?

Two hard, staccato taps. *Ping. Ping.*

He did.

"I was angry. I challenged you."

He taps, an acknowledgment that he heard me.

"That boy had an accident tonight. On the killing floor. His foot was crushed. Even if he doesn't lose it, he won't ever walk without a limp, if at all. It was a terrible injury."

Two taps. And they sound cold now, not sad. Hard.

"Did you do it?" My voice comes out louder than I mean it to, and it echoes faintly in the open space.

There is silence for a long time, long enough for me to wonder if the Ghost has cut the slender thread of sound that connects us, if he's gone off to haunt some other part of the factory.

But then I hear it, in the darkness, in the not-so-quiet. It carries easily over the thrumming din of the killing floor, over the harsh in-out of my own heavy breaths.

Ping.

I relax, sagging a little as I hold on to the pipe. Accidents happen. This was an accident.

Ping.

I drop the shell on the table and sprint down the hall.

⤙◎ Chapter ◎⤚
Five

BY THE TIME I get back to the clinic, Tercan is stirring. My father is by his side, murmuring soothing words the boy will never understand. The gentleness in my father's voice is unmistakable, though, and Tercan relaxes a little, his bony shoulders slumping back to the table. He moans softly. So fragile, this boy. Broken by a ghost.

"He's running a slight fever," my father says. "He'll need a course of antibiotics."

"He won't be able to afford them if he can't work," I say.

"He might die of infection if he doesn't have them." There's no edge to my father's voice, only fatigue. He's sad about what's happened. I don't think he feels the same way about the Noor as the other people around here do. He hasn't treated them differently than he does anyone else. And suddenly I know what he's going to do, because he's done it many times before—he's going to pay for this boy's medicine.

I don't know whether to laugh or cry. Because I challenged the Ghost, my father is going to spend more than a week's worth of wages on medicine for a Noor boy who might not live out the season.

"We could sell some of my dresses," I say. I have a closet full of gowns that I am now ashamed to wear for so many reasons, so as much as it hurts to give them up, it must be done. They're worth something; I know what my mother's clients paid her for dresses, and they were no finer than some of mine. My mother's scent is still detectable in the jade green silk dress, the last one she made before she died. My vision blurs with tears. Would she be proud of me now?

No, I think she would be horrified.

My father lifts his head and searches my face, but then his eyes focus on something behind me. "Melik," he says. "On break?"

I turn slowly to see Melik hovering in the doorway. His brow is furrowed, but his eyes are wide. "You . . . you'll help him pay for this medicine?"

It's all wrong. The way he's looking at me, I know he thinks I'm good. "He needs it," I say in a choked voice.

He's opening his mouth to reply when my father says, "If this is your short break, Melik, you only have a few minutes. You can take him now, but make sure he keeps his foot elevated. He's going to be in a lot of pain, so let him suck on these. Just long enough to relieve the pain, then take them from him."

He hands Melik a paper sack containing some opium sticks, and issues several other instructions I hope Melik understands. As he listens to my father, his gaze keeps flicking in my direction, and it's all I can do not to hide my face.

When my father is finished giving his orders, Melik calls into the hallway, and two other Noor boys come in. The one with the big mole in the center of his cheek is hesitant, but the other, the younger boy with rust-colored hair, looks around with unself-conscious curiosity.

"Sinan," Melik says to him. "This is Dr. Guiren. And this is his daughter, Wen." He nods at me, then gestures back to the boy. "This is my brother."

Sinan's deep blue eyes light on mine, and he tilts his head. "You had a different dress on earlier."

Melik snaps at Sinan in that guttural language of theirs, and he answers back with a laugh before going to Tercan's other side. Sinan and the boy with the mole, whose tan skin has turned ghastly pale, each take a leg. Melik wraps his arms around Tercan's trunk and lifts his body, then gives me one last, questioning glance before he and the other boys disappear down the hallway.

I sink into my father's chair. "How long do you think the company will let him stay?"

My father walks to the clinic door and watches the Noor for a few seconds before shutting it and turning to me. "Not long. I might be able to buy him a little time, maybe a week, but Mugo will be impatient to replace him."

"Right," I murmur. "Feasting season."

"You did well tonight." Father grabs his white antiseptic bottle and wets a cloth.

"Thanks." But I didn't do well. I did the worst thing I've ever done in my whole life, and someone else will be paying for it, maybe with *his* life. I get up to help clean. "Father . . . I wanted to ask you about the Ghost."

My father stops in the middle of wiping down the exam table. "Did Hazzi scare you this morning?"

"Oh, no, he was kind. But he and everyone else think the Ghost is very powerful." I wait, hoping my father will walk through the door I've opened. When he remains silent, I add, "People leave their best offerings at his altar, along with their prayers. They say he answers them."

He chuckles. "People need to believe in something, especially here."

It's not what I expect him to say. He's usually dismissive of this kind of superstition. "Have you ever done it? You know, made a wish?"

Father shakes his head. "My wishes are too big for the Ghost, I think."

"But some aren't?"

He starts wiping again. "Maybe not."

I reach for the bottle to wet my cleaning rag. "Jima said he was a worker who died on the killing floor."

"That is the myth," he says, wringing out his rag in the sink.

"Do you believe in him, Father?"

He looks down at the floor. "No, of course not. I don't believe in ghosts." His voice is trembling, and I have no idea why.

My father opens his pocket watch and makes a small, distressed noise in his throat. "So late. I've had a long day, Wen. I'm going to bed. Would you mind finishing up?"

"No, I can do it."

"Thank you." Without glancing at me again, my father walks up the stairs to our living quarters.

I scrub the remains of Tercan's surgery from my father's examination table, sweep a pile of metal shavings from beneath the bookshelf, and load our cleaning machine with all the tools we used tonight. Above my head the floor creaks with my father's footsteps, and I hear his voice, though I know he's alone up there. I wonder if he's imagining my mother is there with him, if he misses her as much as I do. When she was well, he came home to our cottage on the Hill, at the western end of the Ring, one weekend each month. He was like a friendly stranger to me, asking questions about my schooling while giving me a polite-but-distant smile. And now we see each other every day, and I don't feel much closer to him. We don't talk about my mother. We talk about few things that don't have to do with his patients and his work.

I wish I could talk to him about what I've done, but I don't want him to know. I am alone in this, as I am alone in so much else. It is a crushing feeling with no corners and no edges. Endless and uncontainable. The Ghost seems to understand this feeling. Maybe it is the reason he accepts offerings and answers prayers. Maybe it is why he broke Tercan. Maybe it's why I challenged him to prove he is real in the first place. I bow my head and press the back of my hand to my mouth to hold in my sob as I remember Melik's agonized expression while he watched his friend suffer, as I think of Tercan and his ruined future. I deserve this loneliness now.

I sink to the floor and wrap my arms around myself, holding all my sorrow inside. If I make a sound, my father might hear, and that would never do. I clench my teeth and clamp my lips shut and tremble from the effort. I wait and wait and wait, until my father's voice upstairs falls silent, until I can open my mouth without sobbing. Then, leaving my cleaning only half done, I trudge up to my sleeping pallet, hoping to dream of our cottage on the Hill and wake in my old bed with the scent of my mother's perfume in the air.

I rise a few hours later, eat a breakfast of stale bread, and finish cleaning because I don't want my father to have to do it. I scrub the floors, the sink, the counters, making sure no sign of Tercan remains. Then I sweep the metal shavings from the base of the walls yet again. In one little pile I find a square company coin with a hole in the center, the same kind I offered to the Ghost as a reward for destroying a life. I shiver as I put it in my pocket.

My father comes down the stairs as the shift whistle blows. I put my hands over my ears and wait it out, closing my eyes and hearing the lilt of my mother's voice as she sings to me about a field full of citron, where a boy and girl meet and kiss and dream of a life together.

My father taps me on the shoulder and I lower my hands. He gives me a gentle smile. "Sleep all right?"

No. I lay awake and listened to the strange, soft sounds that come from the air vents. Sometimes, I swear, it sounds like the factory is crying. Or keening softly, like pleas from something long since buried deep. It always comes at night, this whirring, whining, mournful sound, and I lie there, trying to figure out what it could be. Maybe it's the Ghost. "Yes, thanks. Did you?"

He nods. "I need to talk to you about the medicine for Tercan. Were you serious when you said you'd be willing to sell one of your dresses?"

"I was. If you think he needs the medicine, I want to help."

He watches me carefully, like he's trying to figure me out. "That's very generous of you, Wen. And I certainly appreciate it. Your new work dress—" He pauses when he sees the look of horror on my face. "No, dear, don't feel bad. You needed to get it. You couldn't go on wearing those embroidered dresses. It's just, these two expenses coming at once. It would be . . . difficult."

Of course it would be. But despite that, my father would still do it. He would do it even if it meant borrowing from the company against his future income. I wonder how often he's done that, how much he actually owes. He must be in debt, after the way he talked about it yesterday.

"I'll go to the cottage today," I say. "My fanciest dresses are there. They're worth the most." A lump has risen in my throat, and I'm having trouble getting my words around it.

My father begins rearranging the little steel basins stacked on the wire shelves over the washbasin. With his eyes focused on his hands and their meaningless work, he says, "I appreciate it." He pauses for a moment. "And once again, I'm proud of you."

His words hurt so much I almost blurt out my secret right there. But I don't want him to have to share this burden with me. He's already carrying so much. So I smile gratefully at him. Then I bow my head, jam my hand into my pocket, and rub my thumb over the square coin until it aches.

The morning passes quickly. Several workers come in with minor complaints, and it's clear the season of sickness has begun. It always does, as soon as the chill wind from the north begins to blow. My father listens carefully to the quiet symphony inside his patients' bodies, then tells me what to do. I pass out inhaler sticks of dried thorn-apple leaves for breathing troubles, ginger and horehound sucking drops for the coughs, a tonic laced with opium for a sore throat. One fellow accuses me of trying to kill him when I dose him with a mixture of honey, vinegar, and cayenne pepper to relieve his chest congestion, but my father steps in and assures him that when the burning stops, he'll be able to breathe again.

I am more than ready for my lunch break and scoot down to the cafeteria as soon as my father nods that I can go. I want to know if Jima got her wish granted, and if any of the others' wishes got granted too. I'm so distracted that I don't see Underboss Mugo until I crash into him as he walks out of his office.

"Watch where you're going!" he snaps, then clears his throat and hitches an oily grin onto his face when he sees it's me. "Ah, Wen. I'm sorry. You caught me by surprise." He slides a hand over his thinning, greasy black hair.

I curtsy and step to the side, afraid to meet his eyes. My father said I should never invite Mugo's attentions, and here I am, nearly knocking him down in the hallway.

"Please forgive me, Underboss, I wasn't being careful. Have a good day."

His skinny fingers encircle my upper arm, and I want to rip myself away, but that would be a bad idea. Like running from one of the wildcats that live in the woods at the southern edge of the Ring, which fills them with the thrill of the hunt, the possibility of a kill. "Wen, I know this has been a sad time for you, but I hope you're settling in here?"

His breath smells like onions, and my stomach clenches. "Thank you, sir. I'm grateful I've been offered a home."

He smiles, thin lips curling back like a snarl. One of his top teeth is chipped. "How old are you now?"

"Sixteen."

His smile becomes wider, but he releases my arm. "Such a lovely young lady you're becoming. You must surely be turning the heads of the young men around here."

"No, sir," I say in a squeaky voice, because I am well and truly scared now.

He's looking at me with pure calculation, like he's adding up all the parts of me to see what I'm worth. "Well, only a matter of time. You come to me if any of them are improper, all right?"

No words come to me. I can't move.

He leans in. "All right? Promise me. I'll keep them from bothering you."

I jerk my head up and down because it's the only thing that might keep him from getting closer to me. Already I can feel the huff of onion breath on my neck.

He nods back at me, satisfied. "Good girl. Now, I'm sure Vie is waiting for you in the cafeteria."

It's enough to get my feet going. I mutter a thanks and walk away, acutely aware of his eyes on my back. I manage to make it to the cafeteria before the day-shift workers are given their break, so the only people here are my friends. I sigh in relief and scoot through the food line, stopping only to check in with Minny about how her son is doing.

She clacks together her wooden false teeth and grins at me. "Doing so well, Miss Wen. Thank your father for me. He's a miracle worker. He'll be rewarded in heaven for his work here."

My father doesn't believe in heaven, but I would never tell Minny that. I tell her I'll stop by her home to bring her boy some of my special ginger drops, which are his favorite thing and the only way we could get him to choke down the medicine that saved his life. She puts an extra bun on my plate and doesn't charge me for it.

Vie, Jima, and Onya all stare at me as I approach, their expressions a mixture of curiosity and awe. "We heard about the Noor boy," Vie says when I reach the table.

I sit down with my tray. The coin in my pocket suddenly weighs a ton. "He was badly hurt."

Onya's head bobs enthusiastically, the loose strands of her silver and black hair swishing across her round cheeks. "He was the one who lifted your skirt! He deserved what he got!"

"Is that what you asked for?" asks Vie. "That he would get hurt like that?" She's looking at me with hungry curiosity, and I want to cry.

"She didn't," says Jima. "She demanded that the Ghost prove his existence, and I guess he thought having a heavy steel rotor fall on the Noor's foot might do the trick."

I flinch. "That's what happened?"

Onya arches an eyebrow. "Seems you have the Ghost's ear."

"I don't!" I nearly shout, then bow my head when several of the men look in my direction. "I never asked the Ghost to avenge me," I say more quietly.

"He did it all the same," Jima replies, her voice strained. "You're lucky he favors you."

My cheeks burn with shame. "He doesn't."

Onya makes a skeptical noise. "But are you a believer now? You should be. The killing floor gives the Ghost opportunities for kindness and cruelty. It's his favorite place to bless—or strike."

Jima pushes away her tray. Once again she hasn't touched her food. "I told Wen he died there."

"It happened seven years ago this season," says Onya, lowering her voice as she shares her hoarded knowledge.

I gape at her. "So recently?" I had imagined this myth was as old as the slaughterhouse itself. It's certainly grown big in a short time. "How can you be so certain?"

"I was here when it happened. It was just another sad accident at the time, but it wasn't long after his death that unexplained things began to happen. The night-shift workers reported strange noises. The lights in some of the hallways began switching on and off on their own. Little things at first. But on the anniversary of his death all three spinners fell apart at once, in the exact same way. That was when some of the men began to leave offerings to appease him. Old Hazzi carved the altar and set up the candles."

"Why thirteen?" I ask.

Onya looks over my shoulder at the plastic sheeting that marks the passage to the killing floor. "*Men* die on the killing floor. Like my Davir did, rest his soul." She bows her head and wipes her nose on her napkin. "But this one was only a boy. He had a work permit, but most of us knew it was forged."

"But they let him work on the floor?" Then I think of Sinan, Melik's brother. If a boy has his work permit, he has as much right to a job as a man—and probably costs less.

She nods. "Sometimes, but mostly he ran errands and did the odd jobs, even delivered notes for me on occasion. He was a wiry little thing, always sprinting here and there. Very inquisitive, too, constantly asking how things worked, eager to help the maintenance men fix the machines on the killing floor. Many around here remember him. I know Underboss Mugo must, and Boss Jipu, too."

"How did he die, exactly?" asks Vie, who has always loved a lurid tale.

"The same thing that happens too often around here. A terrible accident. This one involved one of the spinners."

I shudder, imagining what the spinners could do to a skinny young boy. As my shoulder bumps against hers, Jima abruptly rises from the table and heads for the door, covering her mouth with her sleeve. Onya gets to her feet, then turns back to me. "If you're so curious about the Ghost now, you should ask your father about him."

I blink at her. "What? Why?"

"Don't be dense, Wen. He was the one who pronounced the boy dead."

Chapter Six

I STARE AFTER Onya as she follows Jima out the door. My father knew the boy, the rumored Ghost? Why wouldn't he have mentioned it?

"Poor Jima," clucks Vie, pulling me from my thoughts. She takes a bite of her bun and glances at Jima's abandoned tray. "Did you read her wish when she took you to the altar yesterday?"

I shake my head. "She covered it with her hand as she wrote. She didn't want me to see. Do you know if the Ghost granted it?"

"Judging by her mood today, I'm thinking he didn't. Perhaps her offering didn't impress him."

I swallow down a small bite of bun that suddenly feels like a stone in my throat. My offering was a tin company coin like the one I found in the metal shavings this morning. It's worth a cup of hot tea and nothing more, but I was given something terrible and huge in return.

Vie finishes chewing and wipes her mouth. "I heard Mugo yelling at Jima earlier because she misplaced some records. He said the meanest things, Wen. I felt so bad for her."

I look down at my food and a wave of nausea rolls over me. "Do you think anyone else's wish was granted by the Ghost?"

Vie swipes the bun off Jima's tray. "Apparently, the slurry machine is running properly again. I heard some of the men talking about it at breakfast. And production yesterday was way up. Despite the accident, I guess the Noor are efficient workers. So it seems to me the Ghost granted many wishes. Your challenge wasn't the only one he answered."

The coil of my guilt doesn't loosen at all. Whatever Jima wished for, she obviously wanted it very badly, and I don't understand why she didn't get it. I manage to finish my bun while Vie talks on and on about how she overheard Ebian, the middle-shift foreman, telling Mugo how he's going to get extra work out of the Noor by charging them exorbitant prices for basic necessities, deepening their debt so they won't protest too much when he shortens their breaks and lengthens their shifts. She whispers to me in gleeful conspiracy, but I feel hollow. I think of Melik, who does not seem to know his place, who dares to stand up straight and strong even when he is surrounded by people who think he is worth nothing. I wonder if his shoulders will be bowed and his back broken by the end of the feasting season at Gochan One.

I shoot to my feet so quickly that I startle Vie, who pauses with her mouth open midgossip. "I have to run an errand," I say, and jog to the door despite the relentless weight of the square coin in my pocket.

I walk straight to the altar of the Ghost and pull the coin out. I set it on the table amidst all the offerings and scribbled prayers, which have already accumulated in thick piles since last night. Several of them are in Onya's handwriting, but these are not her wishes. She told me she makes a little extra money on the side by writing out the prayers of the illiterate. She doesn't charge much, just a single tin coin per prayer, but it is a cost to those who can barely make ends meet. Even hope costs something, I suppose.

Rich or poor, educated or not, people want many things of the Ghost, and so do I. With shaking fingers I pick through the Ghost's presents and find my prize atop a neatly folded square of heavy paper. This must be the wish of Mugo, Jipu, or one of the shift supervisors like Ebian. They are the only ones who can afford to waste paper so fine, and Vie told me each of them scrawls a prayer to the Ghost every day. Resting on the paper is an ink stick, a nice one with a good sharp tip. Surely, the Ghost won't notice if I use it once?

I tear a corner off a thin piece of rice paper upon which is scrawled a prayer for the weather to stay warm until First Holiday, which is next week and marks the official beginning of the feasting season. On this tiny scrap I write my own wish, a real one this time, not a challenge. I scribble my prayer in cramped letters, working hard to fit them on the triangle of paper.

—⊙⦿⊙ ⊙⦿⊙—

Have mercy on the Noor. They should be treated fairly.
Please watch over them.

I blow across the paper until the ink goes from shiny
to dull. When I am certain it won't smear, I roll the paper
into a tight scroll. The tiny coil of paper just fits through
the hole in the square company coin. I set it at the edge
of the altar, behind the first candle on the left, the only
empty space on the table. "I'm back," I whisper. "And I'm
asking for your help."

I listen hard, but it's difficult to hear much of anything
because the cafeteria is filling with voices and shuffling
feet as the workers start their lunch break. Despite that,
I swear I hear a faint metallic scrabbling in the pipes, not
a tapping exactly, but something. Enough. I stroke the
scroll with the tip of my finger, a miniscule offering for an
enormous wish. "Thank you for considering my request."

I don't know why this is so very important to me. All
I know is that it hurts me to think of Melik's shoulders
slumped, of his head bowed, of his back broken with
work, of his spirit broken by Gochan One. I don't want it
to happen. To any of them, really, but especially to him.
I listen and wait for a few more moments, then stand up
and step around the wide column that hides the altar
from the rest of the corridor.

And immediately collide with a rust-haired boy.

He grabs my shoulders to keep me from stumbling,
but his hands fall away immediately. It's not Melik. It's
his little brother, Sinan. Up close, he looks even younger,
and again I'm stunned that he was able to get a work pass.

He has an open, innocent face, one that speaks of jokes and laughter and fun. He is nearly as tall as Melik, but so slender that he looks like he could be snapped in half by a stiff breeze. His hands and feet are huge, though, so I think he will end up big like his brother.

"Sorry about that," he says. He does not speak our language as well as Melik does, but I can understand him easily.

"No, I'm sorry. I seem to be bumping into people today. I need to look where I'm going."

The other Noor are pushing by us, eager to get to the cafeteria line. Their hunger is almost palpable, and I think this must be the first time they've eaten today. I wonder if they can only afford to buy two meals a day from the company.

Sinan smiles politely at me even though his eyes drift with longing to the steaming pile of meat-filled buns Minny has just placed in one of the deep bins in the line. "Thank you for taking care of Tercan," he says.

"How is he?"

His smile falls away and he bites his lip. I wonder if he's translating words in his head. "He is . . . crazy? No. He makes no sense. And sleepy."

"The opium sticks," I say. "They'll make him groggy, and maybe a bit disoriented."

Sinan nods. "We only give them to him for short times. But it is difficult because he hurts so much. Melik is with him now."

One of the older men hollers from the back of the line, and Sinan's head jerks up. He calls out something in Noor and holds up a finger. "I have to get in line. We only have a little time before our shift starts. Foreman Ebian told us we can work longer hours for extra money." He grins as if Ebian has done a good and generous thing for them, and I want to cry at his innocence.

Instead I wave him off. "Go eat, then. I can tell you're hungry."

He spins around and joins the line without a backward glance.

Melik is with him now. This means that Melik is neither eating—nor able to work his shift. I march up the corridor, back to the clinic. I climb the stairs past my father, who is listening to the lungs of one of the slaughterhouse workers. I'm going to ask him about the Ghost, but I must do this first. I pull on my waterproof leather boots and am back out of the clinic in less than a minute, stopping only long enough to have my father write down exactly what I need to get. I stride to the factory gate and settle in for my long walk through the Ring.

The rough cobblestone streets are dotted with horse manure and are clogged with carts, rickshaws, and steam-powered horseless carriages. Here, near the factory complexes, live the shopkeepers and merchants, the ones who provide for all our extra needs. I walk by a row of hair salons. One of them has the pink light on even though it's the middle of the day, and two slaughterhouse workers are walking in, their shoulders hunched and their hats pulled low.

I sniff and turn my face away. My mother was so disdainful of the girls who work in those shops. "They should have learned a proper trade," she used to say. She was beyond disgusted that they would offer their bodies up like that, and more than once said their activities should be banned by the government council that manages the Ring. Every once in a while the local police do raid this section of town, but it never changes things. If a slaughterhouse worker has spare coin and wants female company, there's always at least one shop open.

I walk past the Gochan Two compound, which belches black and yellow smoke, and then past Gochan Three with its acid chemical fumes that blow over the whole town on windy days. Once I leave the factories behind, the streets get wider and cleaner. I turn onto the road that will take me up the Hill on the far western edge, the place that was my home until a few weeks ago.

I keep my eyes on the ground, on the tips of my boots as they peek out from under my skirt with every step. I don't want to see the cottage until I'm right in front of it. Already my chest is tight. Already my eyes are stinging with tears. But I am doing something important, so I carry myself straight up to the front door and twist my key in the lock.

The whole place smells of her, of lotus blossom and apple. It is exactly as she left it, small but neat, beauty in the order of things, power in details. I can't be here long, or I'll collapse on the floor and cry. I run to my little room and fling open my closet. Here they are, the colors of all seasons, each one the product of hours of work under her brightest lamp. Each one is a symbol of how much she loved me. I grab two of them: the soft cotton summer dress that looks like a sunset, and a raw-silk dress the color of a sapphire. She had intended me to wear the silk dress at my presentation into upper-class

Ring society, at the winter banquet that happens at the end of the feasting season, after Third Holiday. It was something my mother wanted for me so badly, but even when she was alive, there was a question of whether my parents could afford to pay for my attendance.

It's definitely not going to happen now, so I don't need this dress.

I neatly pack my treasures into a special garment bag my mother made for transporting her clients' dresses, stare for a moment at my mother's closed bedroom door, and then get out of the house as quickly as possible.

My walk to Khan the tailor's takes only a few minutes. My mother never liked him much, but he's the closest and has the biggest shop. He gives me a sad look as I offer my pretty dresses, and I feel hopeful. Maybe he'll be generous because he feels sorry for what's happened to my family. But no. After taking a moment to offer his condolences, he eyes the dresses critically. He says my sunset orange and red cotton dress is somewhat out of fashion and comments that few girls will want a fancy silk dress that is not custom made for them.

When I start to pack them back up and tell him I'm going to his rival across town, he changes his tune. Maybe someone will want these dresses. And garments like these can always be altered. He offers me a low price, and I haggle my way up to something slightly better, then take my money and leave. I ignore the shearing pain in my chest as another piece of my mother is ripped away from me. She's peeling off me like the layers of an onion, and I wonder how much longer until I'm all alone, naked and raw, exposed to the elements.

The apothecary is frazzled. He groans when he hears the bell over the door ring as I enter his shop. It reeks of garlic and ginger. Cold season. A lot of people are sick out here in the Ring as well. I give the apothecary my father's note and his eyes widen. "The price has gone up. Does Guiren know that? We're almost cleaned out of these antibiotics." He snorts. "High-society ladies want to take them for everything, and they've been stockpiling."

My heart sinks. What if I can't afford this medicine? He tells me the price, and I frantically dig the coins out of my pocket. When I see that I have more than enough, I nearly fall to the floor in relief.

Feeling decadent, I buy two fat meat buns from a street vendor outside the gates to the Gochan Two compound, and then I'm back at Gochan One. My heart is thumping a dizzying rhythm in my chest as I face my final task—getting this medicine to Tercan . . . and maybe seeing Melik again.

I shouldn't be doing this.

It's entirely improper. And possibly dangerous. My mother told me the Noor were hot blooded and violent, always ready to take advantage. But . . . it is because of me and my challenge to the Ghost that Tercan is hurt, that Melik is not eating or working his shift. That neither of them is making money to send to their families. Yes, my mother taught me to be suspicious of the Noor, but she and my father also taught me that it is my responsibility to make amends for the wrongs I have done—that no one will do that for me. So I have to try to fix this, even though I know it's not really possible.

I have to guess where the Noor have been housed, but it isn't that hard. They're in the oldest block of dorms, the ones that stand empty eight months out of the year. My father walked me through them a week or so after I arrived, on a day when he was feeling more attentive and wanting me to learn about how easily sickness is passed from person to person in small, crowded spaces. So I could understand what we were up against, he said.

These dorms have narrow, bare hallways, low ceilings, and small rooms that hold eight men each. Whereas the newer dorms have indoor shower rooms with heated water, these older dorms have no such thing. Out back there are a few spouts lined up along the walls, and that's where the Noor can clean themselves. But in the winter, when the temperature drops and the ground frosts at night, it will be torture for them.

As I near one of the old dorms, I look around to see if anyone's watching. It would not be good for my repu-tation to be seen going into the men's dorms, and espe-cially into this one. But except for the night-shift workers, who are still sleeping, nearly everyone is in the cafete-ria or working the killing floor. The square is deserted. Despite that, my heart skips as I run the last few steps to the dorm, hoping no one is peeking out a window at exactly the wrong time. It takes a few frantic tugs to pull open the thick wooden door at the entrance, and when I do, I am hit with a wave of stale, humid air and the smell of men, of salt and sweat. I can't imagine what it's like in the summer, but fortunately, it's empty then. Even now, in the fall, it's stifling.

I step hesitantly out of the stairwell and into the dimly lit corridor. "Melik? Are you here?"

After I call a few times, his rust-colored head pops out of the last room on the left. "Wen? What are you doing here?"

I hold up the bottle of antibiotics as I walk down the hall. "I have the medicine for Tercan."

He squints at me, leaning out of the doorway enough to give me a glimpse of the pale, untanned skin of his shoulder, and then disappears back into the room. When he emerges, he is pulling on a white undershirt. His overalls hang from his hips, and the buckles clank around his knees as he walks down the hall. For a moment I want to run. My breath comes shallow and quick. He is big, and he's not even properly clothed, and I am all alone in this dorm with him. If someting happens to me, I will be blamed. My reputation will be ruined. I should leave. Now.

But . . . the eagerness in his expression is not greedy or lustful. No, all his attention is focused on the bottle of medicine in my hand. He meets me halfway and takes it from me like it's a hunk of solid gold. "This will make him better?"

"It will keep him from getting sick. With an injury like his, infection would be bad. He could lose his foot. This might help keep that from happening." I don't want to raise his hope too high—but I don't want to steal it away, either.

His jade eyes search my face, and I know they will haunt my dreams. "We will pay you back for this."

I shake my head. "No. You don't have to." He'll be too

busy trying to pay for basic necessities and attempting to scrape a few coins together to send home. He cannot afford this medicine.

He scowls. "We *will* pay for it."

It has been such a long day, and I don't want to argue with this stubborn boy who does not know his place, even though I'm starting to like that about him. "How are you going to manage that? You're not even working right now."

His jaw tightens. "Tercan should not be left alone. We're . . ." His broad shoulders slump. "We're afraid they might come and take him, that they might expel him from the compound or just put him on a train out of town."

They might. Right now Tercan is taking up space an able-bodied worker could occupy. He is eating food meant for people who can make money for the company.

I pull the still-warm buns out of my pocket. "I brought these for you. And for Tercan," I add quickly.

Melik inhales the scent and his stomach growls. He puts a hand over his belly. I offer him a bun. "You haven't eaten all day, have you?"

He shakes his head. "You don't have to do any of this, Wen. Why are you?" He raises his eyes to mine, and I almost tell him. But if I did, he would hate me. He would know how bad I am, and I like the way he's looking at me right *now*.

"Because you're far from home and you deserve some kindness." As it slips out of my mouth, I realize I believe it. "Now go to your shift. I'll sit with Tercan until sundown. No one will come after that." The bosses will all be in their comfortable homes in the Ring, far from the smell of blood and the weight of misery that hangs over this place.

I could get addicted to the way this strange Noor boy is looking at me. It's curious and wondering and warm, like spring. He takes one of the buns from my hand and whispers something in his throat-hitching language. Then his hand moves so quickly, in the sharp, sudden way I associate with the Noor. But when the backs of his fingers brush my cheek, it is a slow and gentle touch, one that both startles and quiets me. It's a moment suspended in time, and I want to dwell in it for a while, at least long enough to help me understand what's happening, but he doesn't give me the chance. He whirls around and runs back down the hall, boots clomping, his head nearly bonking against the low ceiling with every stride.

"Let me get him presentable!" he calls over his shoulder. I walk slowly down the hall, giving him a chance to cover his friend, who I'm sure is almost naked in the humid air of this dorm.

When Melik gives the all clear, I enter the room and sit on the sleep pallet next to Tercan's, which is against the wall beneath the single, tiny window in the room. He is lying on his back, his foot propped up on a rolled-up pallet, deep purple circles under his sleepy eyes. I wonder which of the Noor gave up his bed for Tercan. Probably Melik.

There's a single bare lightbulb suspended from the ceiling, and by its light Melik watches me settle in as he wolfs down his bun. "This is not the place for a girl like you," he says with a full mouth.

OF METAL AND WISHES

He's right, of course, but I can't tell him why I'm willing to risk it. It's not because I'm good or selfless. It's the opposite. I focus on measuring antibiotics into the little dosing cap the apothecary gave me, as if this medicine can turn back time and make Tercan like he was yesterday morning. "Go to work and don't worry about it anymore."

He thanks me and runs off again, to take his place on the killing floor, to wield his long knife. I wonder if the Ghost has received my prayer yet, and if he'll do what I asked. Maybe I should have gotten him a bun too.

Tercan eats half of his bun, then vomits it up. He is pale and sweaty. I go out back and wet a rag with water from one of the spouts. I wash down his face, his arms and legs, trying to make him more comfortable. I peel off the bandage and peek at his foot; it's terribly swollen and bruised, but there are no red streaks, no pus. A hopeful sign.

Tercan's being brave. He stays still, lets me do what I have to do. When I'm finished, he gestures at me, putting his hand on his chest and extending his open palm toward me. I don't know exactly what it means, so I smile at him, hoping that's the reaction he wants. He smiles back, but I can tell from the glaze in his eyes that he is in agony. I let him suck on an opium stick until he is asleep, then I pull it from his mouth and set it next to his bed. I leave after sundown, happy for the cover of darkness as I sneak from the dorm.

I skip dinner and trudge back to the clinic, looking forward to a hot bath to wash away all my regrets and sorrows. I walk through the doorway to find my father waiting for me. His expression is tight, and his skin has a grayish cast to it.

Mugo is standing next to him.

"We have excellent news for you," Mugo tells me, grinning wide and showing his chipped tooth.

I look to my father for some hint of what's going on.

"Underboss Mugo is in need of a new personal secretary," he says in a hoarse voice. He cannot meet my eyes. He holds up a work pass. My name is written on it. "You start on Monday."

Chapter Seven

I SWALLOW MY SCREAM and stay rooted in place, once again remembering the cautionary tales about girls who run from the wildcats in the forest. I bow my head and stick my hands in the pockets of my dress to keep Mugo from seeing them tremble. "As you wish."

Mugo claps his hands. "It's settled, then. Wonderful. I'll see you bright and early on Monday morning," he says to me. He seems to think he's done something great. Either that or he's very excited. He shakes my father's hand and leaves.

My father and I stare at each other for a long time.

"What happened to Jima?" I finally ask. "Did he fire her?"

Father presses his lips together and nods. "This afternoon."

"Why did he choose me? I don't know how to be a secretary."

Father sighs, a heavy, mournful sound. "Mugo says Vie can teach you."

"Did you tell him I can suture? That I can help you? Did you—"

"He said I have no need for an assistant. I'm so sorry, Wen. I had no choice."

It takes a minute for his words to sink in. My father can't afford to have me here, eating company food and wearing company clothes. And Mugo knew this, because he has access to all of the books. "What did he threaten you with?" I whisper.

Father shakes his head firmly. "You don't worry about that. You worry about yourself. Do this job, and earn your keep, and you'll be fine."

It would be so much easier if he sounded like he believed what he's saying. "I have to take a bath," I announce, louder than is necessary in the small space of this clinic.

"Okay," my father says. He's not going to ask me how I'm feeling. And that's all right, because I'd never tell him. That I wanted him to fight for me, that I wanted him to refuse. That I wanted him to protect me.

My mother would have. She may have been a fine lady, but she would have ripped Mugo's hair from his head. She would have slapped him across the face. She would never have allowed this to happen.

Except she did, because she couldn't stay alive, and now I'm here. Another layer of her peels away from me all of a sudden, and I scramble up the stairs and retch into the water basin. When my stomach stops heaving, I take a scalding bath and scrub every inch of my skin until it's red and sore. I braid my wet hair very tightly. I lie in bed in my nightgown, every inch of me hurting, and I welcome it. I'm not screaming out loud, but my body is silently shrieking.

Sleep eludes me. A few hours after my father quietly makes his way into the curtained alcove that serves as his room, I get up. I am not alone; my father is here, but I have been abandoned all the same. The loneliness is suffocating, and I can think of only one being who might understand it. I pull on a dressing gown and my soft woolen shoes, and I pace the corridor. When I can't hold myself back any longer, I creep down to the cafeteria, to the Ghost's altar.

Like last night, the prayers and offerings are gone, including mine. My heart lifts. Maybe the Ghost is going to protect the Noor. Maybe he will do what I ask. I kneel in front of the candles, thinking of everything I've learned about him since I've been here. On my first day here Ebian told me and my father that the Ghost eliminated the rat problem in the grinding room. Onya claims he magically fixed her typewriter. Minny insisted that the Ghost somehow kept her from being fired for missing too much work when her son was ill. So many stories, and though some are of the Ghost's wrath, most of them are tales of how the Ghost made miraculous, wonderful things happen.

"I think you're a nice ghost," I say, testing how it sounds in my mouth. It doesn't quite ring true because Tercan's face flashes through my mind, reminding me that the Ghost has the power to do terrible things. Maybe he is punishing me now, giving Mugo the idea that I should be his secretary.

I slide the tip of my finger through the long tongue of flame coming from one of the tallow candles. "Ghost, are you there?"

I wait for the taps, but they don't come. I curl in on myself, until my forehead rests against the edge of the altar. "I don't have an offering for you, but I do have a need." I close my mouth as soon as I realize how selfish I sound.

As I'm getting up, I hear the metallic scraping coming from my left, from a side hallway I've never been in. "Hello?" I call, straightening my skirt and taking a few steps toward the hall.

There's a spot in the darkness of that hallway that's just a bit denser than the rest of it. "Is someone there?"

The spot doesn't move. But as I inch closer, I am quite certain it's the silhouette of a man—except it isn't shaped quite right. Maybe it's not a man at all. "Ghost?"

The dense spot gasps and moves very fast. A door slams. I don't stop to think—I run. I reach the door and rip it open, then fly down the steps, which are lit only by yellow emergency lamps.

I hear footsteps.

I descend two flights quickly while the air grows colder against my skin and the hairs rise on my neck. Jima said people don't go down to the basement anymore, that the last few who did never returned. It's possible they simply got lost, of course. This place is immense. I pause on the bottom step, trying to get my bearings. There are four hallways, each one going in a different direction, all dark. I should stop right now and go upstairs.

But somewhere nearby someone lets out a breath he's been holding.

I cling to the stair railing. "Come out right now! Why are you hiding?"

My hands grope for the switches on the wall at the base of the stairs. The lighting in three of the hallways comes on, but the hallway to my right stays completely dark. The ever-present pipes line each of these corridors, coiling together in the corners, intersecting across the ceilings, carrying who knows what. The lights flicker in their steel cages, showing barren cement, closed doors—and no movement. So I take a few steps into the dark hallway, until the light around me turns from gray yellow to brown black, stopping before I sink into inky obsidian darkness. I've never been afraid of the dark, though now I wonder if I should be. But when I am rewarded with shuffling up ahead, a faint footfall, a soft clanking, I can't resist.

I move forward slowly, my hands out in front of me, my feet skimming along the ground. "Please, I know you're up there!"

"Stop!" The voice is loud but hoarse, like a door with hinges in dire need of oil. He sounds panicked. "Don't move!"

"I just wanted to talk to you," I say, taking another step. My foot catches on something and there's a noise like a thread's been snapped.

A weighted net drops onto me, tangling around my body and pulling me to the floor. With a startled cry, I try to rip it off, but it's made of some kind of slick material that slides through my fingers like water. From behind me there's a metallic scrape and a scuttling sound, like a crab on a stone.

I manage to turn my head enough to see what's making the noise, and I scream.

There, coming from under the stairs, creeping slowly into a pool of light, is the biggest spider I've ever seen. Its body is the size of a tomcat. It moves stiffly but surely, every step stabbing the ground with a sharp *click*. Its black legs arch around a low, fat body that almost drags on the ground. From behind a coil of pipes beneath the light switches comes another, and yet another emerges from one of the lit hallways. They each have two black, bulbous eyes and a row of six smaller eyes above those. And when they step directly under the light, their abdomens gleam metal-smooth. They're not animals—they're machines. Bloodless and soulless and way too close. I whimper, struggling in my net. Almost in unison, the things slash their curved silver fangs down twice before raising them again—and walking straight toward me.

I crawl with spastic, scrabbling movements into the dark, away from the spiders, which are now lined up in a row and marching down the hallway. Beneath the weight and tangle of this net, I can't get to my feet, let alone jump over them to get back to the stairs. The only way to escape is by going forward, but I only succeed in trapping myself further in the net. It's suffocating me. I am choking on my fear.

Footsteps come toward me through the darkness. "Get *up*," whispers the hoarse voice.

"Help me," I plead, fighting to free my hands. The net

is wrapped around my head. I can't see anything now. But I can hear. The metallic spiders are closer. I kick my legs, the panic making my muscles twitch. I don't want those silver fangs embedded in my skin.

There's a tug on the net, and I'm pulled upright. "This way," the owner of the voice says.

The spiders' footfalls are right behind us. The man pushes me ahead of him, and then he wraps an arm around my waist and he's almost carrying me. My toes are sliding along the ground. "In here."

As I continue to fight hopelessly with the net, my companion shoves me into what appears to be a little nook, possibly used for electrical or emergency access. He presses in behind me, filling my ears with the scraping sound of metal against cement. Is he holding some sort of weapon? "We have to keep out of their way," he says.

"What are those things?" My voice is high and tremulous. I'm about to start screaming and I don't know if I'll be able to stop.

"Security precaution." He smells of green tea, mint, and . . . plum cakes? His body is warm against mine. We're both breathing hard. The scuttling spiders come closer, closer, and I flatten myself against the wall of our cinder-block hiding place. Cold pipes against my chest. Moist stone beneath my hands. The net almost strangling me.

Better than silver fangs buried in the flesh of my calves. I shudder. My companion presses even closer. He's muttering to himself and picking at the net like he's looking for something. Then, as the spiders' clicking footsteps pull up parallel to our hiding spot, he stops moving entirely. We stand silently, waiting, and after a second of pause during which my heart ceases to beat, the spiders continue to walk down the hall, their scuttling reduced to a mere whisper in the dark.

The man's body relaxes and he returns to pulling at the net. "Shouldn't have made it so hard," he mumbles. "They weren't meant for you. Not for you."

A second later he seems to find what he's looking for. He pulls at just the right spot, and the net simply falls away from me. He guides me into the darkened corridor.

"Time for you to go back," he says, dragging me toward the light. "You shouldn't be here."

"Wait." I try to pull my arm loose from his extremely strong grasp. "Who are you?"

He laughs, a quick, impatient sound. "I think you know the answer to that, Wen."

"You know my name."

"Of course I do." He says it like it would be ridiculous of me to expect anything else. His strides are long, but there's a hitch in each step, along with a faint clanking every time he swings his arm. He must be carrying something.

"Are you a thief? Have you stolen something from upstairs?"

"Why would I need to steal anything? People give me their best treasures." He pulls up short before we enter the part of the corridor where a hint of light could reach us. I step forward, but he doesn't follow. "You wanted something from the Ghost tonight," he says from the shadows. "What was it?"

"It's none of your business," I snap, but my voice

breaks in the middle as I recall the terrible loneliness and dread that drove me to the Ghost's altar.

"Are you sure?" And then, in the dark, I hear the pings. Two metallic taps against the pipes. Coming from a few feet behind me.

I gasp. "A joke. You played a trick on me. I thought—I thought the Ghost was—"

"Real?"

I nod.

"I'm real," he says quietly.

"But are you the Ghost?"

"It depends on your definition."

The sadness and solitude in his voice is a language of its own, one I speak fluently. "Are you the boy who died on the killing floor?"

"In a manner of speaking," he whispers.

"But you're alive." I dive back into the dark, and my hands land on his chest. His warm, breathing chest. I can feel the heat and the rapid rise and fall, even through his shirt.

He jerks away from my grasping fingers, sinking farther into the murk with a soft clanking noise. "Not really. I'm not . . ." He curses. "Why did you follow me down here?" he roars. "No one comes down here!"

I stumble backward, away from his anger. "I'm sorry. I wanted to—I don't know. I just . . . needed the Ghost."

The harsh rasp of his breath echoes down the hallway. "You can't come down here again. It's very dangerous. Promise me!"

"I promise!" I blurt out, eager to calm him down. He sounds like a wounded animal there in the dark, and I can't reach him. Can't help him. I know I should run, but I don't want to. The Ghost is alive, has been alive all this time. And he's been alone down here for the past seven years.

"Please," he says. "Don't tell anyone you came down here. Don't tell them you saw me."

"I won't. I swear I won't." I mean it too. I don't want him to be hurt.

"All right," he says, the sawing of his breath quieting a bit. "You can go. Just. Go!"

I bolt for the stairs, almost thinking I can hear those scuttling spiders behind me. I hit the steps and pull my skirt out of the way of my shoes as I go up two at a time. I nearly miss the landing for the main floor and keep going, but manage to slow myself down long enough to wrench open the metal door and stagger into the hallway. With my skirt flying out behind me, I keep sprinting until I burst through the doorway of my father's darkened clinic, dash up the stairs, and dive onto my sleeping pallet, still wearing my shoes and dressing gown.

Then the shaking begins, the trembling that comes from the center of me, which has been tilted from its axis tonight. My Ghost . . . is alive. He's in this factory. He knows its secrets, and some of them are apparently very dangerous. And I . . . I'm afraid I'll never talk to him again.

In chasing him down tonight, I think I've chased him away, right when I wanted to talk to him most. As bizarre as it sounds, I feel like I've lost a friend. In ripping off his disguise of death, I've made him dead to me.

Or possibly very angry at me. This thought sends a chill right through me. I don't know how he did it, but if he was able to crush Tercan's foot on the killing floor, if he's able to do all the things people give him credit for, then he is not someone I want as an enemy.

Chapter Eight

MY FATHER OPENS the curtain and emerges into the parlor that doubles as my bedroom. He watches as I lie flat on my back, limp as an overcooked noodle, not even flinching at the piercing sound of the shift whistle. His own expression is pinched; the lines on his face seem to have deepened overnight. He looks old. Like something vital has been sucked out of him.

It scatters all my plans, the ones I carefully built while I lay awake last night. If the Ghost is actually a live person, then my father must know something about it. Onya told me that my father was the one who pronounced the boy dead. Has Father lied to everyone? Why would he do that? But when I look up at him, I can't ask. He looks so frail to me, and I don't want to see him crumble.

"I'll get our breakfast together," I say, hopping up from my pallet.

As soon as he realizes I'm not utterly broken, his tight expression loosens a bit.

We don't have much of a kitchen, and food is so expensive in the Ring that it's actually cheaper to buy from the cafeteria even though that's not exactly cheap either. But my father keeps a few stashes of grains and dried fruit because he leaves his clinic only when he has to, for fear he won't be here if someone needs him. I heat water in the pot and use some of it to make tea and some to make porridge. It's bland as can be, so I sweeten it with a few drops of honey in each bowl. We eat in silence, and then I go to the washroom and splash cold water on my face.

I have five days until I am offered up to Mugo as a sacrifice.

I plan to keep very busy until then, because otherwise I will run away.

The bell on the clinic door jangles, and I hear my father's footsteps as he descends the rickety stairs. I remove the clasp from the bottom of my braid and brush my hair, then rebraid it neatly and fasten all the stray locks in place with little hairpins. I pull on my brown work dress, which is in dire need of a wash. Its hem is muddy and gray black after my trip through the Ring yesterday. I put on my thick apron over it and tie it tight around my waist.

The sound of the wet, whooping cough reaches me as I walk down the stairs. And then it becomes a duet. No, a trio. I enter the clinic to see three Noor, pale and shivering, sitting side by side on my father's table. My father turns to me and pulls his cloth mask away from his mouth. "It's the flu. Get your mask."

I walk straight across the room and pull my cloth mask out of the drawer, then slip it over my nose and mouth and fasten it behind my ears. "Did they bring it with them from the west?"

"No, I don't think so. Some of them would have been sick on the train. But I checked all of them personally. All were healthy. I've treated a few locals with the flu this week, very mild cases. The Noor might have picked it up here, but these three are much sicker than any I've seen so far this season."

Our eyes lock as we realize how bad this could be. The Noor are crammed into those horrible, tiny, dank rooms with almost no ventilation. "We have to go to the dorms," I say.

My father nods. Every year the flu sweeps through the Ring and the Gochan factories. Most people recover, but we always have our share of deaths, usually the very old and the very young. But if the Noor have no resistance, if their bodies can't fight it . . .

While my father treats the three sick men, I gather supplies. With sign language and a few simple words, the men have managed to convey that they are not the only ones sick. I fill a crate with germ-killing soap, cloth masks, a big sack of cough drops, and our only bottles of eucalyptus and clove oil. Then I run up the stairs and pull out our biggest iron pot. Over the next hour I make an enormous batch of willow bark tea and siphon it into three water jugs.

By the time I get back downstairs, the Noor are gone,

and my father is waiting. "You don't have to come with me, Wen," he says. "The dorms where the Noor are staying are—"

"I was there yesterday to take Tercan his antibiotics," I blurt out, then meet my father's questioning gaze. "I wanted to make sure he had it as soon as possible," I add quietly.

My father stares at me for a moment, but then nods, giving me courage. "You can't carry everything by yourself," I say, hoping he doesn't argue. I need to make sure Melik is all right.

"I'd appreciate the help, then," Father replies, filling me with relief. Together we load the crate and the jugs of tea, along with a few ladles, onto a wooden cart. Father puts a sign on the clinic door indicating that he'll be back in an hour, and then we take the long walk across the compound to the Noor dorms.

As soon as we open the front door, I sense the sickness on the air. Vomit and sweat, the smell of suffering. I position my mask over my nose and mouth, and my father does the same. We carefully lift the heavy cart over the threshold.

"Melik?" my father calls. He's looking for a translator.

Sinan runs down the hall. "Melik is sick. You've come to help him?"

"Yes," I say in a choked whisper at the same time my father briskly says, "Of course. We've come to help all of you. You're not ill?"

Sinan shakes his head.

"How many are?"

Sinan frowns. "Maybe twenty? Twenty very sick. And

many more a little sick." He looks at me, and his fear is easy to read. "Melik is very sick."

"Then you can help us," my father says. "Please spread the word that we're here, and that we're bringing medicine to reduce fever and make the pain in their muscles go away. And when you're done with that, go fetch buckets of water and some rags. Ask the central office for some and say Dr. Guiren sent you."

He's going to help Sinan stay busy, and Sinan is more than willing to accept the distraction. He walks up and down the hall, shouting in the Noor language. My father starts at the first room we come to, but my eyes keep straying down the hall to the last room on the left.

Sinan and my father enlist several of the healthy Noor to dole out tea, cough drops, and chest rub to their sick friends. I watch them, cradling the others' heads, dabbing oil on the chests of the severely congested. I am mesmerized by their care of their brethren. The Itanyai people—*my* people—are not like that. We keep our sentiments and our hands to ourselves. Anyone too touchy is considered *off* somehow. Weak. Especially men. But the Noor, they are not afraid to touch one another, to comfort one another, to stroke hair and to grasp the hand of a sick friend. Their brotherhood shows in their faces, in the hushed words they murmur as they coax tea past the lips of the fevered and aching.

With their help we move down the hallway quickly, but not quickly enough for me. When we are halfway through the long corridor, I give my father a pleading look. "I want to check on Tercan," I say, because that's true, and it's also more acceptable than wanting to check on Melik, whom I have no particular reason to worry about.

My father nods solemnly. "Go ahead. I'm worried about him too."

When I turn the corner into that last room on the left, despite all the kindness I have witnessed this morning, I am still stunned by what I see. Tercan's face is as pale as it was last night. The circles beneath his eyes are just as dark. But he has scooted himself across the small space and is sitting against the wall. It must have been agony for him to move, but I know why he did it.

He wanted to get to Melik.

Melik's head is in his lap. His skin is leached of its tan, but his cheeks are red with the fever. He is breathing very quickly. But he looks asleep. Tercan is singing to him, quiet and broken notes of the most mournful song I've ever heard. A few other Noor boys are gathered around him, listening. One of them is holding Melik's hand. Another is touching Melik's leg. A few of them join their voices with Tercan's, some off key, but the beauty of the melody is not lost.

I don't want to break the moment, to wake Melik from his rest, so I turn my attention to the rest of the room.

Two boys are on their pallets, clearly fevered, each attended by another, healthy boy. It's only a matter of time before the others come down with it. As quietly as I can, I kneel by the sick boys' pallets, touching their burning brows to gauge the severity of their fevers and rubbing a few drops of the pungent oil onto the bony space where their neck meets their chest. I carefully ladle tea into their mouths, and when the other boys see what I'm doing, they want to help, offering me wooden cups to fill so they can take care of their friends. I let them take over and finally make my way to Melik.

"How long has he been like this?" I ask Tercan before I remember we don't speak the same language.

Tercan places his hand across Melik's forehead. "Hot," he says. He holds up the half-empty bottle of antibiotics and looks at me hopefully.

I am filled with both frustration and awe. Tercan has obviously tried to give Melik his medicine. I take the bottle and point at Tercan's foot, and then nod. I point at Melik and shake my head. Antibiotics won't work for this kind of sickness. We've seen that over and over in the last few years. But the way Tercan's looking at me, I don't think he understands, and I decide to leave it for later. I squat next to them and lay my hand against Melik's cheek. He gasps; my skin must feel like ice against his. His eyes fly open. They are glittering with fever.

"Wen?" The weakness in his voice makes me want to cry.

"How are you?"

His eyes fall shut. "Everything hurts. Am I going to die?"

He sounds so resigned. But I am not. "You're going to be fine. I have medicine for you."

His lips curl upward at one corner. "Wen always has medicine." I'm not sure whom he's talking to.

I fill a wooden cup with the tea and gesture to Tercan so he will help me raise Melik's head. Tercan loops his arm below Melik's shoulders and lifts him. I start to give Tercan the cup, but then I realize he is shaking with pain. Caring for his friend is taking an enormous toll on him, right when he needs all of his energy to heal. After a few minutes I manage to get him to move over and let me take his place. I point firmly at his sleeping pallet, and he gets the message. He calls to one of the other boys, who comes over and helps him get back without too much jostling of his broken foot.

And now I am sitting with my back against the wall and Melik's shoulders against my chest, his head lolling in the crook of my neck. This is the closest I have ever been to a boy. His weight on me is crushing, but satisfying in a way I can't explain. The fuzz of his sheared hair tickles my skin. It's so soft, like feather down, like a baby's. If my hair were cut short like this, it would be as stiff as a bristle brush.

"I need you to drink this," I tell him, lifting the cup to his lips.

He takes a sip and grimaces. "It's terrible."

"I know, but you're going to feel so much better if you drink it."

His hand closes over my arm, a firebrand pinning me in place. "Is there enough for everyone? For the others who are sick?"

"More than enough." I hold him tighter as a blazing fierceness coils inside my chest. I will not let this boy die.

He drinks the tea obediently, wincing at its bitterness, and allows me to rub the eucalyptus and clove oil on his skin. His body tenses at the first brush of my fingertips, but almost immediately his breathing comes easier. After I finish, he slowly sinks into a heavy, exhausted sleep. He mumbles something in Noor and nuzzles into my neck, which sends a pleasant shiver down my spine despite the unrelenting heat of his body. His long fingers hold my forearm against his chest, and I am trapped, but for the moment I don't mind. The feel of his muscles going slack, the steady rhythm of his breaths . . . these are enough for me right now. I stare at the cinder-block wall, thinking of that song my mother sang to me, about a girl and boy in the field of citron, and find myself humming along.

Sinan arrives with a bucket and some clean rags. I wipe Melik's face with the cool water. He has a nice face, a strong face. A square jaw, a long nose, maybe a bit too long, but it fits him. I learn his features as I clean the fever sweat from his skin. I bow my head when I realize Sinan is watching me closely, and when I can't bear the weight of his gaze any longer, I say, "Do you want to take over? I should probably get back."

Sinan laughs. "I think he prefers you."

My cheeks burn, but not with fever. "He doesn't know me. You'll be more comforting to him."

Sinan makes a skeptical noise and says something in Noor to the other boys, who chuckle quietly. Then he has mercy on me and comes over to take his brother off my hands. He helps me lower Melik's head onto the pallet without waking him. But when I stand up, it's like Melik's weight hasn't been lifted from me. I feel heavier, rooted to the earth more deeply, like even a typhoon couldn't blow me away. I wonder if this is how Melik feels every day, if this is what allows him to move through a dangerous world so steadily. I wonder if I will ever know him well enough to ask him. The odds are not good.

I join my father out in the hall. He looks tired but satisfied. He tells me that two of the eldest Noor are very sick and may not make it, but that the others should live through it as long as they receive proper nutrition and ventilation. He goes into Melik's room and props open the tiny window, which lets in a cool autumn breeze. After he issues some instructions to Sinan, we go back to the clinic. My father sees a steady trickle of patients all afternoon, and I brew up a second batch of willow bark tea to take to the Noor who are too sick to attend their shifts.

Before dinner my father goes to Underboss Mugo and tells him about the flu outbreak. Mugo agrees that the sick Noor should remain confined to their dorms until their fevers break. He even consents to allow Minny and the other workers to brew up beef broth for the stricken Noor while they recover. The cafeteria workers roll out carts of it in big vats, but only to the middle of the compound's small square. They refuse to take it to the Noor in their dorms, so the Noor must venture out and fetch the broth themselves.

As I leave the cafeteria I hear the whispers: The Noor are being blamed for bringing sickness to Gochan. A few of the men comment that they're going to ask the Ghost to rid this place of them entirely. One stocky man with a gap between his two front teeth holds up a few company coins. "Worth it!" he crows.

My stomach churns as I watch a few men duck behind the pillar to make their offerings and leave their malicious prayers. My wishes will carry no weight with the Ghost now; I'm fairly sure he despises me for tearing the lid off his secrets. I don't want to give him any excuse to cause heavy machinery to fall on me, or whatever it is he does to those who displease him, so I stay away from his altar.

I spend most of the next three days at the Noor dorms. Although many of the men gaze upon me with a mixture of suspicion and amusement, they accept my help with obvious gratitude. Sinan teaches me and my father a few phrases in Noor, enough to allow us to ask where it hurts and to offer medicine. I use them over and over again, and the Noor reward me with encouraging smiles when I do, though I'm sure I'm mangling their language terribly. Several of them make that gesture at me, the one where they place their hand over their heart and then extend their open palm in my direction. I can only assume it means "thank you."

The two eldest Noor are carried away quickly by the illness. But after a bad night and day Melik recovers rapidly. Many of the younger Noor do as well, and they drag themselves up from their beds to help their newly sickened brothers, the ones who gave them tea and held their heads the day before. I cannot help it; I like to watch them together. I cannot reconcile these men who care for one another so tenderly with the image of the Noor fed to me my whole life. Untrustworthy and warlike. Greedy and cutthroat. I don't understand how the two could be so different.

With the help of the healthy ones, I mop the floors and scrub the walls with antiseptic wash. It leaves the whole place smelling astringent and sharp, but that's better than the humid haze of terrible scents that accumulated in here with so many sick, dirty men piled on top of one another. I work late into the night, and then I get up early and start the process again.

By the time Saturday comes, Melik is ready to go back

to work. Many of the Noor are, and my father clears them one by one. A few hours before the shift is set to begin, I walk down to the dorms to check on the ones who are bedridden, armed with my willow bark tea and a new batch of ginger cough drops, which, it turns out, most of the Noor really like. Sinan in particular is crazy for them. Although I am bone weary and sleep deprived, I am almost smiling as I walk down the hall, because this is it—we've gotten the Noor through this with only two casualties, which is much better than we expected. If I still thought the Ghost was a ghost, I might be giving him some of the credit for this. But because he's not, I know the credit belongs to my father, myself, and the rest of the Noor, who took care of one another when almost no one else would.

I arrive at Melik's room. He sits on the floor in his newly washed overalls, looking pale but strong. The look on his face, though, is of pure pain. Tercan's head is in his lap, and Sinan is sprawled out on the pallet next to his. Both boys look desperately ill, sweat-soaked and shivering. The room reeks of vomit.

"Since last night," Melik says in a choked voice.

"Why didn't you come get me?"

He grimaces and looks away. "I tried. Underboss Mugo said you and your father were unavailable, and he sent me back here."

My contempt for Mugo knots my gut. "I'm sorry. I should have come this morning."

I squat and run my fingers over the boys' fevered brows. Tercan's forehead is blazing; his fever is much higher than Sinan's, much hotter than nearly anything

I've felt. I lower my head to Tercan's chest and hear the rattling, wet, labored sounds of lungs filling with fluid. It frightens me, but I try not to let Melik see it. "Can you help me? I want to keep Tercan's foot elevated, but I think he'll breathe better if his head and chest are raised too."

Melik obeys without questioning. "Maybe I should stay," he says. "I don't want to leave them." I think he saw my fear after all.

"You can, but you've missed two whole shifts. You need to earn the money. That's what you came here to do, isn't it?"

He runs a hand over his short hair. I can tell it used to be much longer by the way his fingers flutter, grasping at red-and-rust locks that are long gone. "Something like that. Mugo has informed me that we will be charged for the broth and the supplies we used." His smile is full of bitterness. "Broth is very expensive around here."

Particularly given the fact that the cows are right here in this factory. This is ridiculous. Right then and there I make up my mind to sell more of my dresses to cover some of these costs. But I don't tell Melik that, because I know he will argue. He will insist they can pay for it, because he is proud. Because he does not know his place.

I do not want him to know his place.

"So," I say, settling into the corner between the sick boys, pulling out two wooden cups and pouring the tea, "you'd better get moving. You never know when the shift whistle will go off early."

With a solemn expression he places the palm of his hand over Tercan's heart and says something in Noor, and I wonder if it's a prayer. He does the same thing to Sinan. Then he squats in front of me for a few seconds, looking at me with those pale jade eyes in the way I do not deserve. "We will not forget what you've done for us. *I* will not forget," he says quietly, and then he leaves.

When I recover from that moment, I tend to Sinan and Tercan. I wash their bodies, spoon broth and tea down their throats, rub the last of my eucalyptus and clove oil on their chests, lay cool cloths over their foreheads, and sing them every song I know. Sinan opens his eyes from time to time, sees that I'm there, and falls back into restless sleep. Tercan is much more far gone. There is a faint purple blue cast to his lips, and his breathing is labored and unsteady, like someone is sitting on his chest.

Late in the evening my father comes. He listens to Sinan's chest and nods to himself, answering some question posed inside his own head. Then he does the same with Tercan, but whatever he hears makes him frown. "This is very bad, Wen. He has developed pneumonia."

And with those words I know what I've feared all afternoon is going to come to pass.

Tercan is going to die.

Chapter Nine

I REFUSE TO leave Tercan's side. My father tells me I should get some rest, but he does not argue with me when I say I'm staying. I mop Tercan's brow, hold his hand, even pray to a God I do not believe in. If this boy dies, I have killed him. I will live with this crime forever on my conscience. That knowledge crowds out all the thoughts in my head until the pressure grows unbearable and my eyeballs ache with it. Until my skin stretches tight and hot. Until every part of me hurts with the understanding of what I have done.

Long after night falls I make my confession. I whisper it in Tercan's ear while tears roll down my face. How I never knew the Ghost was real, how I never imagined he would answer my challenge in such a horrible way. How sorry I am, how he does not deserve what has happened.

Melik returns a little after dawn, and by that time I ache so fiercely that I can barely move, but I don't want him to see, don't want him to guess. I release Tercan's limp, clammy hand and slowly stand up. Along the walls flowers bloom orange and red, the color of my sunset cotton dress. I blink slowly; my eyes feel too big and swollen for my head. My conscience is choking me from the inside out.

"How are they?" Melik asks as I get to my feet. His voice comes to me from underwater, and I try to shake my head to clear it, but the effort makes me dizzy and I lean against a wall. I need to tell him about Tercan, how his friend will die because of me. I should give him the chance to hate me properly. But before I can get the words out, his expression changes from serious to frantic. "Wen? Are you feeling all right?"

I brush my hair from my eyes, but my scalp is so sensitive that instead of words, only a whimper comes from my mouth. Melik is in front of me right away, ducking his head to try to get me to look at him. He sticks his fingers under my chin and his eyes go wide. His palm is across my forehead in the next instant. "You're burning up."

"It's all right. I'll go home now," I say.

I take two steps, and suddenly the floor rushes up to greet me. Right before I hit, the world tilts and I'm in Melik's arms. His clothes smell of the killing floor, and my stomach roils. But his shoulder is the perfect resting place for my head, which is good because it's too heavy to hold up right now.

"I'll take you," he says quietly.

The cool morning air is pure relief to my burning

skin. I lick my dry lips and sigh as the light wind caresses my face. Before I'm ready to give up the breeze, we're inside the factory again. The sounds of killing are sharp and painful in my ears, and I cringe against Melik's chest.

"What are you doing with this girl?" The voice is nasal and all weasel. Mugo. He's in early today.

Melik tenses. His arms tighten around my body. "She's sick. I'm taking her to her father."

"He's already out at the south dorm complex. More flu there. Give her to me. I'll take her."

My fingers curl into Melik's shirt, and his grasp on me turns to steel.

"Oh, sir, she has the same flu the others do. This illness is very bad. Two of our group have died from it. Someone as important as you are should not risk catching it." Even through my fevered haze I am able to admire Melik's tact. And to appreciate the way he's holding me like he's never going to give me up.

Mugo makes a contemplative noise. "Very well. You may take her."

Melik thanks Mugo and wishes him a good day before swiftly carrying me down the hall to the clinic. "May I take you to your bed?" he asks. "Or do you want me to put you on the examination table?"

"Bed," I whisper.

He carries me up the stairs and lays me on my pallet. "I shouldn't be up here," he says. But then he gets me a cup of water and holds my head while I drink it. When I'm finished, he gently wipes my face and removes my shoes. He crawls up to my head, and I stretch my fingers to touch his face, to make sure he's real. His skin is cold against my fevered fingertips. He holds still for me until my hands become too heavy and fall back to the pallet.

"I'm going to fetch your father. Tell me, does he have keys to the front door of the clinic?"

I close my eyes and focus. He's asking me something important. "He carries them clipped to his pocket watch chain so he doesn't forget them."

"And does anyone else have the key?"

"I don't think so."

"Good. I'm going to lock the door behind me when I leave."

I'm starting to drift away, but I swear I hear him mutter something about Mugo, and even hearing that name makes me tense up. Then Melik makes me forget everything, because his lips are pressed to my forehead, cool and soothing, and I want to tell him that this could be the only medicine I need.

It's over too soon, and suddenly I'm in a tiny wooden boat adrift in a boiling sea. Nothing above me but yellow sky marbled with red veins that pulse with my fluttering heartbeat. My feet are on fire; I look down to see the bubbling, roiling water seeping between the cracks in the hull. It covers my feet, ankles, knees, and I'm sinking, boiled alive, my skin peeling from me in layer after layer. Finally there's too little of me left to hold the soft parts inside. My black conscience bursts free, slicking the water like oil. I watch it from below, blooming in inky swirls, coalescing to form Tercan's face. His broken, bleeding foot. Melik's eyes shining with tears. And then a silhouette, human, but something not quite right about it. One of the arms thicker and longer than the other, the head tilted in a funny, off-kilter way. My Ghost. My Ghost who is alive, who does awful, wonderful, cruel things.

Then come the spiders, and their fangs are made of fire. They slash at me for ages, and it hurts even though all of me is gone already, tainting the ocean with my darkness. I scream but make no sound. I pray even though I don't believe. I beg for mercy I don't deserve.

Until someone offers it anyway, and I sink into nothingness.

I'm not sure how long it takes me to come back to myself. But at some point I wake up sweating and shivering, and my father is there. He wipes my face with a cool cloth. "You're through the worst of it," he says, squeezing my hand. "All you need to do now is rest."

He leaves me in the dark, and I lie there with my blankets wrapped tight around me. I have no idea what time it is or what day it is.

That's when I hear the scuttling.

I'm so weak I can barely move, which hardly matters because I'm paralyzed with fear. Tangled in my blankets, I listen to the metallic scraping, the rhythmic clicking, the whir of tiny gears. It's coming from the corner, by the air vent, or maybe it's an invention of my fever-crazed brain. The ticking footsteps inch closer, closer, and I imagine those giant spiders with their gleaming, wickedly curved fangs, tearing the meat from my bones.

Then it stops. I lie in a half-mad twilight kind of sleep for a long time, afraid to move, waiting for it to come get me. When the purple pink of the sunrise begins to glow faintly through the window above my pallet, I have gathered enough courage and strength to stick my head out from under my blanket.

No spider is lying in wait for me.

I chuckle to myself, a hollow and dry sound, and rise from my resting place to start the day. I take a bath and wash the sickness away. My brown work dress is hanging in our closet, and I pull it on, noticing both that it's been cleaned and that it's noticeably looser than it was the last time I wore it. I tie my apron on tight, wrapping the strings around my waist twice. I am weak, easily winded, and making myself fit for company nearly drives me back to my pallet. My father stirs in his alcove, making sleepy huffing noises that say he's awake but not happy about it, and I decide to clean up and make breakfast to show him I'm recovered. That he doesn't have to worry. That I won't leave like my mother did.

I start the water heating and grab the broom to tidy up a bit. There's a small pile of those ever-present metal shavings a few feet from the window. As the broom bristles push the shavings and metal scraps across the floor, mingling them with the dirt from our shoes, I see it. It's the size of my thumb, a piece that's bigger than the rest. I pick it up and hold it to the light of the window as the shift whistle blows. I am too mesmerized by the object in my hands to be bothered by it.

It's a girl, a metal girl, tiny scraps soldered or welded together to form her face, her dress, her hands. The finest wire is braided down her back for her hair. I examine her face closely, my heart fluttering uncomfortably.

It's me.

"What are you doing?" my father asks.

I spin around, clutching the tiny metal me tightly in my fist. My mouth opens and closes a few times, but I'm not sure what to say, so I hold the thing out to him.

He blinks several times as he takes her from me. He walks over to the lamp and switches it on, then tilts the figure under the light. She gleams prettily, more beautiful than I'll ever be. My brain is still sluggish from the sickness, and I don't understand why my father seems so perplexed when he looks back at me. "Where did you find this?"

I point to the half-swept pile of metal shavings. "There. When I woke up. I don't know how long it's been there." I glance around the room, as if there's something here that will tell me what day it is.

"It wasn't here last night," he says. "I would have noticed. And I haven't left your side for nearly two days."

"Two days? You mean, it's—"

"Tuesday, yes. I told Mugo you wouldn't be able to start until next week." His face twists. "I also told him this would be a great disappointment to you, and that comforted him. He's agreed not to charge you for your meals until then."

I manage to find myself a chair before I fall down. "Thank you. I could start before then, probably." The sooner I start, the sooner I can begin to help him pay off his debt—and keep him from falling deeper into it for my sake. Who knows what would happen if he did? Mugo might decide to bring in some other doctor. My father wasn't the only one left without work when the crash came. He was lucky to secure this position, and lucky to keep it. And I will not be the reason he loses it. "I could start tomorrow, even."

He shakes his head. "You look much better today, but you'll be tired. You haven't eaten solid food for almost three days, and you were already exhausted when you got sick. I should never have let you spend so much time in the Noor dorms."

"You couldn't have stopped me." It shouldn't be true. I should obey my father, and I usually do, but in this case I couldn't have, not if I wanted to live with myself. Which reminds me of something I wish I could forget. "How's Tercan?" I ask in a small voice.

Father makes a pained face. "He held on for a long time. He wanted to live."

I feel like the metal version of me, unable to expand my lungs to draw breath, caught in one rigid position forever. "When?"

My father gazes at the small figure in his hands. "Last night. Melik discovered him when he returned from his shift."

Melik. He must be devastated. I don't know whether Tercan was related to him or not, but he obviously loved him like a brother. "How are they?" I ask, because I don't want my father to know how much I think about Melik. "That's three they've lost from this. Unless . . ." I can barely breathe—what if Sinan didn't make it?

Father reads me easily. "No, only three. All of them are recovering now. The illness is spreading through the other dorms, though, and there are many bad feelings toward the Noor."

"Because they blame them."

He nods. "You can't tell them otherwise." He gets to his feet and holds the metal figure out to me. "You have an admirer, it seems."

I take it from his hands. It's warm from his skin. "I do?"

I immediately think of Melik, but he could never do something like this. He wouldn't have access to the tools. Plus, he has a million other things to do, life-and-death kinds of things. He has no time to fashion works of art to impress a stupid, selfish girl like me.

My stomach tightens. "It's not Mugo, is it?" He has the money to pay someone to make things like this.

Father's expression darkens. "No, he wouldn't send something like this. You really don't know who might have done it?"

It dawns on me slowly, like water reaching a boil. Yes, I know who might have sent me this. I wonder if my father does too. If he doesn't, I'm not going to be the one to tell him. I promised the Ghost that I would do nothing to give him away. I need to ask my father about it in a way that doesn't reveal what I know, and I'm too tired to do that right now.

I turn the little figure in my hands. Is this how the Ghost sees me? Is this some kind of peace offering? A get-well wish? Does this mean he isn't angry with me? Would he talk to me again?

How did he deliver this present, exactly?

I look at my father and shrug, but my palms are sweating. I cross my arms over my chest to try to hug away the chill.

Father is watching me closely. "Still feverish?"

I shake my head.

He looks at his pocket watch. "I have to go help the Noor dispose of Tercan's body this morning."

His words hit me like the kick of a mule. "Are they burying him?"

"No, they can't afford a burial plot, and they'd never be able to get one anyway, because the people of the Ring would not want their ancestors lying next to a Noor. We have to take him to the furnace."

The furnace is the final resting place of those too poor to be buried. The fire eats their flesh and bones and sends the rest out the chimney stack, into the sky. I actually wouldn't mind that kind of end. It seems better than being stuck in the cold, hard ground. But people who go to temple believe in the sanctity of the body, that even in death it must be preserved. Destroying a body with fire is the height of disrespect because it implies the body—and therefore the person—is unclean somehow. Unnatural. Unworthy of being returned to the earth.

I don't know if the Noor believe that, though. I don't know if they have the luxury of believing anything. "I'm going with you," I announce.

The least I can do is pay my respects to the boy I killed.

Chapter Ten

MY FATHER AND I trudge down to the Noor dorms, our breath huffing white in front of our faces. Even huddled in my overcoat, I am freezing. I think the fever burned away all my insulation, and now I'm just bones and flesh. Sinan is sitting on the front stoop of the dorm, blowing his breath into his hands to warm them. His eyes are a bit swollen, like he's been crying.

"Are they ready?" my father asks him.

"They've been waiting," Sinan says. He will not meet my eyes.

More sorrow awaits us inside. I don't want to see it, don't want to face it. I want to pretend like it never happened. I want to go back in time and skip lunch on that day, or forget to put the tin coin in my pocket that morning . . . or maybe be a better person and never challenge a ghost to avenge me. But I can't do that, so I will do this. I march up the stairs and make my way down the hall.

Before we get to the room, Melik and three other boys come out, carrying the body wrapped in sheets. Melik's eyes are red. But when he sees me, his expression brightens with something like relief. I should lower my eyes, but I don't. I *want* to look at him, and I want him to look at me in that way I don't deserve. So I watch as his brightness fades back into sorrow as quickly as it appeared.

My father asks after the health of a few of the Noor, and then we're escorting Melik and the others across the compound to the southwest entrance of the factory, where the furnace burns off all the parts of the animals we can't use, all our garbage. The smell is of burning meat, day in and day out, charred and acrid if you get too close.

We're too close right now, stepping through the doorway that will take us to the furnace. I stare down the long hallway lined with tangles and coils of pipes, with access panels and little alcoves. As we walk, I hear a faint rhythmic tapping. At first I think it's the random protests of a worn-out set of pipes, but it turns out it's not random at all. Five slow taps, then alternating fast and slow, then three slow and two fast. I hear the pattern three times before we're halfway down the hall, but no one else seems to notice. Except my father. He's listening carefully, his head tilted slightly. After the completion of the fourth repetition of the pattern, he frowns, and his lips become a tight gray line.

Soon the roar of the furnace is too loud for us to hear anything so quiet as tapping. I shed my overcoat because it's already boiling and we're not even in the furnace room yet. All of us are sweating. Some of the Noor look sick, but Melik looks determined. He holds up his hand to the others before we go in. He allows another boy, the one with the mole on his cheek, to take Tercan's shoulders and head.

With tears in his eyes, which are probably as much a product of the bitter fumes as his grief, Melik addresses the Noor. He is not the oldest of them, but it is clear he has some authority here, because they listen to him with absolute attention. As he speaks, the throaty words flowing smoothly off his tongue, I watch the Noor. I see jaws tightening, chins lifting, shoulders shifting from slumped to straight. Eyes brightening, heads nodding. He spreads his arms, his long fingers, and his eyes are blazing. His voice rises to ask the group a question. They all answer in unison. He does it again, a different question. They all answer in unison again, louder. Tears are rolling down some of their faces, but all of them look fierce.

I have no idea what he's said, but I think he's just reminded them who they are.

It's like he's taken off a mask, or maybe put one on, I don't know. This Melik is a man, a warrior, a soul that could never be crushed. Now I see what could be possible if the Noor are pushed too far. They are not weak, not passive. It's only a hint, a glimpse, but there's fire here. My father was wrong; they are not defeated, not completely.

With their heads high, the Noor carry Tercan's body to the furnace. The men who shovel offal and garbage into its flaming mouth all stand back, looking unhappy. My father hovers close to me. I try to focus on the Noor but am distracted by the enormous bins full of animal guts, the stench of rot, of sewage. This will be Tercan's resting place. There is nothing more humiliating, I would think, but the Noor are now impassive as they place his body on the metal plate. Melik himself slides his friend into the fire, and when he turns away, it's still reflected in his eyes.

He looks neither left nor right. He simply strides toward the door, and the other Noor fall in behind him. I've never seen anything like it, this kind of defiance within compliance, refusal to be broken while standing inside a machine that would gladly tear you to bits.

My father nods to the furnace workers and asks one of them how his daughter is feeling. Their expressions relax as they speak to him, as he tries to smooth things over. It takes him a few minutes, and I stand near the exit and wait, unable to take my eyes off the carnage, the bloated coils of intestines, the shattered, bloody bones. My father takes my arm. "You look like you're about to collapse."

I tell him I'm fine, but I'm relieved when he opens the door and we're out in the hallway again, where the air is slightly more breathable. The Noor are gone, back to their dorms to finish their mourning. They're scheduled to work in a few hours, and I wonder if they'll carry their defiant expressions onto the killing floor. For their sake, I hope not.

I take another bath when I get back to the clinic because the smoky smell of death has seeped into my hair and clothes. I'll have to wash my brown dress again and use the strongest soap we have.

I choose the plainest dress in the closet, an unbleached

muslin. With purple thread my mother embroidered a simple, looping pattern around the neck and waistline. I braid my hair and then coil it in a knot at the base of my neck.

When I get to the cafeteria, Vie and Onya are there, and they look happy to see that I'm back on my feet again. I get myself a bun from the cafeteria line and join them at the table.

"You're so pale!" Onya says. "We heard you were on death's doorstep."

"I don't think it was that bad," I say.

Onya humphs. "Those Noor have fixed us up good. Everybody's sick. Production is down. Boss Jipu is in a panic."

I swallow a bite of bun and pray it doesn't come back up. "This happens every feasting season, Onya. I remember my father talking about it last year."

She makes a sour face. "Don't you stick up for them. It's worse this year. They're filthy bad luck, pure and simple."

I open my mouth to argue, but Vie doesn't give me the chance. "When are you starting in Mugo's office?" she says. She looks excited that I'll be joining the ranks of the office girls, and I suppose I should feel that way too, since I'll finally be earning my keep.

"My father insisted I have a chance to recover, so he told Mugo I'd start Monday. I think I'll start sooner, though."

Vie nods eagerly. "You look all right to me."

Onya laughs. "You're so desperate for company that you'd tell her that if her arm was hanging by a thread. She looks like a ghost!"

Vie has the grace to look embarrassed. "Jima's been

gone for a week, and she was the fastest typist."

"What happened?" I ask. Jima is a smart girl and a hard worker. I don't understand why she would be fired. And it doesn't bode well for me, because I can't type my way out of a paper sack.

Vie raises her eyebrow. "The rumor is her extra-curricular activities got her in trouble."

I stare at her. Is she saying Jima was promiscuous? Did Mugo discover her with a boy and fire her for impropriety?

Onya slaps Vie on the arm.

Vie yelps. "What did you do that for?"

"Because you are a stupid girl who doesn't know what she's talking about. And you're lucky, too, that Jipu is your boss and not Mugo." Onya turns to me, and she's shaking with anger. "You watch yourself, Wen. Mind your manners and don't wear fancy little girl clothes like you do. You're asking for trouble."

And with that, she takes the bun from her plate and storms out of the cafeteria, leaving me with blazing cheeks and a lot of questions.

Vie has questions of her own. "Iyzu told me you spent time in the Noor dorms, alone with some of them. Was he right?"

I sigh. Those rumors were bound to circulate, but I'm too tired to worry about it. "All of them were bedridden with fever at the time."

She grimaces. "You're lucky. I can't imagine what they would have done to you if they had the strength. Weren't you terrified?"

"No. I don't think everything we've been told about the Noor is true, Vie."

She gapes at me. "One look at those barbarians tells me everything I need to know. What is wrong with you?"

"They're human beings," I snap. "And they take care of each other." *More than the Itanyai do,* I think.

Vie rolls her eyes. "I take back what I said a minute ago. I think you're still feverish."

"Maybe I should go lie down, then," I say, eager to get away from her. I leave the cafeteria, but instead of going straight back to the clinic, I creep to the Ghost's altar. Two of the slaughterhouse workers are there, reeking of blood, obviously having decided that their wishes are more important than a cup of tea and a moment to sit down.

". . . if not, it's a transfer for me. And you know what that means," mutters the older of the two.

His companion slaps him on the back. "The Ghost will fix it, and then you'll have no trouble making that quota. Have faith."

The older one with the paper folds it up tightly and gives me a suspicious look that makes me take a step back. I find myself wishing I had an ink stick and a piece of paper, something that made me look like I belong here. The two of them brush by me, and I hope I'm imagining it when I hear one of them whisper, "Noor-lover."

I drop to my knees in front of the altar, glancing over today's offerings. A fresh plum cake. A packet of green tea. A few coins. A candle. A small book of homemade paper along with an ink stick. I can almost tell by the cost of the gift what kind of wishes they are, and whom they came from. The women leave pretty gifts, sweet gifts. The men leave presents of cured hard salami. One has left a bottle of beer. Another has left a wish for good health along with a pair of clampers—which I suspect was stolen from my father's clinic. All of these items, all of these wishes. I wonder which ones the Ghost can and will grant.

On impulse I lean over and tap the pipes, a kind of greeting, maybe a thank-you for the little metal statue. I'm not sure if I actually feel thankful for it, but I certainly don't want him to think I'm ungrateful or angry at him. I want us to be at peace with each other.

I want to stop thinking about him, but that's not possible.

"Can you hear me?" I whisper, but there's no answer. No tapping, no sound from the pipes. I peer into the side hallway where I chased him the other night. In the daylight it doesn't look so sinister, just a dim, plain corridor leading to a staircase. I walk its length and place my hand on the metal door. As badly as I want to open it, I don't. He made me promise.

I emerge from the hallway at exactly the wrong time.

"Wen!" Mugo strides over to me, that oily grin on his face. "You look much better than the last time I saw you. Your father said you were very sick. I see now he was exaggerating."

I bow my head, my stomach churning. "My fever broke last night. I'm tired, but recovering, thank you."

"Well, you look lovely as always," he says, and I glance up to see his gaze trace along the neckline of my dress.

I cross my arms over my chest. "You're very kind, sir." I raise my head and say the last thing I want to say. "I can start tomorrow if you like. I know you're in need of a secretary."

His eyes light up. "If you think you're sufficiently recovered, that would be ideal." He licks his lips, and I swallow back my fear.

"Thank you, sir," I manage to say, though my mouth has gone very dry.

He pats my shoulder and heads into the cafeteria, and I stand there, feeling more alone than I ever have. Yes, I am wearing a dress my mother made for me, but right now it has betrayed me. The way Mugo's eyes slid along the purple thread, like it was drawing his attention to me, to my body. That is not what I want. Right now I want my brown dress, the one that hangs from me like a burlap sack.

I have to get it washed so I can wear it tomorrow. The thought gives me new energy. I start down the hall but pull up short as the Noor file in for lunch. Sinan sees me and whispers something to Melik, whose eerie gaze flicks over and lands on me. I expect him to smile, but he doesn't. With a shake of his head, he says something to Sinan. For a moment Sinan protests, but Melik holds up his finger and nails Sinan with a look so fierce that the younger boy backs down quickly, nodding at whatever Melik has told him. Then Melik steps out of line and walks toward me.

We stare at each other for a moment. He must have washed and changed after the trip to the furnace room, because I don't sense the bitter scent of death on him, only the faint smell of lye soap. His face is flecked with red gold stubble. "How are you?" I ask.

"Alive," he says. I have no idea what he means by that.

"I'm so sorry about Tercan," I blurt out. I want to

touch him, to offer some kind of comfort, but it would not be appropriate for me to grab him like that, out in public—or anywhere else, for that matter.

His jaw tightens and he nods. He watches me carefully as he says, "You mourn for the boy who lifted your skirt in the cafeteria? Who exposed your skin for all to see?"

Something inside me shrivels. I hope I'm imagining the edge in his voice. "Yes, I do. He didn't mean it."

"He did. Do you know what he said, Wen? Right before he tripped you?"

I shake my head. I don't want him to tell me.

He does anyway. "He said, 'I'm going to pluck some of the feathers from this pretty peacock.' He said a few other things he wanted to do to you too, but I won't embarrass you by repeating them."

He already is embarrassing me, and he knows it. The heat of shame is rising from my chest, up my neck to my cheeks. I look away to keep him from seeing, but he steps to the side, staying in front of me. "Any normal girl would have wished him harm," he says in a deadly quiet voice.

I can't help it, my gaze shifts to the alcove where the Ghost's altar sits, and Melik notices immediately. He walks over to it and leans around the column that hides the low table from view. His body tenses and he looks over his shoulder at me. "Is that what you did, Wen? Did you wish him harm?"

I can barely speak. My whole body is shaking. How does he know this? How did he figure it out?

I absorb the way Melik's looking at me now, the way he should have been looking at me all along. "Forgive me,"

I say, because I never asked Tercan for it, and because I need it.

"It's not your fault," he says lightly. "Like I said, any normal girl would have done the same." He wishes me a pleasant afternoon and strides into the cafeteria, leaving me staring after him, wanting to cry. His words were kind, of course, but it's what he didn't say that's left me cold.

He didn't say "I forgive you."

⟶⊸❧ Chapter ❧⊷⟵
Eleven

I RESIST THE URGE to chase Melik down and beg him for his forgiveness, because he is so strong, so hard, that if he doesn't want to offer me something, I'll never be able to take it from him by force. I go back to the clinic, not even trying to fight the shudder that grips me as I walk by Mugo's office. Starting tomorrow, I'll be spending eight hours a day trapped in there with him. I promise myself that I'll be strong, that I'll keep my head down and do my best, no matter how much he yells at me or looks at me with those hungry, weaselly eyes of his. I will earn my way, and I won't make my father borrow or beg to support me. I wanted him to protect me, but I think he is too weak for that, too scared of what Mugo might do to him.

Up ahead, my father comes out of the clinic and locks

the door behind him. He's got his medical kit under one arm and a jug in the other. Instead of turning to come down the hall toward the offices or the cafeteria, though, he walks to the rear stairwell. I can't think of why he'd be going down there, I can't—

Yes, I can.

This morning my father was listening to the tapping of the pipes, frowning at whatever he heard. Onya told me that my father pronounced a boy dead, but my hands were against that same boy's very alive body a week ago when he saved me from those terrible spiders. The Ghost could have fooled everyone else in the factory into thinking he was dead—except my father. Around here you're not dead until my father says so. And in this case he said so.

He lied. And now he's sneaking off into the factory basement with valuable supplies.

Perhaps it's anger, knowing my father hid the truth from me, knowing he will give medicine and supplies away without keeping enough to support his daughter. Perhaps it's fear—does my father know the dangers that lurk on the lower floors? Perhaps it's fiery curiosity, my desire to see this living Ghost and talk to him face-to-face. Perhaps . . . perhaps it bothers me that my father knows more about him than I do. Or perhaps it's simple fool-ishness. My feet move before I figure it out, carrying me swiftly down the hall. I catch the slow-swinging metal door to the stairwell before it clicks shut, and I slip onto the landing and let it fall closed behind me. I listen to the sound of my father's footsteps descending quickly, hollow taps on the metal steps. My own feet are much quieter, and my muslin dress is whisper silent as I follow my father at a safe distance.

As the air takes on a chill, my fear of whatever awaits me down here almost conquers me. First of all, the Ghost. He made me promise, and now I'm breaking that promise. His voice was so desperately panicked and angry as he told me never to come down here again. And yet he left me this token, the tiny metal me, so beautiful. I have to believe he doesn't hate me, that he wants something from me. The Ghost isn't the only thing that scares me, though. The net. The spiders. If that's the factory's version of security, there's some kind of evil genius in charge. The spiders are like miniature versions of the war machines made next door, the massive, steam-powered off-road troop carriers and tanks that were used to suppress the Noor so brutally. When my mother told me those stories when I was younger, I felt proud, the kind of pride that comes from growing up in the shadow of something so powerful. Now I am horrified. I've felt only a portion of the terror those things cause, and I would never wish it on another person.

It doesn't stop me, though. I get to the base of the stairs, six flights down, and watch my father's back as he walks slowly down a dank, dimly lit corridor with an arched ceiling. The pipes are thicker here, like fat snakes lying together in the trees, too lazy to strike. Father stops to step carefully over something at his feet, then proceeds.

I follow him, and when I get to the place he was, there is a thin wire stretched across the hallway, no more than a thread. It's about the same gauge used to make the braid of hair on my tiny metal girl. This was the kind of thread I broke that night in the basement, the one that brought a net down on my head and awoke the spiders. My father must know this—where the traps are and how to avoid them. I slowly look up.

And immediately squat low, covering my mouth with both hands to hold in the scream. There, stretched across the ceiling, is not a net. It's one of the spiders, this one with longer legs than the others. The tips are razor-sharp points. Its black, dead eyes, all eight of them, stare down at me. If this pounces, it will punch eight holes through my body like a long knife cuts through a cow's throat. With shaking hands I lift my skirt high and step over the wire, my shoulders hunched to my ears, certain the thing is going to jump on me at any moment.

My father has disappeared from sight, but I can still hear his distant footfalls, and I move as quickly as I can to catch up—which isn't very quick because I have to look for wires strung across my path and spiders lying in wait. Despite my caution, my foot snags on something in the near dark. A dead rat.

It's been sliced to ribbons.

Its little mouth is open wide, and so are its eyes. It looks as terrified as I feel, and I pity it, that its last thoughts were of horror and pain as the spider tore its guts from its body. Two thin, parallel streaks of blood lead away from the carcass. I remember how low the spiders' bodies hang and picture their bloody bellies dragging the floor as they scuttle away from their kill. Near where the trail ends is one of those piles of metal shavings. There are a lot of them down here. The sides of the hallway are lined with debris, like there's a predator down here that eats metal, and these are the crumbs that fall from its mouth. I don't want to meet this predator.

The hallway turns a sharp corner and opens up, becoming wider and much brighter, which is not what I would expect from a place this far underground. Lanterns hang on both sides, casting a silver white glow. My father is far up ahead, pressing a spot on the wall under the tenth lantern on the right before stepping across the hallway and disappearing. He is so focused on his task that he doesn't notice me learning all his tricks.

The walls are made of sheets of hammered metal, enormous panels of it welded together, so shiny that I am almost blinded as they reflect the lantern light. Hundreds, thousands of pale-faced, wide-eyed Wens stare back at me, magnifying my fear. A scared little girl in a white dress.

I move quickly toward the tenth lantern on the right. I'm a few dozen steps away when part of the floor shifts beneath my left foot. My heart drops into my belly. I haven't learned my father's tricks after all. From behind me come several popping noises and the whir of gears. I spin around and see four metal spiders, each the size of a spring melon, crawling toward me with fangs raised. I back up so quickly I bounce off one of the walls, tearing my sleeve on the sharpened sconce of a metal lantern. As the spiders advance on me, spreading out across the hallway to block my escape, I lunge for the tenth lantern. There's a button on the wall below it, and I slap my hand against it and let out a scream as one of the spiders reaches the hem of my dress. Its fangs slash down, tearing the fabric and hitting the floor an inch or so from my wool-covered toes. A door slides open behind me, nearly silent. Only the wave of cold air tells me I have an escape hatch.

With my heart drumming loud enough to drown out the metal clicking of spider feet, I throw myself through the doorway as two of the creatures jump onto my skirt. I must hit the opposite wall just right, though, because the door slides shut on my dress with a brittle metallic crunch. I bat at my dress, at my arms and legs, but it seems the door has saved me, because the spiders are either trapped on the other side with the rest of my dress or crushed to bits by the door itself. For several frantic minutes I fight to free myself, and finally manage to do it by tearing a full tier of muslin off the dress. Now it ends at midcalf, which is not only ridiculous but also horribly immodest. However, I'd rather have a short skirt than be eaten alive by mechanical arachnids.

I'm at the top of another staircase. The walls are made of rough stone. This must be the oldest part of the factory, the ruins on which the rest of it is built. Water trickles between the stones, and black moss clings to it. It feels like I'm in a cave, not a building.

My father's footsteps are long gone now. After all my adventures, I'm well behind him, with no hope of catching up. I am alone deep within the guts of this old factory, knowing full well there are horrors waiting in the dark. If I go forward, I could be slaughtered like that rat. I'm asking for it. But when I hear a scrabbling noise on the other side of the door, I know I have no choice.

I creep down the steps slowly, trying very hard not to touch anything.

There's plenty of light down here. Fine wires streak along the ceiling, an intricate web carrying electricity to lanterns set into metal sconces with sharp, curved ends. They are beautiful, but not in a way that makes me want to touch them. There's something cold about them despite the warmth that emanates from their glowing bellies.

When I emerge from the stone staircase, I look up in awe at the cavernous space around me. I have never been in a place like this. The ceiling is as high as the one on the killing floor. It's supported by thick columns of stone. Enormous metal monstrosities hulk along the walls, heavy gears and giant, spiraling drill bits, surfaces scarred with flames and grimed with oil.

The floor of this old factory room is . . . strange. Parts of it are black and wet looking, like moss on rock, and parts of it are covered in silver gray plates of metal. The metal winds its way through the space, a garden path, branching off into several rooms that have been con- structed with welded metal. But none of that is as bizarre to me as what lines these paths.

Sitting and standing on the black, mossy patches are . . . people.

Metal people. Like my metal girl, only life-size. And I recognize them. Boss Jipu sits by a fork in the path, his broad jaw and narrow forehead giving him away. In the corner, with his arms spread wide around his wea- selly body, is Mugo. A few are children—Minny's son, just a scrap of a boy, squats on a mossy patch a few feet from me. They are so lifelike, and yet completely cold. Beautiful but untouchable. Fascinating but repellent. All of them have the same dead black eyes the spiders have, only these eyes are bigger. They are huge, in fact, rendering each countenance glazed, heartless, distorted.

Some of them are staring at each other.

Some are staring right at me.

I back up until my heels hit the staircase, and right then I hear the metal clicking, which sends a razor blade of fear sliding straight through my body. They're here. The spiders. I burst forward, directionless and panicked.

"They won't hurt you," says an echoing voice, hoarse and tired. It is magnified somehow, and I look up and see a pipe over my head with a flared spout sticking out from it, like a gramophone.

"Where's my father?" I wrap my arms around myself. I wonder if he's been eaten already.

"Come see for yourself, Wen," says the hoarse voice. "Second doorway on the left."

I do as he says, even though I am wound as tight as a spring and ready to run for my life. The second doorway on the left opens up to a darkened room with a metal floor. In the corner, though, is a plush chair and a footrest.

My father is asleep in the chair, a book on his lap. *Stories of Kulchan and His Warriors.* He read me this book when I was younger, and now he has it here.

"Guiren hasn't gotten much sleep lately," says the ravaged voice. "He only made it through a few pages before he faded away."

"Ghost?" I whisper.

"You weren't supposed to come down here, Wen. I told you it was dangerous." He doesn't sound mad. He sounds too sick to be mad.

"I'm sorry. I followed my father." This room isn't very big, but it is rather dark. My father sits by a lit lantern, but the rest of the chamber is in shadow. Still, I can see there is a partition that separates this part of the room from its other half, with only a doorway-size opening at the rear of the room.

The voice is coming from behind the partition.

And it sounds as bad as Melik's did when he was wrung out by fever. "Are you ill?"

"You know, I'm ready for anything. I can stop anyone from coming down here if I want. Except for you." He chuckles, and then coughs.

"Why can't you stop me? It wouldn't be that hard."

"No, it wouldn't. You are so . . ." He lets out a heavy breath, and it echoes through the pipes. There's a creak, and then his voice simply comes to me from across the room, no metallic magnification. "Life was simpler before you came to Gochan, do you know that?"

I laugh; I can't help myself. "For me, too."

My father lets out a soft snort and shifts in the chair. He must feel very safe, or else he would never fall asleep in a place like this. I wonder if he's been coming down here for the last seven years, watching the Ghost build this metal paradise for himself. I wonder if he's helped him, if one of the reasons my father is in so much debt is that he has been feeding and nurturing a ghost for the past seven years.

"He's been good to me, your father," the Ghost says.

"If it weren't for him, I would be long dead." He sounds so tired, like maybe being dead wouldn't be the worst thing right now.

I take a few steps toward the partition.

"Wen, stop," he says quietly. "Please?" His voice cracks.

"But I want to see you."

"You can't," he whispers.

"You're sick," I say, trying to think of a way to get him to allow me to step around the partition, to meet the living dead boy who haunts Gochan One, the one who leaves me presents and protects me from metal spiders. "Do you need anything?"

He's quiet for a moment. "I . . . need . . ." He sighs. "Guiren!"

My father jolts up like he's been goosed with a cattle prod. His mouth drops open when he sees me, and then his face darkens in a way I haven't seen since I carelessly dropped my mother's favorite vase and shattered it into a million pieces. His voice is shaking when he says, "Wen, go wait for me by the staircase. *Now.*"

He doesn't give me a chance to respond, simply takes me by the shoulders and gives me a shove through the doorway.

"Sorry, Wen," the Ghost says through the pipes. He doesn't sound sorry. He sounds exhausted and sad and amused, all at the same time.

By the time my father comes to fetch me, I am chilled to the bone, from both the dank air and the dead-eyed scrutiny of the Ghost's metal friends. My father takes me by the arm and hoists me up, his jaw working. He holds me in a bruising grip as he pushes me up the stairs ahead of him. He doesn't let me go as he opens the sliding metal door, and ignores my spluttering warnings of what might lie on the other side. When he sees the crushed spider parts embedded in the torn bottom section of my dress, which is lying in a heap in the now-empty hallway, he squeezes my arm so hard I cry out. He leads me along the hallway, past the dead rat, over the trip wire that triggers the enormous, sharp-legged spider, and up, up, up the stairs.

He escorts me into the clinic and up to my room, where he orders me to change while he brews a pot of tea on the stove. When I emerge from the washroom, he is waiting for me. "How could you be so stupid, Wen?"

I sit down at the table and put my head on my hands. Melik hates me. Mugo likes me a little too much. The Ghost . . . I have no idea. And my father is on the warpath. I'm too exhausted to be respectful. "I might be stupid, but you're a liar."

He rocks back; I've never spoken to him like this. "I'm not," he says sharply. "I told you I don't believe in ghosts, and that's true."

"You could have told me you knew who he was. That he was alive."

"Why would I do that, Wen? He's been hidden for seven years, and hidden well. No one has even suspected he is alive. And now, within a month of arriving at Gochan, you're threatening all of that."

I raise my head. "What am I threatening, exactly? Why do you keep him hidden like that?"

My father's eyes go wide. "You think I keep him hidden?"

"Onya told me he was just a boy when he died. He couldn't have taken care of himself. Or is that story a total myth?"

Father sits down in the chair across from mine. "It's not a myth at all. There was a boy who came to Gochan with work papers that claimed he was sixteen, though he looked no older than thirteen." He lets out a huff of quiet laughter. "He was a charming kid, and obviously quite bright. When he wasn't doing odd jobs for the bosses, he came to the clinic to visit me. I've never met a child who asked so many questions." He glances at me. "Except for you, actually. But this boy had no schooling at all. He couldn't read or write, but it took him less than a month to learn. I got him some paper and an ink stick, and after that he'd leave his questions in writing. I could tell he'd been reading my medical texts."

"It sounds like you spent a lot of time with him."

"He had no family, or none he would speak of. He was all alone in the world. I gave him what little time I had." There's no apology in my father's voice. "He hadn't been here six months when it happened. He was on the killing floor, delivering a message to one of the workers. His shirt got caught on one of the spinner hooks as he ran by." He scrubs a hand over his face. "It happened very quickly."

"Tell me," I whisper.

"You've seen the spinners, how they clamp to the cows' legs and turn them upside down to present the animals' throats to the butchers. They're very powerful machines." He stares at me like he expects me to look away, but I don't. "Before anyone could help him, he was jerked against the engine's central casing. You know, the part behind the wheel rack?"

I grimace. It's too easy to picture. "He fit right through the opening, didn't he?"

My father nods. "He was very thin. It tore him up, worse than any injury I've ever seen here. It ripped his arm off, but he was still stuck there, held by a thread." He swallows, and I wonder if he feels as nauseated as I do. "His face was pressed against the casing." His eyes meet mine. "It gets very hot when the machines are running."

My heart crumbles. I don't know why I pictured him as whole, as strong and unbroken. "But it didn't kill him?"

"It very nearly did. I thought I was taking care of a dying boy when they brought him to me. I didn't expect him to survive. But then . . ." His eyes widen and he shakes his head. "He kept breathing, kept fighting. He seemed unable to give up."

I think of Tercan, who wanted to live. But even if he had, he would have been turned out into the Ring, penniless and maimed, unable to work, unable to protect himself. Without a lot of help, he would never have survived the frost that comes at night, the ice that freezes the ground. He would have starved or died of exposure. "So after all that, you couldn't let him go."

My father blinks at me, like he's surprised I can grasp this so easily. "There was no way Mugo or Jipu would have let him stay, no matter how fond of him they were when he was whole. As they have said to me many times, this is not a charity. So I told everyone the boy died, and that I'd disposed of his body in the furnace. And then I found a place for him and helped him make it comfortable, somewhere no one would find. Until he was strong enough."

"Strong enough," I murmur.

My father's face twists like he's bitten into a sour apple. "I never expected him to get quite *this* strong."

"If he's so strong, he could live in the real world. You shouldn't hide him."

"You think I'm in control of what he does? Wen, think about it. The Ghost has everything he needs and can keep everything he's frightened of far away. I'm not keeping him hidden. He's doing that to himself. He's never going to leave Gochan One. He's turned this place into his personal playground."

My father reaches for the little object I left on the table this morning, the tiny metal me. He holds it out to me and says in a choked whisper, "I just want to make sure he doesn't decide you're one of his toys."

‑‑◉ Chapter ◉‑‑
Twelve

NEVER HAVE I MET a more diabolical machine. I thought the metal spiders were the worst, but they are nothing compared with what sits in front of me. It must weigh as much as I do. It crouches on the desk, hulking and hostile, and in the last few hours it has nearly reduced me to tears three times. My hands ache fiercely from wrestling with it, the pain starting at my fingertips, throbbing through my knuckles, radiating up my arms.

This typewriter is my enemy.

I punch its keys with absolute malice but barely manage to make it cooperate. Every letter is a battle, and I have to press down with all my might to get the little metal paw to swing forward and ink its letter on the paper. If I hit the wrong one or don't press hard enough, it takes several minutes to correct the mistake.

Next to me sits a thick stack of notes, all in Mugo's tight, precise handwriting, that I must transcribe by the end of the day. I've completed two.

The worst part is when Mugo comes out to check on me, which he does frequently. He's being nice, but his smile frightens me, and so do his fingers, twitching at his sides while his eyes slide over my chest.

As I pull the third completed note from the typewriter, my sore fingers smudge the ink and I stifle a screech of frustration. Mugo chooses exactly this moment to slink out from his office, and he clucks his tongue. "Oh, Wen, what will I do with you?" He says it in such a greasy way, and I'm scared of the answer to his question.

He pats me on the top of the head, like a little girl, but then his hand slides down to my braid. He gives it a sharp tug. "Be more careful. Paper is expensive," he says in a slightly sharper voice. "I would hate to have to deduct the cost from your first paycheck."

"I'm sorry, Underboss Mugo," I mumble, my eyes on the paper in front of me: a note to Minny and her cafeteria staff to cut back on the meat in the beef casserole in order to shave costs. "I'll try harder."

I pick up the next note, one ordering old Hazzi to come in to discuss his impending transfer. I frown— Hazzi's arthritis is getting worse every day. "Sir, is this note correct?"

Mugo leans way too close to read it. "It is. I'm bringing in a young man from the Ring to take his place, and Hazzi's going . . . to a more suitable work environment."

Before I can ask where that place might be, Mugo's fingers slip under my braid and brush the back of my neck, and I shudder. He smiles. "What a pleasure it is to teach a young person a new trade," he says quietly, then strokes my neck, up and down, up and down. "You should wear that white dress tomorrow, the one with the purple thread. This brown dress does nothing for you, and I know you have nicer ones that are more appropriate for someone in your position."

I nod because it is the only thing that will make him go away. He returns to his office, leaving me frozen in my chair, once again contemplating running away. Maybe it would be best for everyone.

When my eight hours are over, I rush out into the chill air of the afternoon, desperate to escape. I take the long walk to my mother's cottage and select a few more dresses I'll never wear again, the petal pink summer muslin and the stately gray winter wool with stark white blossoms lining the cuffs and waist. Khan the tailor is less generous this time, but it's still enough to pay for the supplies the Noor used during the flu outbreak. No matter whether Melik hates me or not, I can't allow the company to swindle them like this, to bring them here and make them work for a pittance, to grind them down and leave them with nothing to show for it but debt. I want them to keep the fire in their eyes, their backs straight, their heads high. Melik is like that, always proud, always . . .

Right in front of me. He comes out of the building a few shops ahead, the collar of his work jacket pulled up high around his neck, his shoulders raised against the icy wind from the north, his rust-colored hair unmistakable. He doesn't see me as he walks swiftly back toward the factory compound.

My mouth goes dry and my eyes sting.

He's just walked out of the salon. The one with a pink light on even though it's not yet dark out. I get to the storefront and peek in. A few empty barber chairs sit forlorn in the front parlor. A door at the rear of the space is slightly ajar, and from behind it glows warm yellow light. In that back room probably sits a whore, happily counting up whatever coin Melik paid to enjoy her company. I reach into my pocket, where the heavy silver coins jingle. The price of letting my mother go. The money I planned to use to ease the burden on the Noor.

Melik obviously does not feel the same obligation. He is paying a woman to pleasure him, and the thought hurts me, much more than I could ever have expected. I bite my lips closed and breathe hard, anything to keep from crying. I am so stupid. I imagined he might still like me, even after he looked at me coldly yesterday. I realize, to my shame, that I have been weaving the delicate threads of a fantasy, one where he holds my hand and maybe even kisses me. *Me*, not just any girl. And certainly not a whore.

But this is the kind of boy he is, and now I know, and it is best that I do. Now I will not waste another second thinking of him. Except . . . I can't pry my eyes from his back as his long strides carry him through the factory gates and back to his dorm.

I trudge through the gates and wave to the guard, a man with a kind face despite the long scar that stripes his right cheek. He tells me a girl as pretty as I am should smile more often, and I try, for him, even though my insides are all acid and bitterness. With my fake grin pasted to my face, I drift to the cafeteria to grab dinner. Several Noor sit a few tables away. They look skinny and pale, maybe from the sickness, maybe from grief. But when they see me, they place their hand on their heart and turn their palm to me. I guess Melik and Sinan have not told them I killed Tercan. I wonder why.

Their gestures, along with their shy smiles, do something to me. The burn and sting inside of me fades slightly, and my hand slips into my pocket again, closing around the silver coins. I pivot on my heel and stalk back to the central office before I can change my mind.

Onya and Vie, who keep later hours because they work for Jipu, look at me like I'm crazy when I announce I'm going to pay for the Noor's supplies. "Think of what else you could do with this money!" Vie says. "You could buy new calfskin boots, or ribbons and soap to last for a year! You could buy yourself another dress!"

"Just take it, please," I reply in a brittle voice.

Vie shakes her head as she takes my coins and crosses out their debt. Onya clucks her tongue when I swear her to secrecy. "You're wasting good money, Wen," she warns.

"Were the other workers charged this much for the supplies they used when *they* were sick?" I snap.

Onya's brows lower. "The others are Itanyai, Wen. *We* are Itanyai. We belong here. The Noor don't. Isn't that what you said? You seemed to understand it then. Perhaps the fever stole your common sense."

I bow my head. Perhaps it did, and I need to shut my mouth or I'll cause more trouble for everyone. I thank them both for their advice—which does nothing to soften their disapproval—and use the few remaining coins to lift a tiny bit of debt off my father's back. It doesn't even come close to covering the food I have eaten over the last month, but it's something.

I leave the office feeling much lighter, not because I am happy, but because there is little left of me. I practically float to the Ghost's altar. I wait for a cafeteria worker who is wider than she is tall to leave her offering of preserved plums in syrup, to leave her wish of . . . I don't know. Maybe she wants the Ghost to make her creaking knees stop hurting, or maybe she wants the oven timer to work properly so she stops burning the meat buns, or perhaps she wants the Ghost to save her from being transferred, since that seems to be what many workers fear. It is clear to me now that people ask him for things it is not within his power to give, and sometimes those things happen anyway, and this is how a ghost is kept alive.

Once the cafeteria worker waddles away, I slip behind the column and kneel before his altar. "I wish you would talk to me," I whisper.

I need his voice to weigh me down. I am alone and emptied out, but I think he could understand this gnawing solitude inside of me, this nakedness that leaves me shivering. My friends seem to think I am wrong somehow, and I wonder if we ever understood one another at all. I have so little of my mother left, and so little of my father as well. He is slipping away from me, changing from a strong, smart man into a weakling, one who cannot protect his daughter from the stroking fingers of Underboss Mugo.

I think he might have been this way all along, and he was just too much of a stranger for me to recognize it.

And then there's Melik, whom I cannot bear to think about, but who slithers into my thoughts anyway. It's painfully easy to picture him kissing another girl, touching her, whispering secret things in Noor as he unbuttons her dress. An invisible hand is crushing my heart to pulp.

The Ghost taps on the pipes, and I cross my arms over my chest, curling in on myself. The pinging is comforting, but it is not enough for me now. "Why won't you show yourself to me?" I whisper. My throat is so tight it hurts. "Please, I . . ." *I have no one else.*

The tapping falls silent, and it is the last abandonment I can take today. Tears slip from my eyes and hit his table, dotting his offerings, smearing the ink on a prayer for strength and virility. With blurred vision, I push myself to my feet and head back to the clinic.

Of course, I nearly crash into Melik as he files in for his shift. "Making another wish?" he asks in that deceptively light tone full of accusation. He steadies me with hands that were sliding over a whore's skin an hour ago.

"Don't touch me," I cry, tearing myself from his grasp. I refuse to look up at him, will *not* gaze into those cruel jade eyes. "My wishes are not your concern."

"Wen—"

"No." I don't want to hear *anything* he has to say. I jog toward the administrative hall, lifting my skirt over my ankles so I don't trip and humiliate myself.

My father is not in the clinic when I arrive. He's probably out at one of the dorms, caring for some of the many workers who have been struck down by the flu. I strip off my clothes and crawl under my blankets, shivering and naked. The scratchy wool abrades my skin, but that's what

I want, to be worn away so the acid inside me seeps out.

"Wen, are you there?"

I sit up straight, holding the blanket tight around me. It's the Ghost's voice; but it's distant and tinny. "Where are you?"

"Same place I was the last time we talked. I've been ill."

"How are you talking to me?"

"Oh, Wen, that would take a long time to explain. Let's just say I know every pipe in this factory, which ones lead where."

"Do you talk to my father like this?"

"Sometimes."

That explains whom he was talking to up here the night Tercan was injured. I lie back down and pull my knees to my chest, the blanket tight around my neck. "I'm sorry you've been ill."

He chuckles. "I'm recovering. Guiren takes good care of me. I rarely get sick because I'm not close enough to people to catch things, but this time . . ."

"Did you catch it from me?"

He's silent for a moment. "Maybe. I don't mind it."

It's my turn to laugh. "You don't mind catching a terrible illness from me? Should I be flattered?"

"You sounded very sad tonight when you came to my altar," he says. I notice that he hasn't answered my question, but I don't press him.

"I'll be all right." I don't know why I'm saying that. It's a total lie. "Actually, I was thinking of running away."

"Really? Where would you go?"

"To the south. I want to see the ocean." It's the only thing I can think of. It's not like I've made a plan.

"That doesn't sound very practical. And I think Guiren would miss you."

"I'm not sure he would," I whisper.

"Would you like to know one of the things that kept me alive when I should have died?"

The question startles me, and it takes me a while to summon the words to tell him I do.

"When I was too hurt to move, when I thought nothing could make the pain go away, your father told me stories. Some were grand, like Kulchan and his warriors, like pirates and genies and treasure and conquest. But others were about the little girl who owned Guiren's heart. How she was full of relentless questions, how she challenged him, how she delighted him with her stubbornness. How she shattered her mother's favorite vase and he had to punish her even though he didn't want to."

I am surprised to find myself smiling. "You could have fooled me."

The Ghost laughs. "I wanted to meet this little girl so badly it made me want to live."

My heart clutches in my chest. I am not that little girl. "My father is a good storyteller."

"Yes, he is. But the best stories are true."

"Why won't you meet me, then?"

"Isn't this enough for now?"

No. "I suppose."

"Good. Now, tell me a story. Tell me about the southern sea."

My fingers find the tip of my braid and play with it. I don't know why I suddenly feel shy. I think it's because

I am realizing that the Ghost knows so much about me, has known me much longer than I've known him. I feel as naked as I actually am, and that thought sends a jolt of anxiety straight through me. "You can't see me, can you?"

"Not right now, no."

"Not now?"

"I can hear you when you're at the altar, but I can see you as well. When you're in the cafeteria and in Mugo's office, too."

I groan. I'll be back there tomorrow morning. "How do you do it? Is it magic?"

"If you consider lenses and mirrors magical, then yes." His voice is less hoarse now, like our conversation has been the oil it needed to run smoothly.

"I don't, but I also don't understand how they help you see."

"Then leave me to my secrets and tell me a story."

So I do. I talk and talk, whispering in the dark, telling him about waves and saltwater on my tongue. About crabs and the sun sinking into the ocean, how I expected it to send steam billowing into the sky and was disappointed when it didn't. He laughs in all the right places, asks questions that tell me he's listening. I talk until I'm the one who's hoarse, until I run low on stories and confide that I am terrified of the morning.

"I will make this better for you," he says softly. "I want to see you smile."

I want to tell him I might, if he were to talk to me face-to-face, but I know he doesn't want that. I think he is ashamed of how he looks, but I can't imagine anyone with a voice as kind as his being ugly. I don't say that, though, because I don't want him to fall silent. So I say, "I'm smiling now."

It's true. I'm no longer hollowed out, no longer alone. His voice has filled in some of the gaps. He's here with me, and I know that now. But I don't know how to say that. I feel stupid even trying.

"I am too," he says. "So this is your offering for tonight. It's more than enough."

With a start I hear my father come into the clinic and drop his satchel on his chair. "My father is home."

"Sleep well, Wen," the Ghost says. I like how he says my name, low and heavy, like it carries weight.

"Ghost?"

"Yes?"

"You know my name—can I know yours?"

"If you ask Onya or Hazzi or even your father, I'm sure they will tell you."

"I want to hear it from you, though."

He chuckles, husky and close, even though I know he is several floors away. "Is that a wish?"

"If you want to call it that."

In the silence I hear my father washing his hands in the sink downstairs. Any moment he will come up. Finally, as the tap switches off, the Ghost says, "My name is Bo."

It's a simple name. A nice name. It brings him near, makes him human. "Can I call you Bo from now on?"

"Please," he breathes, so quiet, as my father's weight makes the steps creak.

"Sleep well then, Bo," is all I have time to say before my father walks through the door.

I pretend to be asleep while my father goes to the washroom and disappears into his alcove. He moves heavily, like the day has sucked him dry. I felt the same way a few hours ago, but now I am the opposite. As I poured out my words to Bo, he gave me something back, and now I am wrapped in the dark, warm and still, all of me quiet.

Long after he has stopped listening, before I drift into dreaming, I whisper my final words to my Ghost. "Bo . . . thank you."

Chapter Thirteen

FATHER WAKES UP EARLY and announces that the clinic will be closed for the next two days. "I need to purchase supplies," he says. "This sickness has nearly emptied us out of willow bark, clove and eucalyptus oil, opium, and antiseptic." He holds up our bottle of topical antiseptic and shakes it, showing me it's nearly drained. "I'm going to go up to Kanong."

The factory gives my father a tiny budget for supplies, but he never says no to anyone, so I can only assume he's already run through the yearly allotment and needs to use his own money to get more. Kanong, a large town nearly a full day's walk away, has a huge black market where supplies can be had much cheaper than in the Ring.

"Be careful," I say as he puts on his hat and coat.

"And pray we don't have any medical emergencies!"

He kisses my forehead and says he'll be back tomorrow night. After he's gone, I drink my tea in the silence he's left behind and get dressed. Mugo told me to wear the white muslin, but I can't bring myself to do it because that would make me feel like a whore. And also because it's missing its bottom tier thanks to those evil spiders. I put on the rather staid cream wool; its only extravagance is the edging of black lace around the waist, cuffs, and hem. I twist my hair in a thick bun at the base of my neck. I think it makes me look older, and I hope that might make Mugo leave me alone.

I have no idea how Bo manages it, how he knows what I need, but when I arrive at Mugo's office, I'm certain he's done something to the evil typewriter. It practically purrs for me. The keys respond to my lightest touch, and the ink is sure and solid on the page. By lunchtime I'm through the stack of notes from yesterday and ready for another.

Mugo is agitated this morning. He paces his office while he talks on the phone to a cattle supplier, hurling curse words and even threats. The rancher wants a better price for the bulls, but Mugo is ruthless. Also, maybe desperate. I can tell by the whine in his voice. Gochan One has not been producing its quota, mostly because of the sick factory workers, and that means the money is not flowing as it should.

Vie peeks in at the lunch hour. I know she thinks I'm an idiot for paying the Noor debt, but she also seems to be in a good mood, and I am happy to see a smiling face. I depart for the cafeteria with her as soon as Mugo allows it.

She is telling me about her latest outing with Iyzu and his parents in the Ring when the Noor file in for their first meal of the day, and my eyes drift to Melik before I can stop them. He looks as hungry as the rest, but he has his arm around Sinan's bony shoulders as they walk to the cafeteria line, and when I see him slip a bun from his own plate onto his brother's, I have to look away. It makes things too confusing.

"You're not listening to me," Vie complains.

"What?" I blink at her. "You were telling me about how Iyzu's going to take you out for First Holiday."

Vie and I have celebrated First Holiday together many times, silly schoolgirls weaving through the crowd, elated to be free of our parents, stuffing our mouths with candied dates and burning our tongues on dumplings ladled straight from the pot, giggling at the strong men flexing their huge muscles, and shrieking at the fire-eaters and sword-swallowers.

Vie rolls her eyes. "I was telling you I have a boy for you, too, and we can all go together." She leans forward and winks. "Lati's had his eye on you for some time."

I swallow a bite of rice and beans. "Wait . . . Lati? What?"

Vie looks at me like I've lost my mind. "Don't tell me you haven't noticed!"

"I've only talked to him once." I can barely get the sentence out, because Melik has risen from his seat and is walking toward us.

Vie keeps chattering at me. "You *are* coming with us tomorrow night. You need to get away from the factory, Wen." She pats my arm, but I don't even look in her direction. I'm too busy staring at Melik, whose jaw is set with determination as he stops in front of our table.

"Can I talk to you for a minute?" he asks me.

Vie's mouth drops open, as if she can't believe the nerve of this Noor who doesn't know his place. She clutches at my hand like she's trying to offer me support. But I don't need it.

"I don't see why I should talk to you about anything," I say, loudly enough for everyone at the surrounding tables to hear.

His cheeks flush a ruddy red. "Please, for a minute."

Everyone is looking at us, and I immediately regret drawing attention to myself. I stand up so he'll be able to hear me as I say from between clenched teeth, "Leave me alone. It hasn't been hard for you lately, so I don't see why it would be a problem for you now."

He tilts his head to the side. "Did you pay our debts?"

"I have no idea what you're talking about," I say, but Vie makes a skeptical noise that gives me away.

Melik's gaze snaps to her and back to me. "You didn't have to. We would have—"

"How will you pay your debts if you're wasting your coin on a whore?" I blurt out before I can think better of it.

Melik's eyes fly wide. "What?" And then his expression changes, dawning with understanding. He looks around nervously, then gestures toward an empty section of the cafeteria. Thinking he's going to make his confession, I follow him until he stops near the far wall, away from ears but not from eyes—everyone in the cafeteria is staring. Vie is gaping like she's never seen anything so scandalous. Iyzu and Lati stand near the food line with their trays piled high, frowning and whispering as they watch us. It's almost enough to set me in motion, but not quite. I want to hear the truth from Melik, even if it hurts.

"Did someone say something to you?" he hisses.

I scoff. My heartbeat is pounding in my temples. "I saw it myself."

His mouth becomes a tight line as he nods at me, and then he speaks in a low voice meant only for my ears. "And you found it so easy to believe I would do something like that."

Actually, it was so hard to believe that it hurt like a blazing brand on my heart, singeing me to ashes. If I'd heard a rumor that Melik had visited a whore, I would not have believed it. But I cannot deny what I saw with my own eyes. "Easier than anything else I did yesterday."

Like paying his debt after he broke my heart.

His jaw is working, like he's grinding his teeth. "Then you're a stupid girl, to judge so quickly. I guess that makes you the same as everyone else around here, though."

"What about you? You blame me for Tercan's death. You had no trouble believing I wanted him to be hurt. I can tell by the way you looked at me."

He crosses his arms over his chest. "Sinan overheard you confessing."

So that's what happened. Tercan was unconscious when I whispered to him, but Sinan might have been awake, listening quietly as I poured out my sorrow and guilt. I can't imagine what he told his brother, but my guess is that it was colorful in the way only teenage boys can manage.

"And you believed so readily," I say. "Do you know

SARAH FINE

what actually happened?" The acid is pouring out of me
now, gushing through the tear in my heart. This has been
brewing inside of me ever since Tercan got hurt, all the
beatings I've given myself over this, all the moments I've
hated myself. The defiance rises from me like a giant
wave, ready to lay waste to everything.

"I didn't believe in the Ghost. I tossed out a tin coin
and told him to prove he was real." My fists are clenched
in my skirt. "I thought nothing of it, and I'm sorry for
all of it. I'll live with the regret for the rest of my life.
But I never told the Ghost to hurt him. I'd *never* . . ." My
voice breaks and I stamp my foot to try to keep control
of myself. "I'm glad you believe me to be so bloodthirsty,
though. I'm happy it was so easy, because that tells me
all I need to know about *you*." I brush my hand over my
shoulder, showing this awful, cruel boy exactly what I
think of him.

Melik steps back as he takes it in. He's gripping his
upper arms so tightly that his fingers are white. His
mouth opens and closes a few times, and then he says
something in Noor that might be a curse, because he
spits it with such venom. He closes his eyes and inhales
sharply, pivots on his heel, and stalks back to his table.

The cafeteria is silent. Melik and I have supplied
today's entertainment, and we are riveting. I smooth
back a lock of my hair that has wormed its way loose from
my bun, straighten my skirt, and walk from the cafeteria
with my head held high. As soon as I leave, the whispers
and guffaws rise from the workers, but I don't care what
they think, or even that Lati, who is apparently my date
for First Holiday, saw the whole thing.

I spend the afternoon typing, thinking of Bo and wondering if he's watching me. He said he could see what happens inside Mugo's office, and so I spend a full hour smiling like an idiot. I daydream for a bit as I file things away, wondering if Bo will talk to me tonight, if he'll tell me something about himself. My musings make the time go fast—and keep me from stewing about Melik and how much I despise him.

As I'm getting ready to leave for the day, Mugo comes out of his office and hands me a note. "Deliver this to Ebian," he instructs. His fingers stroke mine as I take the paper, and I force myself not to snatch my hand away.

I walk slowly to the entrance of the killing floor. I've been there only once, the first day my father was showing me around. I had to flee quickly and find a place to throw up. I really hope that doesn't happen today. It would be hard to clean vomit off this wool dress.

I swing the door open, expecting to be greeted with a crash of sound, but the only thing I hear is the lowing of the cattle from the distant edge of the killing floor. Everything else has stopped. A group of men is gathered around the central machine on the floor, the giant, whirring system that sends the razor-sharp meat hooks flying around the room to pick up the flayed cow carcasses and carry them from station to station to have parts of them hacked off and packaged. In some places the hooks are eye level, carrying the meat past the men with the long knives. But then the hooks flow up, sliding what's left high over the floor, across the vast space to the giant refuse bins. The hooks are still now, and the men gathered around the machine are gazing at a spot about twenty feet off the ground, where the hooks rise to their highest point. A tall, rickety wooden ladder has been propped against the main column.

"What's going on?" I ask one of the workers, a rail-thin man standing next to me, holding a clipboard. He must be one of the meat inspectors, who my father told me are paid mostly to look the other way.

"Something jammed. We turned off the power so he could unblock it," he says, and points to the man on the ladder.

It's Melik.

He climbs steadily, a look of total concentration on his face. Despite myself, despite everything I said to him a few hours ago, despite the fact that we have no use for each other at all, my feet carry me forward until I bounce off Sinan, who is standing at the edge of the crowd, his eyes fixed on his brother.

"Why him?" I whisper.

"He's the tallest," Sinan answers in a very small voice.

Melik reaches the top of the ladder and raises his arms high, trying to catch hold of the metal pipes that run alongside the hooks. He wraps his fingers around one and edges himself to the side. It groans with his weight. His boots are on the top rung of the ladder, but the rest of him is suspended over one of the huge conveyor belts piled high with beef flanks. Melik holds on to the thin pipe with one hand as he reaches for a spot between two empty hooks.

As his fingers stretch, I think of Bo, how his shirt got caught on one of the spinners, how he went from whole to ruined in an instant. Melik pokes at whatever's gummed up the gears. He's biting his lip, leaning far out from the ladder. Sinan scoots closer to me, like he needs an anchor. His fear for Melik is contagious. Or maybe, I hate to admit, I have enough fear for Melik all on my own.

Finally Melik pries a small object from between the thin rubber belts that slide the wickedly curved hooks along. When he pulls it out, it brings a glittering snowfall of metal shavings with it. With it pinched between two fingers, he slowly inches back until his feet are stable on the ladder. He flips the object into his open palm and frowns at it. It is at that exact second that the slaughter machines of the Gochan One killing floor roar to life.

Heads jerk up and a startled shout comes from the workers as the spinner jolts and the belts start to move. Several of the men look around in confusion. Melik clings to the main column as the thunder of the machinery shakes his ladder. His eyes widen as the gears whir— and then send the meat hooks flying right at him.

The moment lasts forever, and every detail is carved into my heart. Melik twists on the ladder. The first hook slides by him, skimming over his shoulder, but the second snags his chest. He is slammed against the column as his blood rains down on the Noor standing below him. Sinan screams like the child he is.

And then Melik loses his balance and flies off the ladder, crashing onto the moving conveyor belt twenty feet below.

Chapter Fourteen

THREE OF THE NOOR try to grab Melik's body before it is shuttled to a different part of the killing floor by the relentless conveyor belt. Ebian rushes over, waving his stumpy arms, all jowls and brows. "Get that filthy Noor off our meat! His blood will contaminate everything!"

Sinan's eyes flash and he lunges for Ebian, but two older Noor grab him by the shoulders and drag him away before Ebian even notices. Ebian keeps yelling at the three boys who are now lifting Melik off the belt. His chest is a mess. His eyes are closed and his face is pale. His wine-red blood drips from his limp fingertips as his friends carry him to an open spot between machines and lay him on the grimy concrete floor. Sinan is crying now, and his pain jolts me from my frozen horror.

"Pick him up and follow me," I bark at the Noor, who seem to understand my body language, if not my words. They hoist Melik up and carry him toward me, and I march straight for the door.

I do not turn around as I head down the hall, but I know by the shuffle and scuff of boots that the Noor are right behind me. Sinan follows them, sobbing. Even with all that noise, the sound that is loudest to me is the faint *pit-pat* of Melik's blood flowing from his body. Of course, this is the day my father is gone. This is the day the clinic is closed. This is the day I am all on my own.

I fling open the clinic door and pull on my apron as the Noor lay Melik on the exam table. As I roll up my sleeves and wash my hands, I breathe—in-out, in-out—forcing myself to maintain a steady rhythm. My hands are swift and sure as I scrub between my fingers and under my nails with the only scrap of germ-killing soap we have left.

The Noor are standing over Melik. One of them has his forehead against Melik's and is whispering to him.

"Go back to your shift," I order. "I'm going to take care of him." I point at the door.

The Noor don't budge. I turn to Sinan, who is hovering in the doorway.

"Did you pray to your Ghost?" he asks, his voice broken and airy. "Did you wish for this to happen?"

I swallow back tears of frustration. It's almost too much, that Sinan would believe I want Melik to be hurt. "I would *never*," I say.

Then, because Melik cannot afford for me to stand here whimpering like a child, I suck in a breath through my nose and yank my apron straight. And when I speak again, my voice is loud and authoritative. "Tell them they won't be able to afford medicine for him if they don't get back to work."

I have no intention of making them pay for Melik's care, but I need them to back off and give me space to work on him. My response must strike Sinan as genuine, because he translates, and then all of them move slowly to the door, their eyes on the bleeding figure on the table. The door clicks shut behind them.

Now it is just me and the boy who needs me to be my absolute best.

I lean my ear close to his face and am relieved to feel the warmth of his breath. He is unconscious but alive, though I don't know how bad it is. He must have hit his head when he fell. If his brain is swelling or if something's broken in there, there is nothing I can do for him.

I begin with his head. My fingers map his skull, searching his scalp for soft spots, and discover a bump the size of a duck's egg on the left side. I lift his eyelids, and his pupils go from giant to tiny immediately, reacting to the light. I think that's good.

I touch him all over, his face, his shoulders, his arms and hands and each of his fingers, his back and hips and belly, his legs and knees, probing and poking. He is strong and whole, everywhere. Everywhere except his chest. But that is more than enough to occupy me.

I retrieve a pair of scissors, a set of clampers, a curved needle, and a spool of suturing thread from one of my father's drawers. I place them on a tray and carry it to the exam table, where I set it next to Melik's head. I cut his torn shirt off his body. The long wound starts at the center of his chest, right over his heart, and traverses the muscle on the left side, ending in a deep puncture wound above his collarbone. That part's burbling blood like a little fountain, and I pack it with cotton gauze.

Melik moans and shifts his feet like he wants to run away. He's too big for this exam table, and his lower legs are hanging over the edge. I'll be thrilled if he doesn't fall off while I'm trying to work.

He's talking now, low and desperate words, but I don't understand anything he's saying because it's all in Noor. I regret sending Sinan away, because he could have helped me. I bend and whisper in his ear, "Melik, it's Wen. I'm here with you." I need him to speak my language. I want to understand him. "I'm going to help you. Can you look at me?"

He lurches away from me and throws up all over the floor.

I lunge for a cup, fill it with water, and help him take small sips. He's staring at the washbasin, at the floor, so dazed, like he can't figure out where he is. "What happened?" he asks.

"You got cut with the hooks, and then you fell," I say. "Now I have to sew you up."

He falls back, grimacing. I turn on the bright lamp and aim it away from his face, focusing on the chest wound. It's fairly neat, a wicked slice rather than a ragged tear, and it's mostly superficial, thankfully. It could have hooked him beneath his ribs, under his collarbone or his chin, and left him dying in agony while it suspended him over the killing floor, out of everyone's reach. Out of my reach. I look him over, my muscles knotting and unknotting with rage and relief, rage and relief, over and over in an exhausting battle for my state of mind. Melik is too beautiful to be ruined, too strong to be torn apart, and I need him to go on and on, because that's just what seems *right*.

"I'm going to get you as near to perfect as I can," I mutter, "but you have to stay still for me."

"Wen always has medicine," he whispers. There's a ghost of a smile on his face, but it's ghastly with strain. I think he is very confused, and also in a lot of pain. I go to the little drawer where we keep our opium, and nearly cry when I see one tiny stick left. It won't be enough. I pluck it from its bed of cotton batting and take it over to him.

"Look at me, Melik." I have to say it a few times, and the third time I stroke his face with the backs of my fingers, and he looks in my direction. "We're going to have to work together."

"You're so angry at me," he says. "I'm sorry."

I shake my head. "Don't worry about that now. Here." I nudge his lips with the opium stick. "Suck on this for a few minutes, and then I'll get started."

He does what I ask, closing his pale lips around the thin stick of purified opium as I prep his wound for suturing. I use the softest cotton I have to smear a few drops of precious antiseptic over it, and Melik's fingers close over the sides of the table and hold on tight. I don't give him long with the stick, maybe two minutes, only enough for his rigid muscles to slacken. It won't get rid of the pain, but it will dull it a bit. I wish I had a soporific sponge, but we ran out of those a few days ago. Plus, I'm not sure I should let him fade into unconsciousness again, because that lump on his head looks nasty.

I secure the suturing thread to the needle, then clip the clampers right in the center of the needle's arc. I lean over Melik, who is dozing now. "I'm starting, okay? Try not to move."

He doesn't speak until I have the needle poised right over his skin. "I didn't buy the favors of a whore in that salon."

I hold my breath and sink the needle straight into his flesh. He tenses a little, and is only just relaxing as I bring it back up through the other side. He says what I am sure are dirty Noor words while I tie a perfect first stitch with steady hands. "It's not like you needed a haircut," I comment, gazing up at his short rust-red hair.

He manages to chuckle, but it's cut off suddenly as I begin my second stitch.

"You are such a confusing girl," he says as I tie my knot.

"I think that's the opium." Another stitch completed. I will not stop or slow down until this wound is closed and he is perfect again. Every stitch will be just right. As long as he keeps still.

But his fingers find my waist, and they scrabble along the black lace there. "Tercan was so awful to you, but a few hours later you were saving his life and selling your beautiful clothes to take care of him. When Sinan told me you had confessed to wishing evil on Tercan, I cuffed him in the head and told him to stop telling lies."

"But then you saw for yourself and couldn't forgive me for it," I say, thinking of the way his body tensed as he saw the Ghost's altar and the guilty look on my face. The way he walked away from me, cold as frost on the ground. I dip the needle in and up. The tenth stitch is completed. Melik's still touching my waist, spanning it with his fingers, rubbing his thumb along the lace. If he weren't so out of it, he would realize he's being terribly inappropriate. I would tell him, but I need this right now, because it means he's alive.

He stops rubbing and grips my waist more firmly than I'd expect. "I didn't know what to think, Wen. I was grieving," he says, and gasps as I slip my needle through his skin to complete the eleventh stitch. "You seemed too good to be true, and I felt stupid for trusting you so completely, for falling so . . ." He groans. He needs more opium, but I can't afford to give it to him right now. He's going to need it after I patch up that puncture wound in his shoulder.

He's gritting his teeth now, and it would be horribly selfish of me to ask what he was going to say. "I felt terrible about Tercan. And I'm sorry I wasn't as good as you thought I was."

I think he means to laugh, but it sounds so pained that I wince. "No, you were better," he says in a tired voice. "You were real." His fingers fall from my waist. "My head hurts."

"I'll get something for you when I'm done with these sutures, all right? Can you hang on?"

It turns out he can—through fifty-five stitches, and as I pour the burning antiseptic straight into that puncture wound and stitch it up. Even though I give him a few moments with the opium stick beforehand, that part sends his head arching back, makes the tendons in his neck stand out as he bites back his cry. Sweat pours from his body under the bright lamp, under the relentless stab of my curved needle. I want to stop; I want to put my arms over his head and murmur soft words in his ear and shelter him from the merciless girl stitching him up. I want to understand the things he's said to me. I want him to say more. But he doesn't and I don't stop, and when I am done, each stitch is perfect, and the wound is closed and neat. I use the very last of the antiseptic to trace a thin line over the sutures, and then I bandage him up. I let him suck on the opium stick for a few more minutes, and it sends him into a restless doze.

There are a few more hours until the Noor's shift is over, and they probably won't come check on him until then. I clean up the pool of sick on the floor, scrub my hands in the sink, then strip off my apron. I allow myself the luxury of stroking my hand over Melik's feather-soft hair and the coarser stubble that dots his cheeks. I pull up a chair and sit next to him, staring at his face and trying to decide what I believe. He said he didn't buy the favors of a whore, but I don't know what that means. It might mean that this is some kind of misunderstanding. Or it might mean she gave herself to him for free.

Why should I care, anyway? What right do I have to be so angry? Melik isn't mine, although I seem to have claimed him in some secret way that even I don't quite get. But . . . he seems to care what I think. He hasn't yet told me it isn't my concern, which is the first thing I expected to fly from his mouth when we fought in the cafeteria. He didn't seem surprised that I was angry at the thought that he would buy his pleasure from the whores in the Ring. He seemed more upset that I had judged him, that I had assumed he would do something like that.

The Noor return for Melik as soon as the whistle blows, and Sinan nearly crumples when Melik stirs and smiles at him. I'd much rather Melik stay here tonight. I don't want to let him out of my sight, but with my father gone, even if Melik is horribly wounded and severely concussed, there would be whispers tomorrow if he and I were in this clinic alone all night. I give Sinan the opium stick and a lot of instructions, most of which involve keeping Melik still, and tell him I'll come to the dorm tomorrow to check on his brother.

Melik is able to rise from the table by himself, which amazes me. I start shouting as the Noor try to duck under his arms to support him, because they come perilously close to tearing the stitches holding him together. I show them how to do it properly, and I let them go. Melik squeezes my hand before he is led away, and I don't know what it means, except that he doesn't hate me.

I drag myself up the stairs and fall into bed, still wearing my cream wool dress, which is speckled and smeared with Melik's blood. He could so easily have died today. If he hadn't moved quickly, if the hook had been a bit sharper, if he had hit the conveyor belt the wrong way, Melik would be gone. We'd be shoving his body into the furnace tomorrow morning.

It hurts me, more than I can put into words. I don't care what he's done; if he leaves my world, I will mourn.

It's a terribly vulnerable feeling, like cradling a robin's egg close to my chest.

"Wen?" Bo's voice comes from the air vent, a whisper in the night.

"I'm here."

"You sound so tired. Are you all right?"

"A boy got hurt on the killing floor today. I just stitched him up."

"He lived?"

"Yes. It could have been so much worse."

He's silent for a few seconds, and then he says, "It was a shame the machinery was switched on before he was safe."

I don't want to think about it anymore. Too many what-ifs and should-haves.

Maybe Bo senses my mood. "Did you notice anything different about your typewriter this morning?"

He's obviously trying to cheer me up, and I do my best to let him. "Did you tame it for me? It went from being a wild beast to a purring kitty."

His laugh is sweet and happy. "Yes. I saw you smiling."

It feels like a hundred years ago. "You'll have to tell me how you did that, but not tonight."

"What do you need tonight?"

I need to know that Melik is all right, but Bo can't give me that. "Tell me something about yourself." I pull my blanket up over my legs and settle in.

"For six of the past seven years, on the night of First Holiday, I've sat on the roof, up by the smokestacks, and watched the fireworks."

"You like fireworks?"

"I love them."

"What did you do the year you didn't watch?"

He lets out a breath. "I . . . ventured into the Ring. To see the sights."

"Do you do that often?"

"Just that once. It was an interesting evening." He pauses, and I wait, but then his tone turns light and joking. "The fireworks are safer."

I laugh, dry and airless. "Tell me why you like them so much."

I drift away to the sound of his voice telling me about the different kinds of ingredients used to make the colored fire that comes bursting forth when the fireworks explode. He knows so much about how things work, how to make and dismantle, how to build and destroy.

And just before I fall asleep completely, a terrible question occurs to me when I think about how shocked all the workers looked as the machinery sprang to life before Melik had a chance to climb down.

Did Bo try to destroy Melik?

Chapter Fifteen

I AM VERY EFFICIENT at work today, even though I am low on sleep. I am determined to do things right so Mugo doesn't keep me late. First Holiday is tonight, and the streets will begin to fill just after the dinner hour. Vie is so excited she can barely do her work. She keeps flitting over from Jipu's office to bother me. She's going to wear her purple velvet dress, the fanciest she has, which I don't think is practical for traipsing around the muddy streets all night. I learned that lesson the year my mother let me wear a dress that made me feel like a walking jewel box—it was stained and ruined, and I never got to wear it again. Practical is not what's on Vie's mind, though. Turning Iyzu's head is. She wants me to dress up too, and keeps asking what I'll be wearing. She doesn't think my brown work dress is up to snuff.

I'm dreading telling her I've already made other plans. I'm going to have to do it at some point, but I keep putting it off. After lunch Mugo comes out of his office and gives me another stack of notes to transcribe. I'm learning so much about how this factory works. Jipu is more of a figurehead. He's from a wealthy family, and his father was the boss before him. Mugo is the guy who keeps the slaughterhouse going. He hires new workers from the Ring or surrounding towns, and he transfers older or less productive workers to another factory to make room . . . though the transfer papers don't ever list its exact location. He also cuts every possible corner. I'm surprised anyone's willing to work here at all. The workers have received wage increases every year . . . but their expenses have gone up as well. Mugo is a details man, so he does it in tiny, barely noticeable ways. A service charge here, a penalty there. I suspect many of the workers haven't even noticed that they aren't bringing more home now than they did last year or the year before.

"You're learning quickly," Mugo says. He's standing right behind me, and I have no idea how long he's been there. I imagine him staring at the back of my neck, and it makes me itchy and squirmy, but I force my fingers to keep typing. He edges closer, so that his legs are touching the back of my chair. "I think it's almost time that I teach you a few new skills."

His fingers dance along my shoulder, and I freeze. They stroke at the boundary between the dress and my skin. His fingers smell of mushrooms and dark, damp places, and my stomach turns. "Oh, sir, I'm barely getting the hang of this typing. I'm not good at anything."

My voice sounds so small, almost a whisper, and it chokes off as he begins stroking up and down my neck in the way that makes me want to cry. I lean away slightly, but his fingers stick to my skin like they're glued there. I want to run, but he would hunt me down, I'm sure. Like those big cats in the southern forest.

He leans down and breathes his onion breath into my ear. "You're such a little girl, Wen, aren't you? Just a little girl." His lips graze my hair, and I shudder.

A thunderous crash from Mugo's office shakes the floor.

Mugo shouts a curse, and I turn to see him running back to his office. I rise from my seat and follow, wondering what on earth could have happened. I turn the corner to see him gaping at the wreckage. His enormous shelving system has collapsed, sending an entire wall of files and accounting books and knickknacks and papers crashing to the floor. It looks like a typhoon has swept through the place. The dusty air glitters with metal shavings as they flutter to the ground like the whirling seeds of elder trees.

Mugo's hands are in his thinning hair, and little growling noises are coming from his throat. "C-c-clean this up!" he shrieks at me.

He vacates the office and leaves me alone for the rest of the day. I am so very thankful, because I have just been handed another day of reprieve from these things he wants to teach me that I don't want to learn.

I clean the mess with a song in my heart, and when it is the end of my workday, I escape as quickly as I can, leaving a note that I'll be in early tomorrow to finish.

Walking out of his office is like shedding a skin; I feel lighter and more powerful. I have a mission today, and I don't have much time.

I have to sell more dresses and make it to the apothecary before he closes for First Holiday. I need to get antibiotics for Melik. I have no idea what foulness was on the meat hook that speared him, but I'm quite sure it will make him very sick unless he has this precious medicine. My legs are like machine pistons as I climb the Hill, select two more of my finest dresses, sell them at cut rate to Khan the tailor, and jog to the apothecary's shop.

The sun is dipping low, a dim yellow ball in the haze of gray smoke on the horizon. The streets are beginning to fill with vendors from the countryside, ready to sell their wares to the people of the Ring. After I wheedle a large bottle of antibiotics from the apothecary, using nearly all my money and what little charm I have, I still have enough to purchase a meat bun from a hunched man with gnarled hands who seems to have the most popular cart on the street. Prizes in hand, I head back to the factory compound, my heart already starting to speed.

I don't recognize Jima at first. She steps out from one of the pink-light salons and pulls a hooded overcoat around her, but then raises her head and waves when she sees me. "Wen!"

"Jima?" She's so pale, and her cheeks are terribly sunken, although it's been less than two weeks since I last saw her. "What are you doing here?"

Her face twists a bit. "My family wouldn't let me come home, so I live here now." She looks up at the top floor of the salon, which leaves me with an uncomfortable twinge in my stomach.

"Why wouldn't your family let you come back?"

Jima looks at me like I am a child. Then she rubs her stomach and looks down at it sadly. "Because they believe I'm an easy girl with loose morals who opens her legs for anyone."

Now I'm confused, because if she's living above the salon, chances are that is exactly what Jima has become. My thoughts must be written all over my face, because Jima pinches my arm with a hard look on her face. "Onya told me you're Mugo's secretary now, so don't look at me like that. If you're not careful, you'll be in my shoes soon enough."

She sniffs and brushes past me, sinking into the crowd before I can summon the words to call her back and apologize. With my thoughts in chaos, I trudge to the factory compound and wave to the guard, who wishes me a happy First Holiday and blows me a kiss. Everyone is a bit crazy on First Holiday.

I am crossing through the compound's square when I see Vie coming toward me, wearing her best purple dress, which hugs her plump, curvy figure. She's flanked by Iyzu and Lati. My *date*. I duck my head and scoot across the square, but Vie is already calling my name. She catches hold of the back of my overcoat a second later.

"Wen! What's wrong with you? We went down to the clinic, but you weren't there. Are you ready to go?"

I bite my lip and look up at Lati, who is eyeing me like I'm a meat bun he's just purchased off a cart. "I can't go tonight. My father's out of town and I have to tend to his patients."

Lati frowns. "His patients? But the men are all over the flu. Jipu was telling me everyone was back at work today except for that Noor . . ." His expression changes from puzzlement to anger.

Vie looks up the path toward the old, ramshackle Noor dorms. "You cannot be serious, Wen."

"You can't go in there," Iyzu says. "They'll rip your dress off and use you up while you scream." He sounds almost eager, like he wishes he could watch.

I stare at him. "No, they won't. I've been there many times, and all they care about is taking care of one another and doing their work."

Lati and Iyzu look at me like I've announced that I work at a pink-light salon. I can only imagine what they're thinking. I'm betting I'll hear about it in the cafeteria tomorrow.

Vie puts her hands on her hips. "Yes, they are such gentlemen. Like the one who tripped you and raised your skirts. Like that rust-haired one who dared to speak to you in front of the whole cafeteria. Why would you help him?"

I cannot seem to hide my thoughts today; they are on my face for all to see. Vie's eyes go wide. "Oh, no. No. You're coming with me." She reaches for my arm.

I back away. "No, I'm not. He needs me, and I'm going."

Lati snatches my bag from my shoulder. "With this? What's in here, anyway?" His thick fingers plunge into my satchel and come out holding the glass bottle of antibiotics.

Everything in me goes still and hard. Melik's life is in that bottle. I cannot allow this stupid boy to take it. "Give that back," I say quietly.

"So you can give it to the Noor? They're pigs, and this is meant for people." He has a weird, cruel smile on his face as he shakes the bottle a bit. I realize his good-natured face hides an ugly, twisted boy underneath.

"They're not pigs, and that is my property. Give it back." My face is hot with anger. I wish I were eight feet tall and just as wide. I want to crush this boy.

He tosses the bottle to Iyzu, who bobbles it in his hands playfully. When I lunge for it, he holds it up over my head.

"Guys," Vie says, and I can tell she feels uncomfortable, but she doesn't say anything else. She doesn't tell them to give it back.

"Oh, man, this is good," Lati says. I whirl around to see him eating the meat bun he's pulled from my bag. "Was this for him too?"

"I'll tell," I say through gritted teeth. "Give it back or I'll tell."

Iyzu leans forward, and I do not miss the menace in his posture. "And who, exactly, would you tell? Your father is just the doctor. He has no authority."

"Mugo." I'm shaking now, my arms, legs, fists. I know what this means, this threat of telling Mugo. It means I would owe him, and that I would have to let him do things to me to make up for his troubles. So I'm hoping this threat doesn't get back to him, and that these idiots are scared of him.

Lati stops midchew, the bun gripped in his meaty fist.

The juice is dripping between his fingers. I think he *is* scared of Mugo. But Iyzu isn't intimidated. Not at all. He laughs. "Underboss Mugo hates the Noor as much as we do."

He tosses the bottle up, high enough for it to disappear into the night sky, and then laughs as I weave back and forth, trying to spot it. He shoves me lightly out of the way and raises his hands to catch it, but grasps empty air as another hand snatches the bottle from space.

"This is hers," Sinan says, tilting his head in my direction. He hands the bottle to me.

For a moment I am terribly afraid for him, this skinny young boy who seems to have no fear except when it comes to his brother's safety. The only thing he has on Lati and Iyzu is height—but they are both twice as wide as he is. They could kill him, and he doesn't even look scared.

Then I see why. We are surrounded.

Chapter Sixteen

WHILE WE'VE BEEN BICKERING, the Noor have emerged from their dorms for their shift, and now there are several dozen of them staring at Lati and Iyzu with set jaws and fire in their eyes. Vie tugs my arm, insistent and desperate. But she's not scared of Lati and Iyzu and their heartlessness—she's scared of the Noor. "Let's go," she hisses.

I rip my arm away from her, wondering why I ever called her a friend. I'm so mad at Vie that I want to slap her. "I'm not going anywhere. I have work to do."

Lati is looking at me so fiercely that I bet he is going to ask the Ghost to give me a terrible disease or make something heavy fall on my head. I'm not afraid of that, though, because I suspect I know the Ghost better than he does. The Noor are watching me with serious faces and chins held high, waiting for my response. I turn my back on Vie and the two cruel, idiot boys, and the Noor step off the path to allow me through. I look over my shoulder to see them closing ranks, blocking me from the view of my supposed friends. They are a solid wall of protection, and the only one who is looking at me is Sinan. Before I turn away, he places his hand on his heart and turns his palm to me.

I lift my skirt and run for the dorms like someone's chasing me, and I don't slow down until I am in Melik's room, because oddly enough, it feels like the safest place in the world right now—which isn't saying very much.

He is propped up against the wall, a sleeping pallet rolled behind him. In his hands is a book, but he closes it quickly and slips it under his pallet as I barge in. It's cool in here tonight, dank. He has a work shirt draped over his shoulders, but beneath it I see the thick bandage dotted with blood. He gives me a questioning look as I step into the room, panting. I must look like a hunted rabbit, and suddenly I'm ashamed for bringing this to his doorstep. I take a deep breath. "Happy First Holiday," I say in a cheerful voice that wavers on the last word. "Do the Noor . . . celebrate it?"

"Happy First Holiday," he murmurs. "And no, we don't. Shouldn't you be out enjoying the festivities?"

I can't stop the crazy laugh that bursts from my throat. "I tried to bring you a meat bun."

He raises an eyebrow but doesn't ask me what happened to it. "My brother brought me some rolls from the cafeteria," he says, holding them up. "They won't let me starve."

Of course they won't. The Noor take care of one another, and they seem to treasure Melik. "I'm glad," I say. "I brought you medicine, and it shouldn't be taken on an empty stomach."

"Wen always has medicine." His smile is wry and has the pull of the moon. Like the tides, I flow straight toward him.

He tries to drag a pallet over for me to sit on, but I bat his hand away. "You'll pull your stitches. I do beautiful work. Don't ruin it." I glare at the spots of blood on his bandage.

He looks down at himself. "I've tried to be careful. When will I be able to go back to work?"

"Well, you have tomorrow off for the holiday, and then we'll see. Can I look?"

He nods and then watches my fingers as they peel back the bandage from his chest. My breath becomes faster as I realize how intimate this is, how close I am to him, how my hands are touching his naked chest. Last night he was half crazed with opium and pain, but right now he's all here, and his skin is radiating warmth. I focus on the stitches, on the injured parts of him rather than the smooth cream-white flesh stretched over hard muscles. Those are none of my business.

"It looks all right," I say, sounding like I've just run the length of the compound.

"You must be an amazing seamstress," he says quietly.

I secure the bandage again and sit back. "How would you know that?"

He shrugs, wincing as it pulls his stitches. "Your dresses. They are so fancy. Like the daughter of a factory boss."

"And not the company doctor."

His eyes linger on the silky roses embroidered into the collar of my overcoat. "Did you make them yourself?"

"My mother did." I slip the coat off to reveal my brown work dress. This is the real me, the Wen-without-her-mother. "She taught me the stitches, but I am not an artist like she was."

His somber expression tells me he understands that she is dead. "That's why you live here with your father."

My smile is small. "Only for the past several weeks. I used to live in the Ring, up on the Hill."

"I've heard of it," he says. "That's where Jipu and Mugo live. Where all the factory bosses live. It's a fine place."

I have no idea why he knows where the bosses live. "They do. I went to school with Jipu's daughter. Our house was never as fine as theirs. It's the smallest cottage, actually, right on the edge of the Western Hills. I used to look up at them and dream of what was on the other side."

Melik touches the bottle of antibiotics. "I wonder how closely your dreams compare to reality."

I watch his hands, callused and hard, and know my dreams were those of a silly little girl. What was on the other side of the Western Hills was him, and his people, and whatever they have been through. "Would you like to tell me?"

"Only if you want to know," he says. His hand slowly travels over to mine, which are curled in my lap. They unfurl for him, and I watch our fingers tangle together, trying to translate the shapes they make. But they speak a language I do not understand, and I'm not sure Melik does either, because he's watching them too, like they are outside of us, not connected to us.

"I want to know you." It is the most real thing I've said all day.

"We are permitted to work the land, but we can never call it ours. Did you know that?"

"I know many of the Noor are farmers and sheepherders." I have heard many a joke about how they breed with the animals, in fact, but now I realize how pathetic and degrading that is.

"That is the work we are allowed to do, but always for others, never for ourselves." His fingers tighten around mine. "And that won't change, because we do not make the rules."

We lock eyes. "I was a little girl when the Noor rebelled. My mother told me they wanted to rule. That they wanted to take over, first the western province, then the entire country."

He chuckles. "I was eight. And we wanted to rule *ourselves*, Wen. Is that wrong, to want that? You see how we're treated here. It's no different on the other side of the hills, no matter that there are more Noor there than Itanyai. We wanted a place in the government." He bows his head. "My father went with elders from other villages to negotiate in the capital city. He kissed me good-bye and told me to take care of my mother. He told me he was going to make sure Sinan and I had a future, that he was going to make sure we could look any man in the eye and know we were worth just as much."

Melik's hand trembles in mine, but not with weakness.

It is a raw, hard unsteadiness, like I am holding his rage between my fingers. I am afraid to speak, so when he whispers, "Would you like to know what happened next?" I can only nod.

"It was a ruse. They had no intention of giving us a seat at the table. When my father and the other Noor elders arrived in the capital, they were greeted with nooses. Hanged in the public square. No discussion. No negotiation. No warning, no trial. That was the beginning of the uprising."

My stomach aches. This is not the story I was told. Our newspapers spun tales of Noor greediness, unreasonable demands, threats, and unjustified attacks. "The government sent war machines."

He nods. He is staring at our hands, mine toasted almond and his ruddy tan, a few shades that make all the difference. "My mother fled with us into the high passes of the Western Hills, and if she hadn't, we would have died like so many in our village did. The machines crushed everything in their paths. Sinan grew up playing in the muddy trenches they made as they destroyed the fields and our village. I'm glad he doesn't remember much about it." He raises his head. "But I do."

"I'm sorry." It is such a stupid thing to say. But I have no other words.

His gaze drifts over my shoulder. "Things were not always like this. A thousand years ago the Noor held the west. It was an empire," he says, staring at the wall like he can see his people's great history. "But that was before the Itanyai decided they wanted it for themselves. They took it from us, so long ago that most have forgotten it was ever ours to begin with." He smiles sadly. "And when we rose up and tried to take it back, we had a few guns, a few bombs supplied by sympathizers. But for the most part our only weapons were sickles and threshers."

And the Itanyai had metal monsters that crush and kill. I pull my fingers from his. It seems wrong to be touching him, this boy who survived so much evil brought down on him and his family by my people.

"Are you remembering the headlines and horror stories about the barbaric Noor?" he asks me. "At least a few of them are true, I'm sure."

"No, I feel awful about all of it. And I don't understand why you . . ." *I don't understand why you look at me—an Itanyai—the way you do.*

Melik recaptures my hand and holds it firmly. "How old did you say you were when all this happened?" There is a hint of amusement in his voice.

"Does it matter? My people did this to yours."

His thumb traces a circle on my palm. "There are millions of Itanyai. Maybe if more of them were like you or your father, none of it would have happened."

"I think my father admires you," I say. "He believes you are educated, and that is what he values."

"My father taught me your language," he explains. "I worked in the fields like the rest, but after he was gone, I also translated when anyone needed medical care or government permits, things like that."

"That's why the men look up to you."

He smiles. "That, and I'm taller than most of them."

That's not why they look up to him. Melik is not loud

about his power; in fact, he is quite quiet about it. But it vibrates from him; it's like electricity, like sound. He can't hide it for too long, because those around him feel it against their skin.

"Why were you willing to come here?" I ask. "Didn't you know it would be just as bad, and maybe worse?"

"I don't suppose you have heard about the drought."

"I heard about how the rains aren't coming." It's why the price of vegetables has doubled in the past year, why there are rumors of food shortages in the bigger cities. I am ashamed that I never considered what it might mean for the farmers.

Melik's finger strokes over my thumb. "I couldn't let my mother starve. I promised my father I would take care of her. I was willing to do almost anything, but Sinan ended up making the decision for us."

We both laugh, because Sinan is a force unto himself. "Is he as young as I think he is?"

Melik's smile is as warm as sunlight as he thinks of his brother. "Yes, he's only thirteen, if you can believe it. I have no idea how he got that work pass and signed up for this job, but when he did, I had no choice. He'd signed a contract, and I couldn't let him come here alone. And the rest of the men, they followed me, drawn by promises of money enough for our families to keep their bellies full." His smile fades quickly. "Now we are stuck here."

I squeeze his hand. "Does Sinan feel guilty? Do the others give him a hard time?"

He shakes his head. "No, Sinan still believes we can make money here. He's only a boy, and the others feel protective of him. And many are as hopeful as he is."

I bite my lip. Sinan could not have known what he was doing to all of them, but Melik does, especially now. He has to have figured out that Mugo will never let them earn enough to send money home. "You should leave," I say, even though my chest feels hollow at the thought.

"I don't think so." Melik's voice is hard. "We will not leave until we are paid what we're owed."

I drag my eyes away from our tangled hands. "What are you talking about?"

He meets my gaze for a moment and then looks away. "I don't know why I said that. You've already paid so many of our debts." He pulls his hand from mine and lifts the bottle, staring at the pale green liquid inside. "And now you've paid for this as well. Should I ask how much it cost you?"

I take it from him and reach into my satchel for the dosing cup. "No. But I can tell you how you'll pay me back."

"Oh?" His eyes spark with mischief. "I hope you'll be creative."

My mouth drops open at his forwardness, but what comes from it is a laugh instead of a reprimand. I pour the medicine into the little cup and hand it to him. He does not take his eyes from my face as he drinks it down, grimacing at its sick-sweet taste. The apothecary adds way too much sugar to cover up the bitterness.

"I don't want you to think about debt and owing," I say. "This is from me to you."

He lowers the cup from his mouth. A tiny bit of medicine clings to the stubble above his upper lip. "A gift," he says.

"A gift," I agree, and reach forward to wipe his lip

SARAH FINE

before I think about it. He catches my hand as soon as my thumb brushes his skin. He gives it the lightest of tugs, but I move like I'm water, like I'm light as air. My hand slides over his uninjured shoulder, and he reaches for me as I rise to my knees. His hands on my waist are a shock, overwhelming, tender and powerful and addictive.

We are nearly nose to nose. His breath smells like antibiotics, sweet and bitter. I'm lost in the jade of his eyes. My heart is beating like the wings of a hummingbird.

There's a moment of stillness between us. We're standing on this threshold, about to step over, and . . . he's waiting for me. His look is expectation, hope, and a glint of nervousness. I have a choice to make. Do I believe that he didn't pay another woman for his pleasure? Do I forgive him? Do I want to share him? Is he worth having?

He senses my hesitation, I think. He takes my face in his hands. "Wen, don't do this unless you believe me. Don't betray yourself like that."

"I know what I saw."

"Did you see me with a woman?"

I shake my head. My cheeks are flaming beneath his palms.

"Because I wouldn't touch anyone else. I don't want to since I met you." He releases me and I sit back. I am amazed by him; he speaks the wishes of his heart so plainly, without any embarrassment at all. He is saying he wants *me*, but that feels like so much. I've never even kissed a boy, and he seems like a man, like someone who understands the world.

He watches me carefully. "It doesn't matter whether you feel the same way or not, but I think you do."

"I believe you," I say, because the alternative, that he is lying, doesn't seem possible to me. Not as I'm looking into his eyes and seeing myself reflected there. "But I've never—I'm just . . ." I raise my arms and let them fall. I don't know how to do any of this.

He catches one of my hands on the way down and laces his fingers with mine again. "Is this okay?"

I nod. I don't know how he knows what I need.

A muted explosion outside startles both of us. Melik looks toward the tiny window, which has been closed against the coming night chill. Purple and yellow blossoms bloom on the glass. "The fireworks," I murmur. "They're starting."

I settle in next to him, much closer than is proper, but I don't care. We're facing the window, and he's holding my hand so tightly that no one could tear me from his side. In this cool, dank room I'm warm because he is near. I put my head on his good shoulder. When I glance over, his eyes are on the lights, and there's a smile on his face, and this is the most perfect moment I have ever experienced.

"Melik?"

I jerk at the sound of my father's voice and scramble back from Melik like he's tried to bite me. I smooth my hair and pick up the bottle and the dosing cup. Melik must grasp my situation, because he closes his eyes and slumps down, looking much more sick and weak than he actually is.

My father turns the corner a second later and freezes as he takes in the tableau in front of him, me holding the medicine in my shaking hands, and Melik looking like he needs a lot more than antibiotics if he's going to live through the night.

"Wen. I thought you'd be out," my father says. He smells of the road, of two days' hard walking. He must have heard about the accident and come straight here without even washing up. "How bad is he?"

The tightness in my chest loosens a bit. If my father's going to give me a hard time about being alone in this room with Melik, he's decided to do it in private, and I'm eternally grateful for that. "He hit his head pretty hard, but he's been responsive and talking today."

My father kneels next to Melik, who greets him groggily. Then Father turns to me. "I'm going to take a look at him. Go ahead, Wen. Have your fun tonight."

He smiles at me, but this is a dismissal. He probably wants Melik to take his shirt off so he can take a good look at the entire injury. As he peels back Melik's bandage, I stand up, gathering my bag and straightening my skirt. I don't look at Melik as I turn to the door. I'm afraid my face will give me away again.

"Wen? One more thing."

I freeze, my hand on the doorjamb. "Yes?"

"You did an excellent job with the sutures. He'll barely have a scar."

"Thank you." I walk down the hall slowly, straining to hear what my father is saying to Melik, but I give up quickly because the fireworks are so loud. I burst into the open air, sucking in a lungful of smoky First Holiday smells, letting the chill cool my heated skin. Something inside me has shifted, and now part of me is not my own. It's Melik's. And part of him belongs to me. Maybe. Sort of. I think. I don't want to consider all the reasons nothing should happen between us. All I want to do is let it be.

I make my way down the path as the fireworks whistle over my head, high above the town. And I can't help it, I think of Bo, how much he loves them, how he goes up to the . . . my eyes drift to the roof of the factory, to a spot next to the smokestacks.

My breath catches in my throat. There, at the edge of the roof, I swear I see a silhouette, flashing black and yellow and red as the fireworks boom. He shimmers beneath the lights, glints like metal, and I rub my eyes and look again, trying to make sense of what I'm seeing. He's so distant, but I can just make him out, slightly off kilter, one arm longer than the other.

I stand in place for a long time, held there by my curiosity, until the fireworks grow dim and all that lights the sky is the harvest moon, fat and orange and eerie. The shadowy man is still there too, and I shiver because I've just realized something. All this time I've been watching him, his face hasn't been turned up to the sky. He hasn't been watching the fireworks.

He's been watching me.

Chapter Seventeen

I SLEEP HARD and dream of Melik's hands around my waist and Bo's silhouette stark against the night sky. The morning shift whistle sends me scrambling because I remember I have to finish cleaning the wreck of Mugo's office. He'll be angry if I don't finish today.

My father had a good trip to Kanong; we're all stocked up with black-market supplies, and he's in an excellent mood as he makes our tea, whistling a strain from a song my mother used to sing. He says Melik should recover completely and he couldn't have done a better job treating him himself. He says maybe I should go to medical school, maybe we should try to save enough to pay for the tuition. I can't bear to tell him that there is only one more dress hanging in that closet in the cottage, and as fine as it is, it won't pay for more than a few weeks' supply of medicine. And also, I've seen his balance sheet in Mugo's office—my tuition would be less costly than what he already owes this company. I will not be going to medical school. Ever.

I wear my memories of last night like armor as I arrive at work. The way Melik looked at me, how I think we were going to kiss but Melik didn't push. How he held my hand and it was perfect. It's First Holiday today, and the killing floor closes at noon. It will be the same on Second and Third Holiday, the only times during the feasting season that the floor falls silent. I'm off at noon too, and wondering if it would be too improper for me to go over to the Noor dorms to check on Melik. Maybe he'll feel well enough to take a walk with me.

Because I am stupidly hopeful, I wear my rose-colored wool dress, warm but pretty, with entwining night-blooming roses and thorns along the hem. I weave a matching ribbon through my braid.

And as soon as Mugo arrives at the office, I regret my choice and wish for my brown work dress. He grins and shows his chipped front tooth. He watches as I crawl across his floor, sweeping up dust and metal shavings, picking up files and papers that crashed to the floor when the shelves collapsed yesterday. I ignore him and think of other things, like the sun and the sea and Melik's smile.

Just before noon I am at my little desk, behind the enormous, tame typewriter that now does my bidding. Mugo comes out of his office and stands there with that oily grin on his face, like he's waiting for something.

Then the knock comes and Melik walks in, and if I didn't know how hurt he was, I'd never be able to guess, because he stands straight as ever. He doesn't spare me a glance as he greets Mugo. "You asked to see me, Underboss?"

"Ah. Melik. Yes, I wanted to talk to you about your absence from work. Your station was left unattended for two nights in a row." Mugo is right behind my chair now, and I sit a little straighter to put some space between us. I wonder if I'm imagining it when I see Melik stiffen.

"I was injured, sir, as you know. I unjammed the meat hooks, but the machinery began to run before I got down." Melik's voice is so calm, so level. But every inch of him is vibrating with tension.

Mugo's hand slips over my shoulder and takes hold of my braid. He slips his finger along the ribbon I weaved through it this morning. Not for him. Not for his fingers or his eyes. I want to jerk myself away, but I won't. I can't. I think of my father and his debt. Mugo could turn us both out into the Ring, penniless, in the middle of winter. He could strap Melik with fines so big he'll never be able to pay them back. I've seen what Mugo can do, the lives he can ruin. I've seen Jima, pregnant and sick and abandoned. She's right; I could be just like her. I sit very, very still.

"It was reported to me that you were loitering in your dorm, unchaperoned, with *this* young woman." Mugo gives my braid a little tug.

Melik clears his throat. "I was receiving medical care. Dr. Guiren can confirm this."

Mugo releases my braid. His mushroomy fingers are on my neck, and then—oh, I want to die—they are on the front of me, stroking down, only a few inches above the neckline of my dress. This is no way to touch a girl. This is private. This is sacred and intimate. I lean back to escape, but I only succeed in trapping myself against his weaselly, damp body. Melik's fists clench. Mugo flattens his palm over my collarbone. The threat is unmistakable. Tears of shame sting my eyes. If this were only about me, I would slap him in the face and storm away, but it's not. So I sit here and allow this disgusting man to fondle me, hating him, hating myself.

"Let me tell you something about Itanyai girls," says Mugo, and there is eagerness in his voice right alongside the menace. "They aren't at all like your Noor sluts, so free with themselves. When you are alone with an Itanyai girl, it has an effect on her reputation. People talk."

"I will remember that in the future, sir," says Melik, deadly quiet. His gaze is riveted to Mugo's hand. His cheeks are flushing a ruddy, angry red. He takes a step back. I don't know whether he's trying to help me or maybe just trying to escape.

Mugo isn't finished, though. "Once you ruin a girl's reputation, the other boys will assume she is fair game. They will assume she doesn't mind if they touch her, if they try to get her alone." I know Mugo can feel the frantic beat of my heart against his hand. He likes how badly he is frightening me. He likes this power, that he can humiliate Melik, the Noor who does not know his place. I can *feel* how much he likes it, because his hips are pressed against my shoulder blade.

I realize the terrible mistake I have made. I should have gone out with my pretend friends for First Holiday. I should have left Melik alone and safe. I should have given

Sinan the medicine to take to him, should have asked my father to check in on him. But in making a spectacle of myself, in making enemies of Iyzu and Lati, in announcing that I was giving up the celebration of First Holiday so I could care for a Noor, I have also gotten Melik in trouble. And that is the last thing he needs.

Mugo's hand slips lower, and his fingers skim the neckline on the front of my dress. I can't take it anymore. I try to squirm away, but Mugo's other hand clamps down painfully on my shoulder, holding me in place.

"Stop," whispers Melik, and I hate the pleading sound of it. This is exactly what Mugo wants.

"But haven't you already claimed this, Noor?" Mugo asks silkily as his fingers curl over my skin, as—

The explosion is deafening. I feel it inside my head, in my chest and belly. The lights go out and I am on the ground as dust billows and metal creaks and men scream and a wave of heat rolls over me. I am under my desk. My chair is overturned.

"Wen!" Melik sounds like he's a million miles away, drowned out by the ringing in my ears.

Another explosion shatters the window outside the office, and somewhere in the darkness Mugo shrieks. Ceiling tiles rain down all around me, shattering on the desk over my head. The dust is in my mouth, my eyes. Strong hands wrap around my waist and pull me up, and I have this stupid thought that Melik is going to pull his stitches, and I open my mouth to tell him so, but I inhale a lungful of acrid smoke and start to cough. Melik shoves me out into the hall and stumbles after me, but I can't see a thing, can't figure out where I am, because everything is upside down and splintered and burning. My foot slips in something, and when I look down, all I see is lumps of charred meat. I don't know if it came from cows or slaughterhouse workers.

I stagger toward a foggy ray of light, and behind me I hear someone, Melik, I think, rasping and whooping, trying to draw air amidst the dust and ash and blood and smoke. I am turning back to make sure he's still walking when a hand wraps around my arm and jerks me into a dark passageway. I can't stop coughing. My eyes are streaming. I am blind and deaf and dumb, and my lungs aren't working. Black and white spots crowd my vision; roaring static fills my ears. I am buried under the earth, and the dirt is suffocating me. I am dead.

No, I'm not. Slowly, reason returns to me. I am being carried, maybe by a person, maybe on a gurney—all I know is it is uncomfortable and hard and unyielding. Creaking. Clanking. Warm and cold at the same time.

The air around me is gradually becoming clearer, cooler, and I can breathe, though my lungs burn with every breath. High above me I hear the faintest thread of sound, sirens from the town, from the local fire regiment. Is the factory on fire?

"Just a small one," says the person carrying me, and I snap to like I've been poked with a cattle prod when I recognize his voice.

"Bo!" I gasp.

"I've decided to grant your wish." He clutches me tight, and it hurts. Like I'm caught in one of the brutal metal spinners. I cry out.

"Sorry," he mutters, and loosens his grip slightly. He

carries me through the darkness, past stone walls and black moss, past hanging lanterns and smooth metal panels. He never hesitates, never wavers. He knows where all the traps are.

And as he walks through a patch of lantern light, I turn my head and see his face for the first time.

Chapter Eighteen

HALF OF BO'S FACE is normal—handsome, even—
with a straight nose and a generous mouth, a walnut
brown eye and long eyelashes, a bold brow and thick
black hair. The other half of his head and face is covered
with molded metal. A gleaming steel mask. And the eye
of the mask is black and dead, like the eyes of all of Bo's
metal creations.

He allows me to stare as he walks along, down the
stone steps and into his home, past the metal figures
of Jipu and Mugo and Jima and my father. Something
catches my eye in the corner. There's a new statue standing near the wall, next to one of the ancient, hulking
machines. I would have noticed him if he'd been here
the first time I visited. He's tall, with broad shoulders,
and he doesn't look like the rest of them. Instead of

grayish steel, his hair is fashioned from copper, and it shines brightly under the lantern light.

It's a dead-eyed metal version of Melik, and for some reason, knowing Bo has noticed him makes my heart clutch with dread.

Bo carries me into one of the rooms he's built and sets me on a chair. He takes a few steps back, giving me a view of all of him. The creaking and clanking, the shape of him . . . it makes sense now.

One of his arms is made of metal. It is a mechanical wonder, gears and cogs and springs, long, nimble fingers that move like they're connected to his brain. The metal arm is slightly longer and thicker than his other arm. It is held to his body with straps around his neck and chest. The arm glints dully in the dim yellow lantern light. The shoulder is rounded, shaped like the muscles of a human arm and roped with veins, but the true workings are pure machine. It is beautiful but also frightening.

He's looking at me like he's thinking the same thing. He seems scared yet hopeful. Like he might run, but he's not sure in which direction.

"What happened?" I ask him, regretting the catch in my voice.

His expression changes, his mouth becoming a flat, grim line. "I created a distraction. Things had gone far enough."

"You were watching."

"I couldn't let him. I tried to stay out of it. I thought maybe he would see the shelves as a bad omen, a warning. But his lust controls him, and I couldn't . . ." His metal fingers click together.

"What did you do?"

He looks down at his mechanical hand. "I blew up the boiler on the west side of the killing floor, the one closest to the administrative offices."

He says it so matter-of-factly, like this is just one of his daily tasks. Like he can do this type of thing anytime he wants to. My stomach twists. It was almost noon. There were still workers on the floor. "Were people hurt?"

He shrugs. "It had to be done. Mugo . . . he is not a good man. He was going to hurt you." He winces. "I saw what he did to Jima."

"Why didn't you stop him?"

He frowns. "I installed the explosives and rigged the shelf just before she was fired."

Poor Jima. Her prayer was answered too late. And, like mine, in a terrible, violent way.

I stare at Bo. I know I should thank him, but all I can picture are young men, strong one moment, broken and burned and ruined the next. And Melik—what happened to him? Was he hurt? I think back, trying to remember. He was up and moving after the explosion. I felt the sure grip of his hands on my waist, shoving me to safety. Surely he got out?

"They'll need help up there," I say. "My father is only one man."

Bo shakes his head. "You said you wanted to meet me, and now you're meeting me. That's what you wanted." His dead black eye stares at me heartlessly, but his warm brown eye is full of questions and hurt. His tone reminds me of a child's, so focused on what it wants, unaware of anything else. But he is not a child.

I take a breath, grimacing at the tightness in my chest. "Yes. I wanted to see you. I'm just worried about what's happening."

"Do you worry about yourself?" His voice is hard. "I brought you down here to keep you safe." Both of his hands, the flesh and the metal, become fists.

"Thank you," I say quietly.

It seems to be what he needs, because he relaxes a bit. "You're welcome."

I look around me, finally taking in my surroundings. We're in a room with corrugated metal walls, arching over us in crazy angles and zigzagging bits, creating tiny nooks in which he has stashed offering upon offering, stacks of paper and ink sticks, a pile of candles, a tangled nest of braided thread bracelets, a row of carved wooden animals, a few bolts of fine fabric. In one nook several prayers are laid out, and I wonder if these are the ones Bo is considering granting. A bright lamp is suspended over a large work table along one side of the room. Scattered over the table are wires, cogs, screws, and nuts . . . and the round, smooth body of a large spider with three spindly legs attached to its sides.

I get up and walk over to it, a bit unsteady on my feet. "You make the spiders."

"Yes." He glances over at me shyly as he joins me at the table. He seems so nervous. But as if they have ideas of their own, his hands are already on the spider. Metal and flesh work together in a kind of automatic dance, a twist of the wrist, a flare of the fingers. It is clear he has done this thousands of times, so often that he doesn't need to think about it. His human and machine hands flip shut the panel on the spider's back, then use a small drill to attach a few more legs to its body. As they do, Bo's expression relaxes a bit, and I . . . understand. This is how I feel when I am suturing or scrubbing. Deep in purposeful work, safe from everything else, from selfish thoughts and worries and hopes.

I find myself drifting closer to him as I watch the elegant movements of his hands, the deft way in which he transforms a piece of steel into a creature that can do terrible, amazing things. Bo's tension has drained from him as he tinkers, and it is clear how soothing this is for him. This is the place he finds himself. Minute by minute, wire by wire, he has created himself a world.

My gaze travels over the table, the tools, the circuitry, things for which I don't have the proper names, but that seem to belong in the future, not here and now. "You built everything here, didn't you?"

Bo raises his head and looks around. "It was a bare stone chamber as big as the killing floor when Guiren first brought me down here. He gave me a pallet and a small stove. A lantern. A chair. Some books." He chuckles. "It wasn't enough for me."

"Where do you get all of this metal?"

He throws his shoulders back and smiles. "Come see." He releases the spider and holds out his hand, the one made of flesh, and I take it. He leads me out of the chamber, into the high-ceilinged factory room, where we walk along a metal path. My wool shoes make hardly any noise, but Bo's hard soles clack and echo. He keeps me on the right side of him, the human side. From this angle he could be any boy leading a girl for a walk down a garden path. We stroll past statues of Minny and Hazzi and Onya, past Ebian and a few others I recognize, and past many I do not.

As we reach the center of the massive floor, I hear it, the whir of tiny gears and the clicking of metal on metal, of sharp, stabbing spider feet. I whirl around, already lifting my skirts above my ankles.

Bo laughs. "What are you doing?"

"The spiders," I say in a choked voice. It is one thing to see one lying half assembled on the table. It is entirely another to hear the sound of its movements, to know it is creeping toward me.

"It won't hurt you. Look." He points to a small opening at the base of a squat metal hive built into one of the central columns. From it marches a metal spider the size of a star fruit, but instead of fangs it has a . . . a . . .

"Is that a bristle brush?"

He gazes fondly at the vicious-looking arachnid. "My personal cleaning service. These are not for security."

I eye it as it walks in a steady rhythm, sliding its brush along the floor in a straight line, then turns and treads a parallel path back to its hive. And now that I know it won't be jumping on my skirt, my fear subsides and I am fascinated. "How does it work?" Surely it can't have a steam engine inside it—it's almost silent. All I hear is clicking.

"Do you know how a watch works?"

"Sort of. I know my father has to wind his every day or it stops."

Bo stands up straighter. "My spiders, most of them, at least, don't have to be wound. All they need is vibrations.

Movement. There's a small weight inside of them, and as they move and shift, it pulls the mainspring tight, so they're always ready."

The spider is still pacing, up and down, up and down, until it's cleaned a large rectangular panel. It's created a tiny pile of debris right in front of its little burrow, and finally, it pushes it in and disappears into its hole. "But . . . these spiders move like they're alive. It looks like magic."

"You are full of compliments," he says, and his face is practically glowing. "They aren't alive, not really." He releases my hand and strides toward another column, beside which stands a metal woman. I think it's one of the cafeteria workers on the day shift, but I'm not completely sure. She has a squarish face and a cleft in her chin, which Bo has rendered in careful detail. He opens a panel in her stomach. "Look in there."

Right where her guts would be, there is a rolled sheet of the thinnest metal, delicate as paper. It's speckled with tiny holes.

"Do you know how a player piano works?" Bo asks. "The holes are punched just so, and when it's powered up, it makes the keys move down in a specific sequence?"

I don't really understand, but I nod vaguely.

There's more clicking by my ankles and I flinch away, but Bo leans down and scoops an orange-size spider up, turning it on its back. Its spindly legs keep moving, stabbing at the air. Set into its body, the part that hangs lowest, is a circular panel that looks like a turntable, with a set of wheels in its center. Bo angles the tip of his metal pointer finger down and taps the spider's abdomen, right between the two wheels. A flap pops open, revealing a punched roll similar to the one in the metal woman's belly. It is whirring along, moving like the cylinder in a music box. Bo closes the hatch and sets the spider on the ground, where it marches away, off to do whatever it was made to do.

"They move in sequences I've set. If they bump into something, like a wall, they reset using the wheels in their bellies and head off in another direction. The security spiders, they're a bit different. If they run into something—"

"They bite it," I say in a small, shaky voice, thinking of the disemboweled rat in the corridor. This is why, despite all its other problems, Gochan One has not had much of an issue with rats in recent years. The Ghost has made sure of it.

He grins. "They are marvelous, aren't they?"

They are. Marvelous and terrifying. "I've seen something like them. In the newspapers. The off-road war machines . . ."

Bo nods and points up ahead, at a metal sliding door. "That's where I got the idea." He leads me to the door and hits a rusty button. There is a familiar noise, a high-pitched keening, and I realize this is what I've been hearing from the vents. It's not a person or a spirit or the factory crying itself to sleep.

It's an elevator.

The door slides open, and I peer inside. It's a heavy metal cage. It must have been a freight elevator when the factory was new, years ago when it was used for who knows what, before it became a slaughterhouse. "This is the only one that works," Bo says. "It's the only one I allow to work."

He ushers me aboard, holding my hand tightly enough that I think he's afraid I might run, which is exactly what I want to do. My breath is rasping in my throat like a saw on a tree branch. The gates crash shut and the cage comes to life, shaking beneath my feet, all around me, and I am going to be buried, crushed, eaten by this metal monster. I can't help it; I tuck myself into Bo's side and throw my arms around his waist, burying my face in the warmth of his shirt, keeping myself as far from the carnivorous, hard steel and rust bars as I possibly can.

After a moment of hesitation Bo wraps his human arm around me and whispers, "I will never allow you to be hurt. You're safe."

I don't feel safe. I feel like I will be gobbled down at any moment. I'm already in this thing's mouth and it will chomp me to bits. We're zooming up, and I feel dizzy. Bo holds me steady, and I can tell by the solid beat of his heart that he's not nervous at all. He is the master of this beast, and it does what he wants it to do.

We jerk to a stop, and I cannot look at him as I let go of his waist. Bo slides the creaking cage doors open on daylight. We must be near the roof of the factory, because there's less cinder block and more glass. Most of it is shattered, and I step carefully around the shards because the larger ones could cut right through my cloth soles. There is a sudden burst of life in front of us, feathers and flapping and the bitter-damp smell of bird droppings.

"They nest up here," Bo says. "Even in the winter it's quite warm because the furnace stack is nearby."

"We're that close to the rear of the factory?"

He points through the filmy, cracked glass. "That's the

stacks." He points just to the left of that. "And that's the roof of Gochan Two."

I peer at the hulking shadows in front of us. The enormous warehouses that make up the Gochan Two complex are much closer to Gochan One than I thought; I've never seen them from this angle. But right here, at the rear of the factory, they are close enough to leap from roof to roof. Or to build a bridge and stroll across. And that's exactly what someone, I assume Bo, has done.

"I get the metal from here," he explains, leading me along the short, wide catwalk. I make the mistake of looking down and my stomach clenches. We are at least four stories off the ground.

"No one sees you walking back and forth?"

Bo scoffs. "Who would see? There aren't any windows in these buildings. And Gochan Two falls silent at night."

Already the noise of Gochan Two is deafening, and we are still on the outside of it. Bo leads me to an improvised hatch cut through the metal roof, and then I hear nothing but crashing. Like a war is going on in our war machine factory. We're in some kind of crawl space, and I cover my ears and squat low, overwhelmed as the noise takes over. Bo touches my shoulder and tugs me over to another door, which leads to a room more insulated from the piercing sounds of metal on metal. Lit from windows cut in the roof, the floor of this chamber is strewn with the same kind of metal debris that lines the hallways and corridors of Gochan One. In the corner is a low table, and spread across it is a sheet of paper, curled at the corners, covered in diagrams and numbers. I point to it. "Is that yours?"

He nods. "I work in here sometimes. From this room I can go anywhere in the factory. I've been doing it for years. It's so quiet at night. Peaceful. I learned most of what I know from the manuals the engineers keep in their offices." He gives me a bashful smile. "I like to think I've improved upon their designs."

I wander over to an opening that's been carved into the floor and covered with a pane of glass. I gasp—we are high above the factory floor of Gochan Two, looking down from the roof, hidden by crisscrossing beams that keep this massive structure from falling in on itself. What I see beneath me is blinding and brutal. I have to squint as the swinging arms of the assembly machines and massive presses catch the glaring overhead lights. Gray-shirted workers look so tiny and vulnerable amidst all this steel and iron and copper, piecing together the heavy steam engines of the war machines, crafting their enormous metal legs and cannons and whatever else helps them kill those who stand against our government. I wince as I think of Sinan playing in the scars these things have left on the land.

When I look up at Bo's half-human, half-machine face, I see that he is entranced. This is his kingdom. This is the size of his world, and it is infinite and sorrowfully tiny at the same time. He pulls his eyes away from the controlled chaos below to gaze at my face.

"You're here," he says quietly, like he doesn't believe it.

I look into his walnut brown eye, the human one, the one that is full of emotions I can't possibly understand. I feel so silly, pitying myself for being alone. People will look for me if I disappear. People are probably looking for me now. But Bo . . . no one is looking for him. He is long dead and buried, and the only time people think of him is when they want a favor from the Ghost. They don't wonder if he's lonely, but I know he is.

"I'm here," I agree. I'm not sure what I can offer him or what he wants from me, and I hope this moment is enough.

He smiles, but its sweetness is tainted by his cruel, black, glaring eye. "You look like you're about to fall over," he says. "Come on. I'll take you home."

My father will be happy to see me, so relieved. I can only imagine what he's going through right now. And Melik—I need to know he's all right. But when we get to the fortresslike lair, Bo doesn't guide me to the set of stone steps that leads upward to my life. He takes me to one of the metal chambers he's built at the edge of the old factory floor. Warm light glows from this room, and inside is a table set with cutlery, plates of plum cakes and candied dates, and a bottle of fruit wine that must have been an offering from Jipu or Mugo, because the stuff is so expensive that no one else can afford it.

Bo's hand slips into mine, and he's shaking a little. He tugs me farther into the room, where I see a carved wooden chair and the most amazing bed I've ever beheld, the headboard intricately fashioned in a spiderweb of metal, the mattress fat and soft looking, and the whole thing is enclosed in gauzy silken fabric.

I look back at him, confused, my heart thrumming against my ribs. "Is this your bedroom?"

He smiles. "No, Wen. It's yours."

~~๑ Chapter ๑~~
Nineteen

I FEEL LIKE I'VE SWALLOWED a metal spider. The outside of me is still, quiet, smooth. The inside of me is being shredded. Because I see the smile on his face, how happy he is, how proud of himself, and I know he's serious. He expects me to stay here with him. He's been planning it. He's prepared this place for me.

I put my hand on my stomach because that metal spider is going to eat right through me and let my screams come pouring out. "I can't stay here, Bo."

He tilts his head to the side. "You have to. You can't go back up there."

"I need to."

He shakes his head. "Then Mugo would just . . . no, I'm sorry. I won't allow that." He sees the tears in my eyes and reaches out to touch my face. I force myself not to flinch, because I know that would upset him. "Are you worried about Guiren? Because he can come visit you!"

He says it like he's offering me a special gift.

"No, that's not enough," I whisper. The metal walls are creeping closer, I swear, they are caving in on me. "I belong up there."

He takes my hand and drags me past other metal chambers, to the one at the very front, nearest the steps. He pulls me into the room, which is wide and bright and . . . appears to be the place where every single pipe in the entire Gochan One factory complex leads. There are hundreds of them descending from the ceiling and along the walls, and they converge along the back of the space, ending in open spouts, all lined up, hundreds of hungry, gaping little mouths.

Bo points at them. "You can see most of the factory from here. What are you missing so much? What do you want to see so badly?"

It's not what. It's who. But I won't say his name out loud. I'm not certain how I know this. Maybe it's instinct, like how a mouse knows to freeze when it senses a predator approaching.

I do not want Bo to know how much Melik means to me.

He yanks me forward, his metal arm swinging up to tap one of the pipes. "Mugo's office? Look! Will you miss this so very much?"

I put my eye to the opening of the pipe and gasp. It's all right there, slightly distorted, but there. Mugo's office. Or what's left of it. My view must be from the vent high above my desk. Shattered glass glitters on every surface. My typewriter lies in pieces on the floor, next to my overturned desk chair. Mugo's balding head glides directly under my vantage point, and I jerk back.

Bo pulls me over to another pipe. "What about this one? The cafeteria? Are your friends in there? The one who lifted your skirt? The one who called you stupid?" Bo's voice is growing sharper, like a blade on a whetting stone.

I peer into the mouth of the pipe and can barely make sense of what I see. The tables do not hold full plates of food. They hold bodies. Bleeding. Burned. Writhing, flailing, crying. My father is scampering up and down these rows, tending to the wounded.

The men who are suffering because Bo couldn't stand to watch Mugo touch me. Saliva fills my mouth; I am going to be sick. I stumble back, sucking deep breaths of the dank air, thinking of bells and citron and crab apples and embroidered roses and anything, *anything* but this. Bo appears shocked at my reaction and peers into the pipe himself.

"Oh," he says. "I guess the clinic is pretty small. Guiren was smart to tend to them there."

I stare at him as he makes his cold assessment. He seems completely disconnected from the fact that *he* did this. He hurt these men. I swallow the spit that has gathered in my mouth. I shake off the cold, ghostly hand gripping my throat.

"Show me something else," I say, because I want to know what's going on up there. I want to know whether Melik got out. I didn't see him among the wounded, but what if he isn't wounded? What if he's dead? No. He was behind me. Right behind me.

"Here's the area outside the cafeteria," Bo says, bending over to look into another pipe. He frowns and curses under his breath.

"What is it?"

"I was hoping they'd assume you were dead."

My heart beats double time. "Someone's looking for me."

"Yes. I think so. They have no idea what they're about to step into."

I rush over. "Can I look? Please?" He moves over and I peek in. I had no idea I could feel both elated and terrified at the same time, but here it is. Melik, uninjured except for the blood smeared at his left temple, is standing with a group of Noor and a few older Itanyai workers at the edge of the open area outside the cafeteria. He's right by the turn to the administrative hallway, and as he talks to all of them, he's pointing down the hall to the area where I stumbled out of Mugo's office. There is fire in his eyes as he argues with Hazzi about something. He gestures across to the dark hallway where I first chased Bo, and several Noor head for it as Hazzi calls after them. As he does, Melik and a few others disappear down the administrative hallway.

It could be nothing. It's impossible to tell what they're actually doing. But when I turn around and look at Bo's face, it's like his inhuman, machine half has taken over, like it's driven its screws and cogs and springs straight into his brain. The warmth of the past hour is absent from his expression, and now there's only ice. "*He's* looking for you," he says quietly. "The red one. The Noor."

My hands fist in my skirts.

OF METAL AND WISHES

Bo's metal fingers close over one of the pipes. "He must have seen me grab you." He laughs, this jittery giggle that freezes my insides. "This is about to get messy."

The Noor haven't heard the stories—or maybe Hazzi tried to tell them and they didn't listen or believe. They don't know what awaits them if they journey below the factory.

"Bo, you have to let me go. Now. *Please.*" The metal spider has eaten all the way through me now, and my panic is unfurling, red and raw.

I dart for the door, but he blocks it with his body and looks at me like I've lost my mind. "Because of *them?* They've been cruel to you, Wen! They're about to get what they deserve, if you ask me."

He seems genuinely baffled, but that's because he's seen only the bad parts. He hasn't seen the Noor the way I have. So I tell him, all about how I cared for them, how they cared for one another, how they shamed me with their decency and their dignity. I am very careful not to mention Melik specifically.

Bo shakes his head, unconvinced, casual, like dozens of men are not about to die at his hands. I thought he knew so much about me, but now I see he knows nothing at all, if he thinks I'll be able to live with this. I glare at Bo, and now mine are the dead black eyes. My expression is metal. Impenetrable. Cold.

"If you keep me here against my will, you are just like Mugo."

His mouth drops open. "What? I am *nothing* like Mugo! I'm protecting you from him!"

"Mugo wants to control me. He wants to own me. He

doesn't care what I want, only what he wants. And that is what you're doing right now." My voice is steady. I do not look away from his face.

"You're wrong." His voice is not so steady. He will not meet my gaze.

"Bo," I say, moving toward him. "You can do amazing things. You have saved me more than once. But if you keep me here, you've rescued me from one cage only to imprison me in another."

He slumps, like my words weigh a thousand pounds. "But . . . I thought you'd want to stay with me." He blinks quickly. "I thought you might . . ." A tear slides from his walnut brown, human eye, and I am once again reminded how alone he has been, how much he must crave warmth and the touch of another person.

I want to say I'm sorry. I really don't want to hurt him. But I mean every word I've just said. "Let me go, and I'll come back and visit you. We need to go now, though, so the men looking for me don't die before they find me."

"They're not important," he says in a raspy voice.

"They're trying to do exactly what you were doing, Bo—they're trying to save me. If you care about me, you should honor that, not punish it."

"But—"

I stamp my foot. "If a single one of them dies," I say, my voice echoing off metal walls, "I will never forgive myself. Or you. Did my father tell you how stubborn I am?"

Finally he looks me in the eye, like he's trying to understand, like I am a problem to solve. "You'll come to see me again if I let you go now?"

"Only if you protect the men who are looking for me."

Bo searches my expression for a few long moments, but then he lunges for the pipe and looks in again. "They're already headed for the stairs." He grabs my hand in his metal one, grinding the stalks of my finger bones together in his punishing grip. I don't cry out, because I'm too filled with relief and fear to complain. I follow him out of the room and up the stone stairs, hoping we're not too late.

As the door at the top of the stairs slides open, Bo turns to me. "Follow me exactly. Step only where I step, and do everything I say." His expression is tight with worry. "We're going to follow the route to the cafeteria."

Melik was in the other group, the one headed toward the administrative hallway.

When Bo sees the look on my face, he grimaces. "If the red Noor saw you disappear, he'll be looking where it happened, right by Jipu's office. But it will take them much longer to find their way below because that entrance is hidden."

Satisfied that Melik might not find his way to danger before I reach the factory floor, I move to follow Bo, and he frowns. I wonder if it's because my selfish thoughts of Melik are written all over my face. For a second I'm scared Bo will change his mind, but he simply reminds me again to match his steps and strides forward. It's a determined, intricate dance through the metal hallway, and then a race along the long, narrow corridor, past a few rat carcasses and piles of bloody metal shavings, over trip wires, inching around odd protrusions in the wall that will trigger Bo-only-knows-what kind of terrors. He is muttering to himself about circuits and kill switches.

We don't go down the hallway where the enormous, sharp-legged spider waits to fall upon the first poor soul who breaks the wire beneath its web. Instead we take a series of turns and go up a flight of stairs. Bo makes me skip every third one. The light is so dim, only the glow of the scant yellow emergency lanterns, but I see those spiders everywhere I look. The dull black glint of an eye, or the faint silver gleam of a leg, or the smooth, bulbous swell of a belly. Between coils of pipes, nested in snarls of wires, peeking from holes in the cinder block, crouching in the air vents. I could be wrong. It could be my imagination. But the way Bo is weaving through this maze beneath the factory, I think it's real, and I begin to suspect he's as scared of them as I am, which is the most frightening thought of all.

"I can hear them, up ahead," he finally says. I hear nothing, but he knows the gurgles and whispers of this factory much better than I do. "If they go much farther, I won't be able to save them."

It might be because I'm picturing Melik snapping a trip wire, the spiders descending on his shoulders and crawling up his legs, doing damage I'd never be able to repair. It might be because Bo is remembering my promise to visit him only if he protects the search party. He lets go of my hand and begins to run, and I forget to match his steps. I'm not sure exactly what my mistake is. Maybe my foot lands on the wrong spot. Maybe I don't hold my skirts high enough. Maybe I brush the wrong place on the wall with my elbows.

But when I hear the whirring of tiny gears and the click of metal feet, I know I've awakened the spiders.

The first one, the size of a fat spring melon, pops out from under a pipe running along the wall. It lands on the cement floor in front of me, its dead black eyes fixed on my skirts. "Bo?" I call, just a squeak of terror.

He whirls around. "Back up, back up, back up," he chants, running toward me. "Now!"

I leap back as another spider drops from the ceiling and lands right where I was standing. I press myself against the wall to get away from it, but my skirts brush its face, and that is all it needs to know it has found its prey.

With an echoing click, it leaps onto my skirt, sinking its fangs into the layers of wool and lace over my knees. My scream unfolds in that narrow corridor, tearing at the silence. I shake my skirts, desperately trying to jar the thing loose, but its sharp legs are buried in the folds of my dress, and it is slashing its way through, crawling up to my waist.

Bo charges up the corridor and kicks the spring-melon spider to the side. It crashes into the wall and bounces off, its fangs rising and falling like a butcher's cleaver. It scrabbles around in a circle because several of its legs are hanging limp from its body. It still seems dangerous, but Bo ignores it because his eyes are on the spider on my dress. "Don't move," he barks.

There's so much noise here. High-pitched gasps; heavy, dizzying thuds; roaring and ringing in my ears. The sounds of my body fighting death. But something else, too. Someone is calling my name. I don't recognize the voice, but I'm sure I hear it, distant and faint.

Bo's expression is grim as he buries his machine hand in my skirts and wrenches the squirming metal creature away from me. Parts of my dress are hanging from its fangs. "I'm sorry," Bo whispers.

It takes me a moment to realize he's not talking to me.

He holds the thing with his gleaming metal fingers. The spider has no chance—its legs and fangs meet nothing but open air as it tries to do what Bo made it to do. With sorrow in his eyes, Bo reaches with his flesh-and-bone fingers, pressing a spot on the spider's back. The spider stops moving for a split second and then begins to vibrate like the machines on the factory floor. At first I think it's purring, and I can't understand why Bo looks so stricken.

Then the spider just . . . disintegrates.

I watch the glittering cloud of metal shavings fall to the floor, and it's like an icy finger stroking along my spine. This is Bo's calling card. Spread along the floors of the factory. In little piles along the walls of my home—next to my sleeping pallet. In Mugo's office after his shelves collapsed. And on the killing floor, falling from the hook system right after Melik unjammed it. The metal shavings aren't coming from Gochan Two, blown through our vents from their factory. They're coming from right here in Gochan One. They're what's left after a spider has done its job and run its course.

Bo hits the kill switch on the other spider before it finds its way to my skirts. He has a hard time, because even though it is broken, this one is bigger and seems more determined to rip us apart. It is nothing when caught in the grip of Bo's mechanical arm, though. It reminds me of the machinery of Gochan Two, the machines that make the machines. That's what Bo is, and this is how he controls his vicious creations.

He looks down at his fingers, shimmering with delicate metal scales, all that's left of this creature he built with his own hands. "I had to have a way to prevent them from being detected," he says. "They fall apart on their own once they complete their job. The switch just makes it happen immediately."

"You tried to kill Melik." My voice is as cold as the rest of me.

His metal fingers click together as his flesh hand brushes the remains of the spider away. "He hurt you. He insulted you. I could see the pain on your face."

I stare at him. "Is that why?"

He turns his machine side toward me. "He doesn't deserve you. He can't have you." He says it petulantly, like I'm a toy he doesn't want to share.

I keep my words level and calm. "Promise me you won't hurt him again. If you care for me, you have to promise."

He wipes something from his human cheek. A shaving of metal, maybe, or possibly a tear. Whatever it is, he won't let me see. "I promise I will not hurt him. You promise you will come to see me again."

He reaches for my hand, and I let him take it. "I waited so long," he says. "And then I ruined it, didn't I?"

I squeeze his fingers. "Help me now, all right? Help me now."

He nods. "Will you come? Will you promise?"

Some of the tension leaks from me. "I promise."

He raises his head and looks down the hall that will take us to the stairs, to the factory floor, to my life, to—

A piercing cry of terror echoing down the corridor.

‑‑∞⊙ Chapter ⊙∞‑‑
Twenty

BO CLUTCHES MY HAND and we race forward together. I am so desperate to reach the person whose cries go on and on that Bo has to push me behind him to keep me from blundering ahead. He leaps over a trip wire and lifts me over as well, and then we're around a corner where the power's been cut and the darkness is thick around us. I glance over at Bo to see that his black eye is glowing now, a light in the darkness. His steps are sure as he charges toward the struggling mound halfway down the corridor. It's a man. He's on the floor up ahead, all in a heap.

From a few hallways away several others call this man's name, Ugur or something like that, and their desperation matches his. He calls back to them, speaking Noor in short, panicked bursts.

"The net," Bo says as he runs ahead of me. "He's caught in the net. They're almost on him."

The spiders are coming, then. The big ones, with bodies the size of tomcats, with legs as long as my arms. Everything in me screams to run the other way, but I know it's no safer behind me. One wrong step and I'll be sliced to bits.

Bo shoves me into the shallow alcove where he saved me the night I stumbled into the same trap Ugur's in right now. "Stay here, and I'll get him."

A few seconds later a squirming body is pressed against me. It's not Bo. This one's covered in a net and has two human arms. He stinks of urine and sweat, of animal fear, and is shaking and struggling hard, like a fish on a hook. He must have seen what was coming for him. And it probably reminded him of the war machines that destroyed his village, erasing the years between now and then, dragging him back to relive whatever happened to him when the Itanyai crushed the Noor rebellion.

"After they pass, you can go," Bo says. "I have to stop the Noor coming down through the administrative hallway before they get themselves into trouble. Remember your promise." He pulls at the net, and it falls away from Ugur's body.

I put my arms around Ugur's waist and try to lean around him so I can see Bo, but it's no use. I can already hear the soft clanking of Bo's machine arm as he sprints down the hall, away from the advancing spiders.

Ugur is crying, trembling. He is not a man in this moment; he is a child who has lost his way in a dark forest. I pull his face to mine and whisper soothing words, partly in an attempt to drown out the metal clicking of spider feet that must sound like bomb blasts in his ears. I shrink back against the damp walls and try to bring him with me. The Noor are still calling for him, closer now than before. They must have gone down the other hallways, the ones that are safer because they don't lead directly to Bo's home. Ugur was the unlucky one today.

Or maybe not. I have his face in my hands, and I won't let him go. He is quieting, and his struggling is slowing. "Wen?" he whispers.

"It's me, Ugur," I say, even though I have no idea who this man is, only that he is Noor. I try to tell him to press himself closer to me, deeper into the nook, but I don't think he understands me, because he moves away from me a little, like he's trying to keep a respectful distance.

He starts talking to me in that throat-catching language of theirs, and I shush him because I want to hear if the spiders have passed, and also because I don't understand him anyway. Finally I put my hand over his mouth, and that seems to be a signal he comprehends, because he shuts up.

And so have the spiders. They are silent. Have they passed already? I sag in relief.

That's when Ugur starts to scream. He reels back into the hallway, arching and writhing. He's a dark windstorm in this tunnel, a patch of shrieking blackness. There's a metal crunch, and I think he might have stepped on one of the spiders, but his shrieks go on and on and on—and then fall silent, suddenly, utterly. I hear a slide and a thud—and a muffled, wet clicking. I peek out of my alcove as three Noor round the corner and hold up their lanterns. I search their forms and faces. Melik is not among them. Their identical looks of horror freeze me to the bone. I slowly turn my head.

There is blood everywhere.

The Noor run toward us, shouting Ugur's name. When their lantern light reaches him, my stomach heaves. He is on his back, a few feet from our alcove. One of the spiders is on his belly, and it has shredded him. The pink and purple coils of his intestines are wrapped around the spider's body and legs as it burrows deeper inside of him.

One of the Noor throws up against the wall. The others stand silently, staring at Ugur, who is unmistakably dead. His eyes are wide and his mouth is open, and now I can see that he is caught in a spider's embrace. One of his legs must have been within a spider's reach as it stalked down the hall, enough to give it a foothold and allow it to scuttle up his back. Its legs are wrapped around his head and neck. The tips of its feet are on his cheeks. I do not want to see the back of his head, but I know this is why his screams fell silent so suddenly.

I sink to the floor, clutching my stomach. One of the Noor grabs for the spider that has buried itself in Ugur's guts, and I practically tackle him. If he pulls it out, the thing might attack him. I wrap one of my arms around his hands and reach for the spider myself, for that kill switch on its back. Its head is deep inside Ugur, but its back is exposed and vulnerable. My fingers slide through blood and tissue, scrabbling over the smooth metal of the spider's body, prodding and pressing. And then I find it. The spider starts to vibrate, sending warm droplets of

Ugur misting into the air. I lean back as it falls apart, leaving only glinting silver and red bits.

My hands are covered in blood. My face, too, I have no doubt. The Noor are speaking among themselves, but it is nothing but noise as I stare at Ugur's wide, glazed eyes. He has a mole on his face. He was the boy standing next to Melik that day in the furnace room. Now Melik has another of his friends to mourn. Because of me.

One of the Noor crouches next to me and I look up into his pale face. His sorrow and horror are deeper than the shadows around us. "Wen," he says. "Come."

He takes my arm, tugs me up, and says something to the others in a low voice. Then he leads me away from Ugur, away from the carnage, toward the stairs. He does not let go of me as we walk, but I don't sense anger from him, or suspicion. Or anything, really, except the exhaustion that comes with something so terrible that you can't even fight against it.

He pulls me to a stop right in front of the door to the open area by the cafeteria. He takes my hands and rubs them against his shirt, then swipes his sleeve over my face. The rough fabric reeks of meat and death, and I try to squirm away, but he holds me steady and keeps wiping.

"Melik," he says by way of explanation, and I understand. He's worried what Melik will think if I am brought back to him covered in blood. It is strangely tender, the way this Noor cares about that kind of thing.

When he is finished, he's a bloody mess, but I am slightly cleaner. There is still blood between my fingers, under my fingernails, on my bodice and skirt, but this Noor seems to think I look better, because he nods and opens the door that leads to the main floor. I am suddenly hesitant. Everything that has happened is because of me, and I'm not sure I can bear it. With leaden feet I trudge down the hall. My bloody Noor companion heads back down the stairs to his friends.

At the end of the hallway there are men, some Noor and some not, milling about, their brows furrowed. They are probably waiting for those in the cafeteria, the ones who couldn't simply walk away from the blast. I look for my father among the crowd, but he must be in the cafeteria too, seeing to the wounded. I wonder if he believes I am dead, if he worries, or if he suspects the truth. For a moment I stand among these men, who barely seem to notice my presence. I am another casualty of today's accident, no more and no less. I am not particularly important to anyone here.

But then . . . old Hazzi catches sight of me, and he shouts to someone in the administrative hallway. Melik comes around the corner a moment later, his eyes wild and searching. He spots me easily, the flash of ruined pink among the mass of brown overalls and work shirts, and he comes straight for me like there is no one else here. I am suddenly aware of my beating heart, of the tears in my eyes, of the blood in my veins as it calls to him.

Perhaps it is his size, or maybe the heat in his eyes, but the men move out of the way for him. He still has blood on his left temple, and some of it is smeared on his work shirt. There are patches of black and gray on his clothes and face from the explosion and its aftermath. But he is here and he is whole, and when he gets to me, he doesn't stop to assess, and he obviously doesn't think about what is proper. Neither do I. As he reaches for me, I raise my arms, and then my feet aren't touching the ground. He scoops me up, bowing his head into the crook of my neck. He squeezes me so tightly I can barely breathe. Soft, desperate words are whispered against my skin, and even though I don't understand them, I think I can translate. *You are alive. You are here. You are mine.*

I am dimly aware that there are others around us, but I cannot force myself to care. "I was afraid for you," I whisper, and hold on tight as a wrenching sound comes from deep in his chest at the sound of my voice.

"I knew you were alive. I knew it. I knew it." His hand is in my hair, and his forehead is against mine, and—

The touch of his lips is shocking to me. Not because it is completely inappropriate, although it is, and not because I am afraid people are watching, although I should be. What shocks me is how much I want it, after all these hours of worry and all these days of wishing. What shocks me is my hunger for him. Melik's mouth is on mine, and it is soft and warm and overwhelming and delicious. He is everywhere, all around me, holding me against his lean, hard-muscled body. He smells of ashes and sweat and it's him and I need it. We breathe together, eyes wide open, unwilling to allow the other to disappear again.

Then he freezes for a moment and puts me down abruptly, clearing his throat and jamming his hands in his pockets. It's like he's come back to himself, remembered everything I've forgotten—this kind of thing is not allowed here, and it puts us both in danger. He glances around us, then down at me. "I'm sorry," he whispers.

I can do nothing but smooth my trembling hands over my bloody, torn skirt. "It's all right," I manage to say, even though it's not, for so many reasons. Because I have ruined what was left of my reputation. Because everyone in this room saw a Noor completely forget his place. Because Ugur is dead and Melik doesn't even know yet. Because Bo might have been watching. My heart is beating so hard that I have to put my hand over it, just to keep it where it is.

"Wen?"

At the sound of my father's voice I whirl around. Sweat rings his armpits and sorrow shadows his face. "I was so worried," he says hoarsely, and welcomes me into his arms.

He hugs me tight, his wiry arms shaking. "Melik told me he thought he saw someone grab you, and then you disappeared," he mutters.

I lean back so he can see my face, and nod. His answering look is all understanding. He knows I was with Bo. "A lot of people were hurt in the explosion," he tells me, "but no one died."

I sag in his arms, thankful for small mercies. Then I remember he's wrong. Someone *did* die. I want to look at Melik, to talk to him, to warn him about what is coming up from the basement. But when I try to turn, my father's grip tightens, and he shakes his head as he watches the people around us. I bow my head. The men in this room are no doubt staring, their gazes full of cold disapproval.

My father speaks to the top of my head. "The Noor sent a search party. Down below. They would not listen when

Hazzi told them it was dangerous—" His head jerks up at the commotion coming from the hallway behind us.

That is when the Noor carry Ugur into the open. Several of the men gasp, and a few make deep retching noises that turn my stomach. Hazzi stares at the dead Noor boy with genuine sadness, then turns away. The Noor have closed Ugur's eyes and his mouth. One of them has donated his work shirt to cover the gaping hole in Ugur's belly where the other spider tore him open. Still, it doesn't matter. Despite their efforts, it is immediately clear that Ugur died a horrific, painful death.

My father holds me firmly as I watch the blood drain from Melik's face while his friends make their explanations over the body of their dead companion. The men around me are talking too, about the Ghost and the dangers that lurk in the bowels of the factory, about how the Noor have clearly stirred something deadly, how they are bad luck for the rest of us.

Melik raises his head and looks at me, and his expression is no longer one of relief and joy. All that lies there is torment and confusion. His gaze slides down the front of my dress, landing on every bloody patch and smear, on the torn mess of my skirt, like he's noticing it for the first time. He takes a step toward me, and my father pulls me back.

"I need your help in the cafeteria," Father says to me.

I glance up at him and see him glaring at Melik. *Stay back*, he's saying. *Take care of your own.*

Melik must heed his silent warning, because when I gather the courage to look, all I see is his back as he and the Noor carry Ugur's body away.

Chapter Twenty-one

MY FATHER ESCORTS the Noor to the furnace room that night, but he does not allow me to go. I keep expecting him to talk to me about what happened with Melik, to scold me or comfort me or anything in between, but instead he avoids the topic completely, like he wants to pretend it never happened.

After another scalding bath, I lie on my pallet and listen to the keening sounds of the elevator. Bo does not try to speak to me. Strangely, I wish he would. But no one is speaking to me right now, so why would he?

Suddenly I need the sky. I need the moon. I need to be away from here because I feel like I'm being buried alive, eaten by a monster of metal and brick. This factory feels like a grave, and I need to rise from the dead. I pull on my dressing gown and shoes and flee.

The first gulp of night air stings and burns my fragile lungs. The frost will come in a few hours, and woe to anyone who must spend the night on the streets. The abandoned, the homeless, the ones who have been used up by the Gochan factories and discarded like trash, the ones too weak or unskilled to transfer to that other factory, wherever it is. There are many out there, like Jima, like Tercan might have been, had he lived. The winter always cuts them down, culls their numbers, but there are always more to take their places on the street corners, in the alleys.

I walk to the compound's fence and stroke my fingers over the links, poking them through the little holes in the thick mesh. This fence is the thin boundary between me and them, between nestling warm in the belly of this beast and getting spit out of its mouth. I peer through the metal links, out to the pink-light salon on the corner. There is a small crowd of men outside of it, speaking in loud voices, looking back at Gochan One with hard, angry expressions.

Snatches of their conversations reach me, piercing this metal bubble and making me press my face to the fence. They are not talking about the whores or the frost or the holidays.

". . . had enough . . ."

". . . last straw . . ."

". . . can't go on like this . . ."

". . . it's not right . . ."

On and on they talk, speaking words of outrage. The explosion today was more than a distraction. It has lit a fuse. More men are coming out of the pink-light salon now, pulling their collars up against the chill in the air. Hazzi is among them, his swollen hands wrapped in a scarf. One of them is slightly taller than the rest, and when he steps into the light of a streetlamp, his hair gleams like copper. Melik speaks in our language, enunciating the words in his hard-edged accent, agreeing with these men, adding his own rage to the roiling pot. He talks of a strike, of demands, of rights. His power is clear tonight. He is not trying to hide it. He is using it, the weight of his words, the strength that vibrates from him like a current. They slap him on the back, and he returns the gesture. I am shocked. These men, several of whom I recognize as slaughterhouse workers, are not looking at Melik with hatred or suspicion or condescension. Tonight they are his allies. He is one of them.

It is suddenly very clear to me that all these men are not going to the salon to visit the whores.

They have found themselves a meeting place to start a revolution.

"What are you doing out here so late?"

I spin around with a startled shriek. Foreman Ebian is standing in the compound's square with his hands on his hips. The fleshy swell under his chin makes him look like a toad. His cold amphibian eyes are on me, and in them I read exactly what he thinks of me. This must be how men look at whores, with an ugly mixture of hunger and disgust.

"I was taking a walk," I say. "I needed some air." I clutch my dressing gown tight around me.

"What were you looking at?" he asks, striding toward me on his thick, stumpy legs.

I step away from the fence quickly. I am so stupid. If he looks through the thick wire mesh, he's going to see the men outside the pink-light salon, and they're going to be in trouble. He might even lock the fence early to keep them out. "I was just watching the . . . I wanted to see if the apothecary was open."

Not good enough, not even by half. Ebian shoulders me out of the way and puts his face to the fence. Every muscle in my body tenses. Then Ebian starts to laugh, a huffing *ugh-ugh-ugh* sound that carries no joy, only cruelty. "Of course you would be looking at them."

I gape at him. He doesn't seem mad at all. He's smiling and leering at me. His meaty hand wraps around the back of my neck and pulls me toward him, close enough to smell the cheap rice wine on his breath. He jams my face against the fence.

"Your next place of employment, eh?" he chortles.

I don't bother to struggle because he will only hurt me. I stare in horror through the hole and am hit with a tidal wave of relief.

The only people standing outside the pink-light salon are women. Three of them, their voluptuous bodies casting curvy shadows on the cobblestone streets. They laugh and wave at a passing horseless carriage. The men, Melik included, are nowhere in sight.

"I . . . I was curious," I stammer, my eyes raking the streets for any sign of the workers. I don't know how they disappeared so quickly.

Ebian laughs, and his hand falls away from my neck. For a moment I believe I am free, but then I hear the tinkle of metal and realize he's fumbling with his belt.

I backtrack but step on the hem of my dressing gown. My bottom hits the concrete ground, hard, knocking the wind out of me. Ebian shuffles forward, working at the zipper on his pants.

"Come here, little Wen. I'm going to satisfy your curiosity," he says.

I glance around me and know there will be no help for me tonight. We're outside, beyond Bo's eyes and ears. Melik has disappeared. My father is probably sleeping in his alcove, dreaming of my mother.

I am alone, and I must take care of myself. I suck in a painful breath, trying to coax the air into my poor lungs and clever thoughts into my frazzled brain. I am not going to let this man touch me.

"Foreman Ebian, you are very courteous," I say.

Ebian stops, his hands tucked into his pants. He squints at me. This is not the response he expected. "I am?"

I smile at him, wishing suddenly that I had metal fangs instead of blunt little teeth. "Indeed. Underboss Mugo will be delighted, I am sure, to hear of this."

He frowns as my words work their way into his drunken thoughts. Mugo. Who has the power to destroy Ebian. Who is not known for sharing. While he ponders this, I get to my feet and dust off my dressing gown. I am bruised and panting, but my face is no longer at the level of his crotch, and that alone makes me feel more confident.

"What would you like to teach me, Foreman Ebian? The underboss has promised to teach me too, but he has not yet had the opportunity. I know he will be thrilled to hear that you provided me with my first lessons."

Ah, this puts a look of fear on Ebian's face. He doubtless

knows Mugo likes his girls pure and untouched so he can ruin them himself. "But the Noor," he says, watching me with narrowed eyes.

I wave my hand to dismiss Melik like I might a gnat, and I hope Ebian doesn't notice how much it is shaking. "Oh, no, I would never defy the underboss. We all know how much power he has!" I cannot believe I am discussing my virginity like this, so casually, so callously.

Ebian removes his hands from his pants with a grunt because he knows I'm right. I will never be glad of Mugo's attention to me, but in this moment I'm not sorry for it either.

"Better get back inside before you catch a cold, then," he says, watching me regretfully, like I'm a juicy meat bun he's accidentally dropped on the muddy ground.

I curtsy to him and he walks away quickly, heading for the compound fence, maybe to visit a pink-light salon and work off some of his frustration. I think a silent apology toward whichever poor woman ends up with him as a customer. I hope it's not Jima. It was so easy to feel contempt for those women when I imagined I would never be like them, when I assumed I'd always have what I needed and further assumed that I deserved as much. Now I understand how foolish that was. I feel sympathy for them and what they must do to put food on their tables. I realize how fortunate I will be if I can avoid that fate.

When Ebian disappears from my sight, I sink down on a bench at the edge of the square. I can see the entrance to the factory easily from here, and I am ready to bolt if another man appears. It is stupid of me to be out here alone, but I can't bear to go back in and walk past Mugo's wrecked office now, because it will remind me that it is only a matter of time before he decides he is tired of waiting. He is the giant cat with me trapped like a rabbit between his enormous paws. He is playing with me before he gets bored and bites my head off. And after that it will be over, and I will be ruined for real. No one will want me, but anyone will be able to claim me.

Bo is right. He cannot be allowed to do that. It will kill me. But I cannot refuse Mugo. What about my father? What would Mugo do to him? Would he send him penniless into the Ring—or would he transfer him? Suddenly I realize how Bo must have thought of this too, how he arranged the perfect setup to protect my father from Mugo's wrath. If everyone believed me to be dead, Mugo would have no reason to punish my father. And despite knowing my father has sold me into this, that he is silently turning his head while Mugo does what he wants, I still don't want him to suffer. I think my father is too fragile to survive it.

Maybe if I run away, Mugo will spare my father, too. But only if he thinks Father didn't know about it. Which means Father cannot know about it.

I have no idea how long I sit there in the dark, on that hard bench, how many silly schemes I dream up, how many plans I make and discard. My fingers are numb and so is my face. I am beyond shivering, but I am still not ready to walk into the belly of the factory, to let it eat me up. It is only when the voice speaks to me in the darkness that I realize there is someone sitting next to me on the bench.

"You saved us tonight, you know," Melik says.

I look over at him, puzzled.

"Your scream."

"Oh. Ebian . . ."

He crosses his arms over his chest and jams his hands into his armpits. "I climbed over the fence to get to you. By the time I made it over, he was walking away. He didn't . . . ?"

My laugh is humorless. "Oh, no—see, I belong to Mugo, so Ebian can't touch me. Not yet, at least."

Beside me, Melik's body winds tight as a spring. "I've been watching you, sitting here, for the longest time. I was waiting for you to get cold and go inside, but you aren't going to, are you?"

I shake my head. My plan right now is to sit here until I freeze to death.

Melik sighs. "Wen . . ."

"I don't know how everything became so messed up," I say. "I can't seem to do anything right. I'm sorry about Ugur."

Melik is quiet for a long time. "Halim, Baris, and Zeki aren't sure what they saw. Only that they heard Ugur's cries and ran to him, but when they found him, it was already too late. They said you were there too, and you knew how to make the silver demons that attacked him disappear."

That's about as accurate an assessment of what happened as any I could come up with.

"I saw someone grab you," he says. "I fell behind, and I couldn't reach you."

He's giving me an opening. Trying not to judge or jump to conclusions. I am grateful but also resentful.

I don't want to talk about this right now. Still, Melik is more important to me than that, and he deserves more than silence.

"You know about the Ghost who haunts the factory."

He shifts on the bench so he can look at my face. "People make wishes, and apparently, sometimes he grants them. And he is the one you challenged after Tercan lifted your skirts." There is bitterness in his voice that makes my heart shrivel. "Hazzi warned us not to trifle with him."

"Today the Ghost was protecting me from Mugo. He could see what was happening, what was about to happen, and so he stopped it."

I dare to look Melik in the eye, and I see neither anger nor disbelief there. "Then, he did better for you than I could," he says softly. "All I seem capable of doing is getting you in trouble."

"I was thinking the same thing—I've caused you nothing but grief since you came here."

Melik moves slowly, giving me all the time in the world to pull away, and takes my hands between his. He holds them low on the bench between us, hidden beneath a fold in his coat. "We are bad for each other, I think," he says, and there is the smallest of sad smiles on his face.

"Obviously." I am squeezing his hands so hard I am surprised it doesn't hurt him. And he is squeezing back.

"Mugo was right, you know. The rules are different where I come from."

"Oh?"

"A Noor woman has the right to choose who she wants, to be with who she wants. And if she is with someone, she can touch him when she pleases."

I smile in spite of myself. "And kiss him in public?"

"Of course." His fingers trace over my palm. "These things are not frowned upon. We don't hide how we feel."

I think of how the Noor touch one another, even the men. They communicate their sentiments with their fingers and hands, with their expressions and gestures and voices. Melik is right—they don't hide. "Isn't anything private?"

He keeps his eyes on me as he strokes the insides of my wrists, lighting a flame low in my belly. "Some things."

I pull my hands back and wrap my arms around me. I don't know what he is doing to me, but I know we shouldn't be doing it here. It's too much, meant for a dark room and a slow-burning fire, and I should not want that right now. "But Mugo was also right when he said that, here, if a girl is free with her affections, any man will think he has the right to touch her."

The sound that comes from him is perilously close to a growl. "I know that now. And even if I didn't before, your friend Jima took care of that."

"You saw her?"

He nods, his expression somber. "The workers' group has pooled some money to make sure she has a safe place to live and enough food to eat. It is not a good life, but she won't be on the streets." He sighs. "But one of the men teased me about you tonight, and she overheard. She gave me an earful. She doesn't want her fate to become yours."

I stare at the stone walkway that leads to the factory gates. I do not deserve Jima's concern. Melik touches my hand, drawing it back into the warmth of his. "I felt so powerless this afternoon. I didn't know how to save you, but I wanted to so badly. And this is why I owe a thank-you to the Ghost."

I don't tell him that I think the Ghost would like to touch me too, but maybe he understands that, because he says, "You were gone for hours. You were with him?" He reads my expression and his own turns grim. "He must be more than air and smoke if he can make all these things happen."

"He is more than air and smoke."

"Can you tell me what happened to Ugur?" I can tell he's trying to keep his voice level and calm. "Did he anger your Ghost?"

"No, the Ghost didn't want him to die, and neither did I." I shiver. "There are . . . things . . . below the factory. Security devices. Ugur triggered one of them, and they attacked. I tried to keep him safe, but I couldn't."

"Security devices . . . this factory is full of secrets, and so are you."

"I'm not the only one," I say, raising my head.

"You saw us tonight, didn't you?"

I nod.

"Many of us, and not just the Noor, are angry at how the workers are treated. I met with a group of them right after Tercan died."

"At the pink-light salon."

He gives me a rueful look. "I was told that is the only place in town where men can slip in and out without others watching too closely. Well. Without *most* others watching."

"You're going to get yourself in trouble." It bursts out of me before I can snap my mouth shut.

The sound that comes from him is all exasperation. "Wen, we're already in trouble. If we fall further into debt, Mugo has the right to sell us to the labor camps. Did you know that?"

My throat goes very dry. They are called labor camps, but they are really death camps. That is where criminals are sent, but now that I think about it, being unable to pay a debt *is* a crime, should the person you owe choose to report it. Is that what my father is facing too?

Melik scoots a little closer to me on the bench. "It was part of the contract we signed. Every worker here has. If you can't pay your debts but you can still work, Mugo can either keep you here or sell you. He owns us, Wen. He owns you, too."

My stomach turns. "The transfers." This is what those mysterious orders are, the ones for the older workers and those who displease him. No wonder they are so terrified. Mugo isn't moving them to another factory. He's selling them. Like slaves.

Melik must see that I believe him. "Mugo plans to sell us after the feasting season is over," he tells me. "Hazzi— who is being transferred in a week—warned me, and one of the others had heard Mugo talking about it. He has no intention of letting us go home."

"Run," I say. "There is a path through the Western Hills. You can follow it all the way to where you come from." Melik could never be a slave. He should never be broken.

"No," he says, and leans closer still. "I will stay here, and I will fight for what is mine."

I am caught by the fire in his words, by the sheer beauty of his face, by the silent power he seems to wield so effortlessly. I am afraid for him and amazed by him at the same time. He shames me, this boy who does not know his place—he is facing slavery and he will not run, while all *I* want to do is run, with little regard for whom I leave behind. "I will stay too," I say, "but I am scared."

He laughs quietly. "There's nothing wrong with being scared. It only means something important is at stake."

He is close enough for me to lean into, and I do, even though I shouldn't. I want to be like one of those Noor women, who can touch whom they please. Because right now I need to touch Melik so badly that I'm willing to risk everything to do it. I duck my head into the crook of his neck and press my forehead against his throat. I curl my hands into his shirt, careful of the long wound that lies beneath the fabric. For this moment it is only us, and the world is the size of this bench. He wraps his arms around me, cradling the back of my head in his palm. He murmurs in Noor, quiet words meant only for us.

"Are you scared?" I whisper against his skin.

He kisses my forehead and holds me so tight that I think I will never be cold again. "Wen, what is at stake is more important to me than anything in this world. I am terrified."

"That's good, Noor," says a hard voice from behind us. "Because you should be."

Chapter Twenty-two

MELIK'S ARMS TURN to steel around me. The pulse in his neck kicks hard against my cheek. Slowly we turn to see Iyzu standing behind our bench, and Lati next to him.

Melik takes my hand as he rises. "It's very late," he says. "Wen was just going inside." He pulls me to my feet and gives me a gentle push toward the main entrance of the factory.

I am too horrified to speak. With my cheeks burning and my head down, I begin to move toward the door, but Iyzu steps into my path.

Lati snorts. "If you're done with her, maybe she'd like to entertain us for a while. It will save us from having to pay for it."

"That will never happen," Melik says calmly.

Iyzu and Lati close the distance between us, exchanging the same kind of teasing, cruel look they shared the night they tried to take Melik's medicine. "You don't have all your Noor friends to protect you and your little slut tonight," Iyzu says to Melik, his voice silky and poisonous, "so how will you stop us?"

Melik smiles and holds his hands out at his sides. "That's right. I'm all alone." There is a brightness in his tone and expression that catches me, something eager yet cold.

Lati, stupid as he is, does not sense it. He grabs for my arm. But he doesn't even get close, because Melik buries his fist in Lati's soft middle, doubling him over. Melik hisses something to him in Noor and knees him in the face before he can straighten up. Lati crumples, moaning like a dying cow, blood gushing from his nose.

Iyzu charges Melik before his friend hits the ground, plowing into him with the full force of his body. My hands flutter at my sides and tears start in my eyes. Melik nearly died two days ago. His wounds aren't yet healed. He loses his balance and falls, with Iyzu on top of him. Iyzu punches at him furiously, raining blows on his face and body. But then I catch a glimpse of Melik's expression.

He does not look scared. Or hurt. He looks . . . satisfied. His mask has dropped away again, and there is fire in his eyes. Iyzu and Lati have given him the opportunity to hit back.

And he is very good at it.

He catches Iyzu around the neck and drives his elbow into Iyzu's shoulder. Iyzu grunts and attempts to roll away. But Melik grabs him by the hair and rises to his knees before shooting a vicious punch to Iyzu's throat. Iyzu's eyes go round as saucers as he tries and fails to draw breath. Melik leans down so that his face is close to Iyzu's, his eyes alight with the flames of hatred.

"Call her a slut again," he invites in a deadly whisper. "Threaten her again."

"Melik," I say. "You're going to get in trouble. You need to go back to your dorm."

He ignores me. He is staring intently at Iyzu, waiting for the boy's response. "Come now," he croons. "I am all alone, so how will I stop you?"

Iyzu lets out a choked whimper. Melik releases his hair and lets him collapse onto the stones while he turns his attention to Lati, who is trying to crawl away. Unhurried, loose limbed, like one of those big cats in the forest, Melik stalks over to him. There is blood on his hands.

"Please stop," I say, but my voice is so small, and it is dwarfed by his rage. I can't let him do this, though. If Lati and Iyzu tell, Melik will be arrested. It won't matter who started it.

I stumble forward right as Melik reaches Lati and blocks his escape route. He nudges Lati's shoulder with his boot. "A moment ago you were looking for entertainment," he says. "Is that still the case?"

Lati shakes his head desperately and Melik's brittle, frightening smile disappears. His jaw goes rigid. "Stand up," he orders.

He wants them to face him like men, but they are only boys. They are almost as big as he is, and they think they are tough only because no one has ever challenged them.

They believe Melik is weak because he and the Noor keep their heads down and have done their best to stay out of trouble. But Iyzu and Lati did not grow up with sickles and threshers in their hands. They are soft boys who, even though they work in this factory, have been given the easy jobs. They are future foremen, like Ebian.

They are nothing compared with Melik.

Fierce pride sparks in my chest, but it is immediately extinguished by my fear. Iyzu has gotten to his feet. And now he is holding a knife.

"Melik!" I cry as Iyzu charges.

Melik's boot connects with Lati's side, kicking him into Iyzu's path. Iyzu tries to jump over his thickset friend, but he doesn't quite manage it, and as he falls, Melik's hand whips out and grabs Iyzu's wrist. He strips the knife from Iyzu and deftly flips it in his palm. And I can see it in his eyes: He wants to kill. He wants to flay Iyzu and Lati like the beef carcasses that pass by his carving station. He wants payment for all the humiliation he and his Noor have suffered. His knuckles turn white as he grips the knife's bone handle, and the blade glints under the moonlight. He looks like he's considering which one of them to gut first.

My terror—for him . . . *of* him—renders me mute.

"Stop. All of you."

My father is standing in the doorway to the factory, and his posture is stiff with fury. It shakes his voice as he says, "Melik, step back."

Melik freezes, the knife still in his hand. He raises his head and his eyes find mine. The fire has faded, banked by uncertainty.

My father marches down the path. He is wearing his dressing gown. He must have woken up and saw that I was gone. "Are you hurt?" he asks, eyeing Melik's chest.

Melik blinks and looks down at himself. He is breathing hard, but apart from his hands, which are smeared with Lati's blood, he appears whole and strong. He touches his shoulder. "Not really, but I—"

"Go back to your dorm," my father snaps. "I will come check your wound within the hour."

Melik nods. His gaze shifts to me again, but my father steps between us. "Go *now*," he says in a voice that tells me he's trying not to yell but wants to in the worst way.

Melik spares Iyzu and Lati one last, cold glance, and then he heads back to his dorm, his shoulders straight and his head high, the bone-handled knife clutched in his fist.

Iyzu pushes himself to his feet. "The Noor assaulted us," he says in a wheezy voice. "We will be filing charges in the morning."

A rustling laugh comes from Father. "I witnessed the entire incident, including your attempt to attack an unarmed man with a knife. I may not have authority around here, but people know me to be an honest man."

"Look what he did to Lati!" Iyzu rasps, jabbing his finger at the round-shouldered boy who is sobbing wetly and has his hands cupped around his nose.

"I see that," my father says coldly. "I would hate for word to spread that the two of you cannot handle a single, injured Noor."

Iyzu's mouth snaps shut.

"Help Lati back to your dorm," Father instructs. "I will be there shortly to tend to his nose. Come, Wen." He puts his hand on my shoulder and guides me to the entrance of the factory.

"How could you?" he asks as soon as we reach the administrative hallway. "Do you have any idea what they will say about you?" His voice trembles with anger and shame.

"I didn't go out to meet Melik. I swear."

"It doesn't matter," he barks. "Almost nothing you do matters now. You kissed a man in public, for all to see. A Noor, no less. And now you have been out at night with him, unchaperoned."

The disgust in his voice strikes a match of defiance within me. "We did nothing improper!" I shriek. "I care about him, Father! And he cares about me!"

"He obviously doesn't care very much for your reputation!" he roars, shoving me through the doorway of the clinic.

"And you do?" The fire of disobedience is not hot, as it turns out. It is as cold as the wind from the north. I imagine each of my words is a shard of ice, shooting from my mouth to stab at his skin, at his heart. "Or are you only saving me for Underboss Mugo?"

My father steps back like he's felt the sting of every frigid splinter. He covers his mouth and bows his head. Without looking at me again, he walks up the stairs.

I spend an hour sweeping the clinic floor and scrubbing the exam table, unwilling to look at him again tonight. When I finally go upstairs, my father is snoring softly in his alcove.

I take my time in the washroom. I stare at my face in the dented, chipped mirror, wondering if I will look different when Mugo is done with me. Will my eyes be shadowed with dark circles? Will my cheeks be sunken like Jima's? When I am used up, will decent men pool their money to keep me off the streets, or will they turn their backs on me?

I clench my teeth to hold the sobs inside. My hands become fists. I—

"Some of the workers are planning to strike."

I gasp at the tinny sound of Bo's voice and step into the parlor. "How do you know that?" I whisper.

"Wen, you should learn not to underestimate me," Bo says. The words are spoken gently enough, but I feel the warning in them.

"Why are you telling me this?"

"Because I want you to be safe."

"Is a strike dangerous?"

His laugh echoes through the pipes. "This one will be."

I sink to my pallet and pull my blanket tight around me. "Remember your promise," I say.

"Remember yours," he replies.

The killing floor is closed for three full days for repairs. The factory is quiet, but it is not peaceful. It is thick with tension and unhappiness. I keep to the clinic, mostly, cleaning already-clean things, keeping my eye out for metal shavings to tell me if Bo is checking up on me. He talks to me through the vent at night, whispering that something is coming . . . something is coming . . . that I should be careful . . . and that I should keep my promise

OF METAL AND WISHES

to come see him. Sometimes I cover my head with my pillow so I can't hear him.

I see Melik only in the cafeteria. He does not try to approach me or speak to me. And he is never alone. The Noor surround him like a personal guard. Iyzu and Lati watch them with absolute loathing. Their faces are bruised, and their cheeks darken with rage whenever Melik comes near. Many of the other Itanyai watch him with suspicion too, like he might attack with the slightest provocation. I can only imagine the lies Iyzu and Lati have woven to protect their own reputations.

The entire compound feels like a tinderbox, stuffed tight and ready to burn.

The day before the floor is set to open again, I return to work to help Mugo set the office suite straight. The underboss is in a terrible mood, and he takes it out on me.

"Haven't you found those balance sheets and contracts yet, stupid girl?"

I peek over the pile of rubble in which I've been digging. My brown work dress is already tan with ash. "No, sir, I'm still trying to find them."

The explosion wreaked havoc with his organizational system. The enormous file cabinets were blown over by the blast, and they spilled their guts all over the floor. I've been rummaging through ceiling tiles and plaster to get to them, and I swear I've inhaled a bucketful of dust since breakfast.

He paces next to the rubble pile, occasionally tossing a chunk of ceiling tile my way just to be spiteful. I barely care. It's better than him putting his mushroomy fingers on me. "Well, tell me as soon as you do."

He walks back to his office, mumbling about quotas and ridiculous worker demands. Between the holiday, the flu, and this latest accident, it's not a good feasting season at Gochan One, and it's going to fall squarely on his shoulders. Worse than any of that, this morning a group of workers, including the Noor, delivered a list of demands—and it came with the threat of a strike. The deadline has been set—tonight at midnight, when the factory is scheduled to reopen. Mugo is seething. He has been on the phone all morning, talking to bosses from other factories and to the local police. He caught me listening earlier and slammed the door.

At lunch I eat in silence with Onya and Vie, but only because there is nowhere else to sit. They tolerate me, but neither of them is sympathetic. In fact, I think they believe I am partially to blame for what's happened. The men have segregated themselves into camps—on one side sit Ebian, Lati, Iyzu, and those I assume are allied with Mugo. They are mostly the career workers, the ones from the more privileged families who are hoping to be foremen and underbosses someday, as well as the ones who hope to seek favor from them. On the other side sit the Noor, along with many of the older Itanyai workers like Hazzi, the ones most likely to be transferred, the ones most likely to be crushed by this factory. They are a skinny, gnarled, slumped bunch, apart from the Noor, who are younger and sit straight, staring across the cafeteria at their adversaries. It is understood that they are truly enemies now, even though no one has said anything out loud. But it has gotten worse, and now I know that something is going to happen tonight when the

OF METAL AND WISHES

strike deadline comes. It scares me to death.

My eyes keep flicking toward Melik, even though I keep my head down. Finally Vie slaps my hand. "I have no idea why you're trying to be shy about it. Half the compound saw you with him the day of the explosion. Lati said it was disgusting."

"Lati is disgusting, so I hardly think he has the right to judge," I snap. And then, because the silent strain of the last few days has simply been too much, I stand up and brush my hand over my shoulder at her. Vie's mouth drops wide open at the insult, and she doesn't recover before I walk away. Melik and I lock eyes as I stride from the cafeteria, and I relive the seconds I've spent in his arms. It's enough to carry me straight to Bo's altar. Because of what's at stake. Because *everything* is at stake. I kneel in front of it.

"I'm ready to keep my promise," I say. "But I can't come to you." I'm quite sure I wouldn't make it without being gutted by the spiders.

"Meet me, then," he whispers through the grate, and it sounds like he's right there, close enough to breathe in my ear. He gives me my instructions, and we make our plans.

I feel grimly powerful as I continue to dig through the rubble in Mugo's office this afternoon, because I am protecting what is mine. Bo has promised not to harm the people I care about as long as I visit him, and it is the one thing I can offer the Noor, this protection. It might be nothing, and it might be everything. It really depends on Bo.

I am in the depths of these thoughts when there is

a knock at the entrance of Mugo's office suite. I look up to see Melik walk in, his jaw set. Mugo emerges from his office to see who's arrived. "What do you want?" he snaps. "I've already received your stupid demands."

Melik's brow furrows. "You sent for me." He holds up a note, and it looks exactly like the ones I deliver all the time to various unlucky workers. But I didn't deliver anything to anyone this afternoon.

Mugo puts his hands on his skinny hips. "I didn't send for you, idiot, so get back to your dorm."

Melik frowns. "But it says—"

Mugo snatches the note from his hand. "I don't care what it says!" he shouts. "Do I look like I have time to help you figure out where you should be?"

Melik looks down at me, his eyes full of questions, but I can't answer any of them. I shrug helplessly.

"Quit looking at Wen like she knows more than I do!" Mugo rushes over to me and pulls me up hard by the arm. It hurts too much for me to keep silent and still, and I try to wrench myself away, but that only seems to anger him more. He slaps my hip.

Melik steps forward so quickly that Mugo flinches. "Let her go, now. You have no right to hit her."

"Get out!" Mugo shrieks, and his fear is apparent to all of us, which completely enrages him. Droplets of spittle fly from his gaping mouth. Veins stick out on his forehead. "You'll be lucky if I don't transfer you by morning! Get! Out!" he roars.

But he's let go of me, and I scoot out of his reach. Melik looks at me like he's afraid to leave, but I nod him away because Mugo might transfer Melik right now if he doesn't obey. These demands . . . the workers are simply trying to get what's fair, but as soon as Mugo finds his balance sheets and their signed contracts, he'll have proof of their debt. A strike may only make it easier for him to sell them to the camps.

Melik reluctantly backs himself out the door. The underboss's fit has drawn the attention of the workers cleaning up the last of the boiler explosion debris. They stare at Melik as he pivots on his heel and walks away, and then they all turn their heads to me and Mugo.

"Get back to work!" Mugo shouts. His face is as red as a beet. "Get back to work or you'll be fined for inefficiency!"

That clears everyone out pretty quickly. And fortunately for me, Mugo seems too upset to deal with me and disappears into his office, slamming the door again. I finish my shift and tiptoe out, grateful to have escaped with only a bruised arm and hip.

I wipe myself down with a wet cloth, trying to rid myself of the plaster dust and ash. I change into my deep purple wool dress with grape leaves curling along the sleeves and neckline. This is one of my last untouched dresses, and maybe I shouldn't even be wearing it, seeing as I might need to sell it to Khan sometime soon, but I don't want to go to Bo looking like a servant girl. I want him to see me well, because I think that is what is best for him—and everyone else in the factory.

My father is in his clinic when I descend the stairs. "Going out?"

"For a walk," I say, surprised at his attention. He and I have barely spoken to each other since that night in the square.

He doesn't look up from his medical text. "How was work?"

His play at fatherly concern sends a hard jolt of anger through me, and I finally say the words that have been eating at my heart. "It was a transfer, wasn't it? Mugo threatened to transfer you to a labor camp if you didn't allow me to work for him."

That brings my father's head up. His mouth opens and closes a few times. "How did you know about the transfers?"

"Melik told me." My fists are clenched. I would never want my father to be sent to a labor camp—but knowing he was willing to sell my virginity and maybe my future to avoid that fate *hurts.*

"Wen, I . . ." He closes his eyes and rubs his hand over his face.

It's enough. As good as a confession. Unable to spend another minute with him, I storm out of the room.

Chapter Twenty-three

I WRENCH THE STAIRWELL door open, and instead of going down, I climb. Bo reassured me that there are no traps on the upper floors, so I move quickly. He told me to meet him for the dinner hour, and it's just started. I open the door to the fourth floor and walk across a narrow room lined on both sides with huge pipes. I reach a door that takes me to another staircase, this one rickety and metal. The air is cool here, and I'm glad for my wool dress and overcoat.

The next door opens onto the roof. There is a railing along the edge. I tread gingerly and am careful not to look down. I love the smoky open air, which is fresher than the stale killing smells inside of the factory, but I do not want to see how far I could fall. As I approach the rear of the factory, where the smokestacks jut into the sky, the roof flattens out and opens up.

I can see all of the Ring from here, and it is beautiful in the smoggy sunset, just starting to glow in the evening dim. I understand why Bo likes being up here. I look around, expecting to see him.

He's not here.

I turn in place and spot a table and chairs nestled at the base of a smokestack. I can tell they are Bo's. The chairs are beautifully wrought, all metal, of course, but there are plump cushions on each of them, probably lifted from the textile factory. I sit down in one of them and look out on the Ring. The streetlamps and pink lights are flaring to life. Decorations from First Holiday hang from every post and pole, the red and green and yellow garlands, the papier-mâché dragon heads that ward off the evil spirits that come with the cold north wind.

I shiver and pull my overcoat tight around my body, wondering if Bo could have forgotten me. When I can't sit still any longer, I get up and stroll to the edge of the roof, bidding my good-byes to the view so I can go back inside and take a hot bath, and prepare myself for whatever's coming late tonight when the strike deadline arrives. If something happens, my father's clinic will fill up quickly, and no matter how I feel about him, I will help him take care of the injured.

A door slams in the distance and hard-heeled foot-steps clomp along the rooftop. Bo stops when he sees there's no one at the table, but then he spots me and jogs over. His metal arm is encased in a shirtsleeve tonight. He's wearing slacks and a dark button-up shirt, like he's one of the bosses' sons who live on the Hill. But when he turns his head, his black eye glows within his metal half-face.

"I'm so sorry," he says, slightly out of breath. "I was working on something new, and the time got away from me."

"It's all right," I say. "I needed to get out of the clinic anyway."

"Did Guiren have a particularly gory patient?" He draws a deep breath and clicks his metal fingers together. I shudder because it reminds me of the spiders, and the clicking stops.

"No, that kind of thing doesn't bother me."

Bo chuckles. "You are a very unusual girl. I was talking to Guiren the other day, and he's got it in his head that you should go to medical school."

I scoff, but really, the mention of medical school stings. "My father is a smart man, but not a very practical one."

"He said you have the mind for it."

"But not the money. Didn't he tell you? Mugo owns him. He threatened to transfer my father to a labor camp."

"You think Guiren sold you." Bo's black eye nearly blinds me with its light as he turns to me. "You're wrong, Wen. Mugo didn't threaten to send your father to the labor camps." He nudges my chin up with his fingers. "He threatened to send *you.*"

I reach for the railing as my understanding of my father shifts on its axis. "Me?"

Bo nods, and the moonlight bounces off his metal face. "Guiren agonized over it. Mugo gave him a choice—you as his secretary or you shipped to a labor camp at sixteen."

I am choking on my guilt. I can't speak.

"He wanted to keep you with him. He decided this might be the lesser of two evils, though truly, I think he might regret it."

"Why?" Because I am such a brat? Because I only think of myself, and not what this is like for my father? Who could blame him if he thinks that?

"Because he has to watch you go through it. Every day he wonders if Mugo will ruin you. He's been waiting for it. It's killing him, but he doesn't want to burden you with his own fear. He doesn't know how to talk to you about it."

I cover my face with my hands. I cannot bear the weight of this on top of my own terror.

"Neither you nor Guiren should worry. I promised you I would keep you safe," he says fiercely, but it isn't enough for me, only another reminder that the danger is real, that the clock is ticking.

Bo is quiet. I think he's waiting for me to look up, to thank him, to relax, but I can't. Then he sighs and says quietly, "I love this view."

He has changed the shape of the conversation in exactly the way I need.

I slowly remove my hands and gaze out at the Ring, only patterns of yellow light in the darkness now. "It's lovely." I look up at his human side, at the warm smile on his face. "Do you ever think of actually . . . going out there?"

The smile dims. "I think of it, sure."

"And where do you dream of going?"

He moves a little closer to me. "I dream of the sea-shore, and it's all your fault."

We laugh a bit, a few musical notes carried on the fog of our breath. "There's nothing stopping you, Bo, not really."

He makes a regretful sound. "Only the fact that I'm dead."

I slip my arm through his because I do not want him to feel alone in this moment. "Surely a ghost who has done such amazing things can manage to resurrect himself."

I gaze at his full face, and in the moonlight it is beautiful. Hesitantly he takes my hand, and his is warm and real, full of might-have-beens. "You make me want to," he says. "You make me want too many things, Wen."

It hurts him, I know, when I bow my head. I can't say what he needs to hear: that I want the same things he wants. In another time and place, maybe, but not here, not now, not with Melik ruling my dreams with his jade eyes and the electric strength that rolls from him even when he is quiet and still. Bo has a different kind of power and is just as strong, but his is a restless and dangerous energy, too prone to cruelty, too childlike to make me feel safe.

"I'm sorry," I say.

He squeezes my hand. "I know," he whispers, and lets me go, turning to look out at the Ring. "It's late. You should get back."

I am shamefully relieved that he is letting me go so easily, that he doesn't require any more from me tonight. "Good night, Bo," I say, and I leave him there, lit by the moon, and return to the clinic.

My father is still at his desk, hunched over something he holds in his hands. I pull off my overcoat and stand over him. "Can I make you some tea?"

He blinks at me. "That would be nice."

I lean over and kiss his forehead, right on top of the worry lines that crease his brow. He sits back, and I see he is cradling a portrait of my mother. She smiles up at me—a heart-shaped face, a wide forehead and slightly pointed chin just like mine, and a winsome playfulness that I lack. She is beautiful, my mother.

She was beautiful.

"When she got sick, I offered to take a leave from this job to take care of her," he whispers. "She wouldn't let me. She didn't want our debts to rise any higher."

I swallow, and my throat hurts. My fingers flutter at my neck. That's where the sickness was, the cancer, my father called it. It stole her voice and made it hard for her to breathe. Then, at the end, it was everywhere. She couldn't walk, couldn't eat, couldn't do anything but try to hold her moans inside. She wanted to keep her dignity. She wanted to be a fine lady to the end.

But I wanted to keep my mother with me. My father and I conspired to sneak each of her lovely dresses out of her bedroom while she was sleeping, selling them to Khan to buy her the dried reishi mushrooms and foxglove root and dozens of other herbs we hoped would cure her, as well as the opium to ease her suffering. My father sent me instructions, and I followed them to the letter, slipping medicine into her tea, making poultices and vapor baths. Still she didn't get better. My father did take a whole week off right at the end, and until the last hour I believed he might save her, that he could do something I couldn't.

"Could you have healed her, if she'd let you come

earlier?" I'm whispering too. This is too painful to talk about in full voice.

He shakes his head. "No, I don't think so. And she wouldn't go to the hospital. She never did like those places." He chuckles sadly. "Rather ironic, I always thought."

I touch his shoulder. "She wanted to be at home. She felt best there. She told me that."

He strokes his thumb along her face. "She was a strong woman, and it was hard to stop her when she had her mind set on something. You are very much like her in that way." His bony frame trembles beneath my fingers. "I miss her so much, Wen," he says in a halting voice. His hand fumbles up to clutch my arm and pull me to him. "I feel like I'm failing her. And I know I'm failing you."

I put my arms around him, trying to hold him together even though we're both shaking with sobs we don't want to let loose. "It's all right," I say, my voice cracking.

He lets out a wheezy laugh. "We both know nothing could be further from the truth."

That's how we're standing, awkwardly hugging, when Ebian bursts into the clinic. He reeks of vomit and it's dripping from his chin.

"Dr. Guiren," he pants, clutching at his chest. "You have to come. I . . . just . . . you have to . . ."

My father stands up, hastily wiping at his eyes. "Of course, Foreman Ebian. What's happened? Are you ill? Injured?" He pulls out his pocket watch and glances at it. I know why—it's still a few hours to midnight. We didn't expect violence before then.

Ebian shakes his head. His toasted-almond skin is

almost green. "It's not me. Not me." His stomach heaves and he doubles over, retching. "You have to come."

"Has there been an accident?" My father has grabbed the medical kit he takes with him on his rounds to dorms, but judging from the way Ebian is acting, I don't think a few opium sticks and bandages are going to be enough. "Where are we going?"

"The killing floor," says Ebian, already in the doorway.

My father gestures to me to grab the other end of the stretcher we keep for cases where we might have to transport the patient, and I obey. "I thought no one was allowed on the killing floor until midnight," he says.

"No one is. It's not one of the workers."

We stare at him.

Ebian wipes his mouth and grimaces. "It's Mugo."

Chapter Twenty-four

MY FATHER AND I JOG down the hall with the stretcher, and I focus on my strides because it feels like my legs have turned to jelly. A group of men waits at the end of the hallway, and they are all talking at once. Ebian waves his arms as we approach, and they part for us. I bow my head. From behind me, I hear a low hiss, and I know it is directed at me. This is Ebian's crew, the ones who hate the Noor and hate me, too, because I am the Noor-lover.

The door to the killing floor has been propped open with a cattle prod. As we approach it, Ebian says to my father, "We don't know how to get him down."

As I turn the corner and peer through the doorway, the first thing I notice is how abandoned it looks, how quiet. My father stops dead and looks up, and so do I.

Mugo is hanging from the meat hooks.

I back up a step. He's been cut open from neck to groin, and this is not the work of any spider. It's a neat incision, not a messy tear. His head is tilted back, looking up at the ceiling, like he can't bear what's going on below. But really, he's not bearing anything. He's obviously dead.

"You need to call the regional police," my father says to Ebian. "There is nothing I can do for him. When did you find him?"

Ebian speaks from just outside the door; I think he's at risk for vomiting again. "I was in the cafeteria and heard the system fire up; I came in here because I was afraid of sabotage, and there he was. He was moving, I think. Could he still be alive?"

My father shakes his head and points to the floor below Mugo. His finger is trembling even though his voice is steady. "If his heart were beating, he'd be bleeding. It looks like he was already dead when he was hung up there, because there's no mess on the floor. Only that."

"What are you talking about?" asks Ebian as he steps past my father to see what he's pointing at. I peek around my father's back. Written in big block letters on the killing floor, in what I assume is Mugo's blood, it says:

THIS IS TYRANNY'S REWARD. BOSSES BEWARE.

Behind me I feel the heat of the men's bodies as they crowd the doorway. At first everything is quiet, but then their voices rise slowly, repeating the phrase over and over like a sparking flame traveling along a fuse.

And then it explodes.

"It's the Noor!" yells one man. "They did this!"

A shout erupts from the knot of workers, and at first Ebian actually tries to calm things down. "We have to call the regional police! This is a murder!"

"They'll take a day to arrive!" Iyzu is standing at the front of the group, red faced. He glances at me with pure contempt, his lips curled into a snarl. "We know exactly who did this!"

"Call the others!" Lati shouts, his bruised face flushed with excitement. "We'll search their dorms ourselves!"

The men have become a mob, yelling among themselves, making plans to gather their numbers and storm the Noor dorms.

Then I hear something that freezes my insides completely. "We saw the red one fighting with Mugo this afternoon!"

As the arguing goes on, whipping their rage into a frenzy, I turn to my father, who is ashen faced and wide eyed, and say the only thing in my mind. "I have to go."

"No," he says, reaching for me. "This is too dangerous."

"I have to." I run before he can grab me.

I don't even try to plow through the mob, because I know they would stop me. They are so busy bickering and planning, though, that I have no trouble skirting around the side of the killing floor and going through the plastic flaps to the little room between the floor and the cafeteria. There's no one here except for a few cafeteria workers, including Minny, who gives me a startled look as I run past the empty tables, out to the area by Bo's altar, around the back of the crowd, and out the door. I lift my skirts and sprint through the square, up the path to the Noor dorms.

I don't know if they did this. I can't even begin to think of who would be angry enough at Mugo to kill him like that. Or maybe there are so many people that I can't think of who wouldn't. But justice won't be done like this, with a mob gathering to destroy the Noor.

I wrench the door to the dorm open and run along the hallway, shouting, "Get up, get up!"

The Noor appear in their doorways, peering at me with curiosity. They don't try to stop me as I barge along. "Melik! Sinan!" I call.

They step out of their room at the end of the hall, and Melik pushes through a few of the others to get to me. "What's wrong?"

"Mugo's been murdered. They think one of you did it. There's a crowd and they're gathering more. They're coming for you."

I watch him carefully, but he gives me nothing to hold on to, no sign of innocence or guilt. He simply lifts his head and shouts in Noor, and all of them stop for a second, staring at him. He waves his arms to set them into motion and pushes Sinan ahead of him, then grabs the sleeve of one of the older Noor and barks an order at him. The older Noor puts his arm over Sinan's shoulders and whisks him down the hallway.

Melik turns back to me. "We're going. There is no way we will find justice here." He pauses, like he's at war with himself, like for once he is not sure of his words. And then he just says, "Go."

OF METAL AND WISHES

He hustles me down the corridor toward the exit, but the Noor are knotted together in the narrow space, tossing one another supplies, shouting instructions back and forth, all trying to go at once. Melik and I are all the way at the back, and we are trapped. He spins and looks around him. "I have to get you out," he mutters.

From the front of the building we hear the first sounds of fighting, shouts and cries and heavy thuds. Melik pushes me behind him and backtracks.

"Do you think you could fit through one of the windows?" he asks.

He puts his arm around me and swings me into one of the rooms as the fighting outside goes on. It sounds like the entire ramshackle building is going to come down around our ears. If the mob thought they could roll through the Noor like a tidal wave, they were very mistaken.

Melik yanks on the metal frame of the window, but I will never fit through that tiny space. "Don't," I say. "It won't work."

He snaps something in Noor and grabs for my hand, tugging me back into the hallway. Most of the Noor are out, but the sounds of men fighting are right outside the door. It's a full-scale riot. The factory square is a battleground.

"Stay behind me, and when we get out into the open, run," Melik says, and leads me toward the stairwell.

That's when we hear the crash behind us.

The mob has found another way in, through a window, maybe, or a back doorway. Iyzu and Lati are at the front, and their gazes immediately land on Melik. Their eyes are alight with viciousness as they shout for the others to seize him, and when I see what's in their hands, I know it is all but over for us.

They are armed with the sparking electric cattle prods from the killing floor.

Melik sees them too, and with a new urgency he shoves me forward again as they charge down the hall. We make it to the front stairs, and I feel the cool night air on my face. Melik's hands are on my waist, and just as I am thinking we might actually get out, he jerks away from me. Iyzu has caught up with us. Melik evades Iyzu's first jab with the cattle prod and punches him in the jaw. Iyzu's head snaps back, but he jerks the prod up as Melik descends on him. The shock sends Melik arching backward, his mouth open in a silent shout that echoes like an explosion in my head. He collapses onto the landing, and Iyzu jabs him with the prod again and again, then presses it into Melik's shoulder and doesn't let up. All I hear is the flopping of Melik's limbs; he is unable to make a sound. The acrid smell of burning cloth and flesh fills the stairwell. I dive for him, only to be ripped away by Lati.

"Bring them both to his room," says Iyzu, and he steps back to let the others drag Melik, who is limp and twitching from the voltage running through his body.

Lati wrestles me along the floor, my feet barely touching the ground. He twists my arm behind me, and the shearing agony makes me scream. "I'll break it if you keep fighting me," he says, and clutches me against him so tightly that I have trouble breathing.

The men dump Melik on the floor of his room. Ebian walks in, somber faced. "Search it," he says.

And they do, tossing around the Noor's possessions, their meager clothing, their sleeping pallets. Melik is lying facedown, and all I can do is watch him, will him to keep breathing.

One of the workers stands up abruptly, holding Melik's sleeping pallet in one hand. "Found something," he grunts, and points to the floor.

There lies a small book, one I remember seeing him read the night I came to his room to check his stitches. On its cover I can easily read the title in block letters: THE PRICE OF TYRANNY.

Next to it lies the bone-handled knife, blood crusted over its razor-sharp blade.

Chapter Twenty-five

THEY ALLOW ME to return to the clinic but post guards outside the door. My father and I are both confined here, awaiting the regional police, who must come all the way from Kanong. As I pace the cramped exam room, my father tells me what he knows. Apparently, all of the Noor, including Sinan, escaped the compound and fled into the Ring. They left a few dozen badly beaten factory workers in their wake. The local police are hunting them, but the police are so incompetent and inefficient that my father has no doubt the Noor will be high in the Western Hills by dawn.

Melik is not with them. We were dragged across the compound, and the last I saw of him, Ebian ordered him locked in one of the refrigerator rooms just off the killing floor.

It is hard for me to think right now because Melik's silent screams are still echoing in my head.

I have no idea what time it is when my father finally orders me to go to my room and try to sleep. He looks like he has aged twenty years in the past few hours, and I know I have done this to him. Judging by the way he is looking at me, I am in a great deal of trouble.

I sit on my pallet and stare. Did Melik really do this? I saw the knife, the blood clotted along its wicked blade. It could easily cut a man down the middle when wielded by a strong hand. And by the way Melik held it that night in the square, it was clear he knew how to use it.

And that book, the one about tyranny, I saw Melik reading it. I heard his words that night outside of the pink-light salon. Strong words, meant to foment a revolution. Was this what he had planned all along? Did the fight with Iyzu and Lati drive him to it? Or did the argument with Mugo this afternoon snap the wire and trigger his rage?

The regional police are coming to figure it out.

I'm not sure the mob is going to give them that much time.

"Bo, can you hear me?"

I hold my breath until he answers. "I can, Wen. Are you all right?"

"No." It comes out of me as a sob.

"Did they hurt you?"

I sniffle. "Not really. But they hurt *him*." I can't hold it in anymore. Melik is too loud in my head, too big in my thoughts. I shouldn't be talking about this with Bo, but he is the only one I can think of who might help me.

"The red Noor did a terrible thing," he says quietly.

My heart sinks. "Did you see him do it?" I demand. "How do you know?"

He is quiet for several seconds. "Ebian thinks he did it. So do all his men."

"That's not enough proof for me," I cry.

An exasperated huff flows through the vent. "They found the murder weapon."

"He's smart. If he's actually guilty, why would he hide it under his sleeping pallet?"

"How do you know Mugo was the only one he wanted to kill? The red Noor certainly had the motive, and who's to say he didn't want to take out Jipu or Ebian, too? What about those boys he beat up? Maybe he was just getting started."

I pause, remembering how Melik knew where Mugo and Jipu lived, like he'd looked into it. What if he *was* going after the bosses?

Bo sighs. "He's aligned with a group of men who want to unionize, which Mugo would never allow. They are naive if they think they will end up anywhere but on a train headed for the camps."

"You know an awful lot about this."

"You're upset with me," he says.

I scrub my hand over my face. This is no way to talk to someone I want to help me. "No. I'm sorry. I just . . . I can't believe Melik would do something like this. He seems so much . . . *better* than this."

Bo laughs, all derision. "He's a Noor! They're little better than barbarians!"

"He's a good man," I snap. But deep inside of me

there is a seed of doubt. Melik is good, yes. But he is also a warrior. He keeps it hidden, but I have seen what happens when his mask falls away.

"You deserve better." Bo grinds out every word. Then he draws a breath and cools the heat in his voice. "You've had such a long day and a horrible night, Wen. Please get some rest."

"Good night," I whisper, because I know I have ruined any chance of getting help for Melik from Bo, if there was ever any chance to begin with.

Once again I'm alone in the darkness. I lie still as my father trudges up the stairs and stands over my bed. I lie still as he brushes his teeth and washes his face. I lie still as he creeps into his alcove and pulls the curtain shut, and I don't move until his quiet snores reach me.

But then I'm up. I can't stand to be still anymore. I slip on my woolen shoes and my dressing gown, and I tread down the stairs so lightly that they don't even creak. I don't turn on the light in the clinic; I don't need to. I know where everything is, and I prepare my supplies and fill the pockets of my dressing gown with the things I might need.

When I'm done, I put my ear to the door and listen.

The guards are outside, and they are breathing heavily. They expect no trouble from us, and it is the deepest hours of the morning. Silently I twist the knob and pull the door open, just a crack. One of the guards is sitting against the wall, his head hanging back, his mouth wide open.

He will be my first victim.

I crouch low and pull a soporific sponge from my

pocket, careful to keep it far from my own nose, and slide my arm out the door. The guard twitches a bit as I lower it over his face, but it takes no more than a few seconds for his breathing to deepen even further, for the drool to drip from his gaping mouth. He will not be waking up anytime soon.

I pull the door open a little farther and see the other guard sitting across the hall. His thick arms are crossed over his middle, and his head hangs forward. I am tempted to leave him there, but if he wakes up before I'm back, he might raise the alarm. I emerge into the hallway and close the door behind me, careful to hold the knob and release it slowly, but the click echoes down the hall like cannon fire.

The thick-armed guard raises his head, blinking and confused.

I am caught.

"What are you doing out here?" he asks stupidly.

"I was hungry," I say, as if that should be obvious. And even though I want to run, I walk straight toward him like one of Bo's spiders. I am activated and will follow this sequence of movements, this plan I've already set in motion.

The guard doesn't expect this. He expects me to be scared of him, to shrink back against the door like I've done something wrong. I don't. I advance on him without hesitation, and he doesn't know what to do with me.

"I might have a bun if you're really starving," he mumbles, because he reads something on my face that tells him I am serious, that I am not leaving until I get what I want.

"That might do," I say, and now I am only steps from him. My hand dips into my pocket.

And when he reaches for his satchel, I pull out the syringe and stab it into his upper arm. He jerks, but I'm ready, and I move with him as he tries to evade me, managing to depress the plunger and fill him with opium before he knocks me away. I hit the wall and bounce off, but find my balance quickly and watch him. He will not be coming after me, even though he's trying to do exactly that.

He lifts his arm and it falls back into his lap. "Whatcha," he says. "Whatcha munding . . . bicklind . . . purpsy . . ." He falls off his chair and lands on his side.

I put his satchel under his head so he's not resting on cold concrete.

I'm not entirely heartless.

My guards will be sleeping until someone comes to relieve them, probably at the day shift whistle. I have until then to get what I need.

My footsteps are completely silent as I jog down the hallway. I climb through a shattered window into Mugo's office. It's pitch black in here, and I won't be able to find my way through the maze of piled debris. I pull a candle from my pocket and light it, because it is easily covered and not as noticeable as the bright electric lights. The suite of rooms is in disarray, but I weave around the ceiling tiles and piles of rubble to the inner office. Mugo kept his master key in the locked bottom drawer of his desk. As my candle's faint light sweeps over the desk, the sight of Melik's name draws me up short. I hold the candle over the crumpled note.

MELIK,

I NEED TO DISCUSS YOUR BROTHER'S ILLEGALLY OBTAINED WORK PASS AND THE NECESSARY PENALTIES. THIS IS A MATTER OF THE UTMOST URGENCY.

UNDERBOSS MUGO

This is exactly the kind of note Mugo liked to write, the kind that struck fear into the heart of every worker in the compound. And when Melik got this, I'm certain it made his stomach drop to his shoes. Sinan is the most important person in the world to him, and if Melik believed he was under threat, he would do anything to protect him. Mugo would have loved that, to bring Melik low.

The thing is, this note is not in Mugo's handwriting.

Usually he made me type his notes, but when he needed to dash one off, he wrote it himself, and his handwriting was tiny and perfect and neat. This note is written in block letters, and there's a certain flare to them, a boldness, that Mugo's writing did not have. The *S* at the end of "PENALTIES" is like a lightning strike, stabbed into the page. It is vaguely familiar to me, but I can't pull the why or where to the front of my mind right now.

I tuck the note into my pocket and pull my father's scalpel out. It's a fiercely sharp little blade, and a few years ago, thanks to my intense curiosity about my father's tiny study in the cottage on the Hill, I learned it is also excellent at picking simple locks. It takes me no time to spring the lock on Mugo's drawer. I swipe the master key and climb back through the window. I press myself against the wall for a moment, catching my breath and listening hard. The administrative hallway is silent, but people are awake at the front of the factory, near the cafeteria. I hear the low, angry buzz of voices. Probably men waiting for the regional police to arrive or recovering in the aftermath of the brawl with the Noor. They are, no doubt, in dangerous moods. But that's all right. That's not where I'm going.

I slide my feet along the floor, sheltering my guttering candle with my hand, and peek through the filmy window to the killing floor. With careful, slow movements I use Mugo's key to unlock the door. Even in the yawning darkness of the enormous chamber I can see that Mugo's body is gone. I inch the door open and slip inside, where the dark letters still mar the floor. I raise my candle to read them again, trying to picture Melik writing them in blood.

But as I stand over them, I see "BOSSES"—each *S* is shaped like a lightning strike. I pull the forged note out of my pocket and hold it up, comparing the two.

I think back to this afternoon, how Melik walked in at the exact wrong time. How it happened when a group of men was cleaning up the mess out in the corridor. So many people saw Melik exchanging words with Mugo, saw Mugo screaming at him. Someone lured Melik here for this confrontation. The same person who wrote these words on the killing floor. Maybe the same person—or *people*—who knew he had a bone-handled knife in his possession.

Melik has been framed.

I'm not sure which emotion is bigger, the rage or the relief, but they've both sunk their teeth into me. If I'm good—very, very good—this will be the key to freeing Melik. This will be the—

"I knew I heard something!"

I jam the note into my pocket and reach for another syringe, my heart nearly bursting from my chest. I turn around slowly as Lati walks forward, a smug smile on his face. Iyzu is right behind him. "Did you come to try to free your boyfriend?" Lati asks.

Yes. "No," I say, taking a few steps back. "But he is innocent."

Lati laughs. "Innocent." He says it like a curse. "Wait until I tell the police how he attacked me. How he threatened me and Iyzu with the very knife he used to cut Mugo open."

"I'm going back to the clinic now," I say. But Iyzu and Lati don't move away from the door.

Iyzu shakes his head. "I don't think so. Did you help your Noor lover, Wen?" He looks me up and down. "Are you just a stupid whore, or are you a murderer?"

"Are you?" I snap.

"Why would we want to kill Mugo?" Iyzu asks with a chilly smile. He walks toward me with a strange, vicious look on his face. I swear, he wants me to pay for the humiliation he suffered at Melik's hands. I can already tell the price will be very high.

My fingers tighten over my second opium syringe, but I know it's hopeless, because there are two of them, and both are twice as strong as I am. If I try to use the syringe or the scalpel, it's more likely they'll turn one or the other against me. So I reach for the only thing I have left. "Have you ever made a wish to the Ghost?"

Lati and Iyzu stare at me.

"I know you have," I say. "Has he ever granted one?"

They look at me like I'm crazy, but Lati tries to recover control of the conversation. "Why, did you *wish* to satisfy both of us at once in exchange for your freedom?"

I am choking on my fear. Part of me is tempted to jam this opium syringe into my own thigh, because at least I won't be awake while they hurt me. But until I'm sure I've been abandoned, until I'm certain I'm completely alone, I won't give up. "I wish . . ." I look around, and then I blow out my candle. "It's a little too dark in here. I wish for some light," I say.

Iyzu strides forward. "You are the dumbest girl on the—"

We all blink as the killing floor lights up as bright as day, every single bulb in the place snapping on at once.

Chapter Twenty-six

BO HAS NOT abandoned me. I start to step around them, hoping they'll let me return to the clinic, but that is too much to ask for. Lati snatches me by the arm.

"I don't know how you did that, but I'm not impressed." He grinds his fingers against my arm bones and grabs a handful of my hair, but as he twists my head back, Iyzu stops him.

"Lati, I think we should hold off," he says, glancing up nervously at the glaring lights. He may not have been scared of Mugo, but he is smart enough to fear the Ghost.

"What are we supposed to do with her?" Lati whines. His fingers are inching up my ribs, and I feel like I'm going to be sick.

Iyzu's smile is hideous. "Let her keep the Noor warm. They deserve each other."

Lati doesn't seem to like that idea. Judging by his suspicious frown and questing fingers, I think he'd rather keep me for himself, but Iyzu is the leader between them, so he drags me across the killing floor to the refrigerated chamber way in the back. I look around, hoping Bo will appear and rescue me, but when Iyzu orders Lati to go fetch a group of men to post outside the door on this side and the one that opens to the cafeteria kitchen, I suspect there are few things my Ghost can do for me now.

Iyzu pulls a set of keys from his pocket and unlocks the chamber, then shoves me inside. "Try not to freeze to death," he says brightly, and then he slams the door.

I am familiar with darkness, but this one is complete. Black and cold. "Melik?"

From across the room comes a low moan, but it is the best sound I have ever heard. I take a step and run into something hard and pointy.

That's when I remember I still have a candle clutched in my fist. I light my only remaining match on the concrete floor, and when my tiny flame gutters to life, I hold it up.

This is a terrible place.

It's as cold as the winter frost. Piles of meat, ribs, hindquarters, and ground chuck are all around me in huge bins. Dead cow and metal and my own fogged breath. But over in the corner is what I'm looking for, and I weave through beef and bins and boxes to get to him. He is curled on his side, his knees pulled to his chest, and he is shaking, shivering, losing his battle against the cold. I drop to the floor and lean over him.

"Melik," I whisper against the side of his face, stroking my hand down his arm.

"Wen always has medicine," he mutters thickly, and then chuckles, like what he's said is incredibly funny.

I think he has hypothermia.

I lift my candle so I can see him better. There's a blackened mark on his shoulder where the cattle prod burned through his shirt and cauterized his pale flesh. His face is deeply bruised, and blood trickles from his nose. They've beaten him. Tried to put him in his place. It fills me with an anger so deep it boils from my skin, enough to keep us both warm.

I get up again and use one of the enormous scoops to dig a heaping lump of ground chuck from a nearby bin. I plop it to the floor and sculpt it into a mound in front of Melik's knees, and then I stick the base of my candle in it to secure it. I sit down next to the candle, strip off my dressing gown, and slide it over us like a tent. My mother made me this gown for cool winter nights, and it will hold the heat of the candle in and keep us alive. Of course, that leaves me in only my thin cotton nightgown, but this isn't really the time to worry about modesty. I'm more worried about freezing.

While I wait for the space to warm up, I rub Melik's frozen hands and talk to him, telling him stupid stories from my childhood, singing him songs my mother used to sing, telling him all the things I wish for, even my dream that I will go to medical school and be a doctor like my father. I don't think it matters too much what I say, but I hope Melik will find his way back to my voice, that he will wake and know he is with me, that we are together. I wish

I could tell him he is safe, but that is far from true.

"I know you didn't do it," I say when I finally run out of mundane things to talk about. "I have proof."

"Iyzu and Lati have proof too," he replies, his voice barely above a whisper.

He's awake, and I have no idea how long he's been listening to me prattle on about myself. I scoot closer, nudging up against his knees, and he raises his head and wipes the blood from his nose with the back of his sleeve. But he doesn't smile at me. In fact, he looks extremely unhappy. "Why are you in here with me? What did you do?"

I shrug. "I'd rather be in here than out there. Lati and Iyzu caught me on the killing floor. They probably don't want me to be able to tell anyone that they framed you."

He squints at me in the dim light of the candle. "You shouldn't be here. This is the last place you should be."

I know that. But I can't regret it. "You shouldn't be here either."

"Do you know if my brother got away?" His voice is so full of fear that it hurts me.

I inch forward on my knees, careful not to set my nightgown on fire. "He did. The local police are looking for your friends, but the last I heard, they had all escaped into the Ring."

I touch his face, a brush of his cheek. Because while I am here, I may as well pretend that I am a Noor woman and I can touch whomever I please. He closes his eyes and winces as my fingers slide down his face. "That hurts." I pull my hand away, but he catches hold of my palm and tugs me back. "I didn't say I wanted you to stop."

SARAH FINE

After a few minutes like that, just the simplest of touches, he opens his eyes, and they are full of want and wish and sorrow. "When they open that door," he says, "they will take me away, and that will be the last you see of me."

"That's not true."

He cups my face with his palm. "You know it is. There's no way I'll have a fair trial. I'll be lucky if I *have* a trial."

"The regional police are coming to investigate. I have evidence that you were set up."

His laugh is as bitter as lye. "I'm a Noor, Wen. Most people in this country hardly think we're worth something as expensive as an investigation."

His words slip into my heart and crush it from the inside. I will try; I will wave the forged note and scream of his innocence, but no one else will stand up for him, and I have no power of my own. Iyzu and Lati are good Itanyai boys. No one will believe Melik over them. The tears sting my eyes. I am going to lose him. This boy is going to die, and there isn't anything I can do about it. "Then, what shall we do with this time?" I ask in a strangled voice.

He smiles, and the candlelight glints in his pale jade eyes. I see so many things there. Fear. Resignation. Sadness. And mischief. "Stay warm."

He pulls my face to his, one of those sudden movements I don't expect. But his kiss is only a touch of his lips to mine, a test, a request. I give him my answer when I fall into him, and he is ready and catches me. His hands are around my waist and his mouth is soft and I don't know what I'm doing but he doesn't seem to mind. He is playful and gentle, and in each of his kisses there is a whispered secret meant only for me. He tells me I am the one good thing he has left, that he does not regret any of the moments we have been together, that if things were different . . . if things were different . . . we would be in another dark room, and there would be a slow-burning fire, and he would be teaching me things I desperately want to learn from him. He doesn't have to say a word; he weaves me wishes with his fingers and lips, with his sighs, with the way he finally decides he needs more and pulls me hard against him.

The candle burns low, and sometime later it sputters and dies. Now it is Melik and me in the dark and cold, with nothing but ourselves to keep each other warm. He coils his arms around me and sits with me curled between his knees, his legs arched up like a fortress around me. "I wanted to take you with me," he whispers into my hair. "When you came to warn me, when I told everyone to run, I wanted you to run with me."

"Why didn't you ask?"

"Because you deserve better than anything I could have offered you."

I would have gone. If he had asked me, I would have said yes. But it doesn't matter now, because neither of us is going anywhere. I nestle my head against the skin of his throat and lift my chin so I can kiss his neck. I am so tired right now, and the chill has crept into my bones and made them ache. But I will not fall asleep; no, I will sit here with this boy who does not know his place, and I will be with him until our time runs out.

"You're wrong" is all I say, so quietly that I'm not sure

he hears me. I burrow into the fading warmth of his arms, and he wraps himself around me, whispering all his secrets against my hair and skin in a language I no longer need to translate.

And that is where we are when the cafeteria-side door to the chamber slams open and we are blinded by lantern light.

When the hands reach for me and pull me up, I sigh with relief because of the warmth on my skin. But my sluggish brain awakens quickly, and I look around to see that we are not surrounded by the regional police, or the local police.

We are surrounded by a mob.

Behind me, Melik is struggling. He grunts as someone punches him. Someone else has me by the arms, and I twist this way and that until I see it is Iyzu. They drag us through the kitchens and into the dining area of the cafeteria where all the men have gathered. Up ahead, Ebian is standing near the entrance, looking on with a blank expression. He frowns when he sees me and gestures to someone on my other side. My dressing gown is shoved into my hands a moment later, and I quickly put it on so that I am not on full display. My eyes search the crowd, which has grown huge during the night. The workers of the day shift are here and have obviously just heard of what has happened. There is hatred in their eyes as they see Melik hauled into their midst, pale and bloodied.

I call to Ebian, for he is the one person who could possibly stop this. "He was framed," I yell, but I am not able to say any more because Iyzu's hand clamps down hard over my mouth.

"We just received word that the regional police will not be arriving for at least a week," Iyzu tells me. "There are food riots in Kanong they must suppress. So we're having our own trial, right now."

Someone has told the regional police that a Noor is to blame, and they will offer him no rights, no protection.

Iyzu wrenches me forward, through the mob packed shoulder to shoulder in this cafeteria. He stops in front of Ebian, awaiting orders. Ebian nods over at Melik. It is taking four men to hold him down—he knows he is fighting for his life.

"Take him to the killing floor," says Ebian, and a shout goes up from the mob. This is exactly what they were hoping for.

At least a hundred grasping, groping, yelling men carry Melik and me through the open area by Bo's altar and onto the killing floor, where Mugo's blood still decorates the concrete. All is chaos and shouting, and I can't reach Melik because I can't move. I can't breathe. I still struggle, though, until one of the men jabs me with a cattle prod and I lose control of my body as liquid pain flows through my veins.

A rope is thrown up into the air and looped over the metal braces that hold the hook system to the ceiling. It falls back into the crowd, and one man seizes it and begins to coil and knot it.

He's making a noose.

The scream comes from me, rising high over the shouting. I claw and kick until someone shocks me again and I arch back and become nothing but agony. Iyzu holds me tight as the men clear a space around the noose, which hangs in front of the conveyor belt. Two of them climb onto the belt and pull the rope back over it. Melik is jerked forward and dragged up to stand between the two men.

He's not struggling anymore.

He sees that it is pointless.

The men wrench the noose over his head while he searches the crowd until he finds me. His face crumples when he sees the shape I'm in, so I stop fighting Iyzu and stand as straight as I can.

Ebian says something to Melik, who shakes his head. He squares his shoulders and looks back at me again. For a moment everything is quiet, because I think everyone expects Melik to beg for his life or make some final, defiant statement of his innocence.

He does none of that.

With his gaze fixed on mine, he places his hand over his heart and then turns his palm to me.

The men grab his arms and yank them behind his back. As they tie his hands together, Melik stares at me, and I stare at him, silently promising that I will be with him until the very end.

When I hear the whirring noise, at first I believe someone has turned on the factory machines. So do the others. They look around, puzzled, toward the circuit box at the edge of the floor. But none of the machines are moving.

That's when I see Bo.

He is standing on the second-level catwalk, though how he got up there, I have no idea. He is looking right at me, and I read something in his face that I do not expect to see.

Guilt.

"I'm sorry," he mouths, and glances down at the red letters on the killing floor, then at the bloody hooks suspended above them. I gape at him, absorbing the truth of his confession.

Iyzu and Lati didn't kill Mugo.

They didn't frame Melik.

Bo did. He kept his promise; he didn't hurt Melik. He set it up so others would do it for him. Just another of his traps.

Rage roars through me, destroying all my fear. "Did you come to watch him die?" I shout above the crowd, but my words are nothing compared with the chanting from the men, who all want to see Melik swing.

Bo seems to hear me, though. His lips become a tight white line, and he shakes his head. He presses a button on the forearm of his machine self, and the buzz of electricity streaks along his hand and flashes between his fingers in a sudden, popping spark.

Then two things happen at the exact same time.

Someone kicks Melik forward, so that he falls off the conveyor belt, his legs jerking three feet above the ground.

And the Ghost of Gochan One brings his spider army to life.

Chapter Twenty-seven

THE CREATURES EMERGE from the machines with a clicking, clattering sound that is loud enough to draw people's attention away from Melik, who is dying right in front of them. It becomes so quiet that all I hear is the sound of spider feet and Melik's legs flapping against the side of the conveyor belt. Iyzu breaks the silence first, screaming like a girl when he sees the melon-size spider crawl out from under the slurry machine, followed by three others, their fangs slashing. And then they are everywhere, swarming over the hook system, unfolding from their spots between conveyor belts, along the wall, among the wires . . . the floor is a roiling chaos of panic in no time.

Iyzu releases me so he can run toward the exit, but his way is blocked by at least fifty men who are trying to do the same thing. Now that I'm free, I could run too. Or I could wait for Bo to help me. But I won't. I am the only person who can save Melik now, and I cannot wait for someone else to come to my aid. I have to be enough. I shove around men as they scramble past, pulling the scalpel from my dressing gown pocket. I lift my skirts, skipping over two plum-size spiders scuttling across the floor, and plant my foot on the gears under the conveyor belt. Clumsily I heave myself onto the belt, yanking my nightgown when it snags on a crank. Then, with a strength I did not have before I watched Melik start to die, I lunge and grab the rope, hacking at it furiously with my tiny blade, until Melik's weight takes over and it snaps, sending him to the floor, purple faced and choking. Choking. Which means he is breathing. Alive.

But he's not safe, nor am I. A few machines away blood soaks the floor as two of the largest spiders I've yet seen gnaw their way through the spines of two of the slaughterhouse workers, who drop like beef carcasses onto the conveyor belts, their eyes glazed with horror.

Men are clogging the exits, knocking one another down, and when the ones at the back fall, their Achilles tendons cut away by spider fangs, they cling to the clothes of the ones in front as they scream.

"Wen!" Bo shouts, and I reel around to see an enormous spider climbing down the central column, where Melik got caught by the hook. "You're on its path!"

I jump from the conveyor belt right as the stabbing spider feet step off the column and march my way. I land in a heap right next to Melik and cut through the rope that binds his hands, almost slashing his scrabbling fingers in the process. With a wrenching tug I pull the noose off his neck, wincing at the bloody, bruised, torn mess of his throat.

"What's happening?" he rasps. The whites of his eyes are bright red with the blood of burst vessels.

"We have to get out. Now. Can you get up?"

"I don't know," he mouths, then coughs and coughs and coughs, curling into himself.

Over the broad span of his back I see a spider approaching, the size of a kitten, on delicate legs, fangs raised and ready to kill. I throw myself over Melik's body and bat at it with the noose. It leaps onto the rope and clamps down with its fangs, and I sling it away. It hits the stone column with a crunch.

Melik gets to his hands and knees, but he's struggling. His face is a deep red, and it's like he's trying to lure thoughts back into his brain with every breath. He raises his head and looks around, because the sounds of slaughter surround us. Men are lying dead or dying just a few feet away, spiders digging into their guts or spines or heads or chests. One man streaks by with a spider clinging to each arm. His shirtsleeves are soaked in blood.

As I put my arm around Melik's waist and help him to his feet, I glance around me, seeking an exit. But everywhere I look, the spiders are marching across the floor, searching for prey. They keep coming from every conceivable crevice, and I know that Bo has been sneaking in here night after night during the quiet season, setting up these self-winding killers so they could hibernate in the vibrating machines until he chose the perfect moment to wake them and wreak havoc.

Bleeding workers are piled against the metal doors of the main exit. Some of the men beat feebly against them, but their friends, in a frenzied panic, have slammed the doors shut and left the rest of us to die. I start to lead Melik toward the plastic flaps that will take us through the passage to the cafeteria, but stop dead as no less than six spiders traipse down the metal doorframe and form a line in front of the archway, blocking our escape. My shoes are too soft to kick them without having my toes detached, and Melik is in no shape to jump over them, seeing as they are as large as lapdogs.

A small thud and telltale clicking on my back has me twisting frantically. It's on me, one of the spiders, and any second it will snap its legs around my head and cut through my skull. I hear my own gasps and shrieks as Melik stumbles away and crashes into the conveyor belt, still weak and off-balance. And then . . . my head is lighter, and on the concrete floor is a spider feasting on what's left of my braid. My hair has saved me, but now most of it is gone. The rest of it flies around my face as I grab for Melik, right as a spider scuttles across the belt toward him.

Everywhere I look, there are killers, large and small, digging their metal teeth into flesh and bone and brain and guts. The killing floor is exactly that today, and Melik and I are about to become part of the carnage.

Bo lands with a crash on the conveyor belt. "Here," he says, pressing a cattle prod into my hands. His arm is bleeding and torn, and there's a wound on his thigh as well. His pants are a bloody, shredded mess. He's been attacked by his own creations. "If you shock them, it triggers the kill switch."

Melik looks up at Bo, at his half-machine face, at his mechanical wonder of an arm. He doesn't look scared or awed, perhaps because of the oxygen deprivation of the last few minutes. "You must be the Ghost," he comments hoarsely.

Bo's expression turns rigid and he looks away.

"I owe you a thank-you," Melik says.

Bo gazes at Melik, at his rust-colored hair and torn neck, and at his arm, which rests heavily around my shoulders as he leans on me for support. "Trust me, Noor, you don't."

He twists in place and jams his metal index finger into the back of a spider that is less than a second from leaping onto my dressing gown. It vibrates and shakes itself into a pile of metal shavings. "Come on. There's another way out."

Melik and I follow him as quickly as we can. I have to keep stopping to shock the spiders that come at us. A few of them manage to leap onto the hem of my nightgown, but the cattle prod is amazingly effective. They flop onto their backs, spindly legs stabbing at the air, and we move on before they fall apart. Bo leads us past the refrigerator chamber, through the grinding room, to a locked door at the very rear of the killing floor. "I know you have the key," he says to me.

I do. But as much as I don't want to be here, I'm not sure I want to go with Bo. He is a master of death, and he's already tried to kill Melik twice. And now Melik is pale and weak, at his most vulnerable. I won't survive watching him die again.

Over Bo's shoulder something catches my eye—a spark. No, a flame. The bitter smell of burning rubber is filling the air, which grows hazier each second. The spiders are chewing through the wires, and I can hear the pops and sputters of electrical fires breaking out. Bo glances behind him, and then he looks at Melik, who is leaning against the wall with his eyes closed, focused on drawing breath into his lungs.

"I can keep you safe, Wen," Bo says. "I can keep you both safe."

I look into his brown eye, into his human, warm, kinder self, and I nod. He takes the key from me, unlocks the door, flings it wide, and shoves Melik through it. The last thing I see before he yanks me through the doorway and slams the door behind us is the killing floor erupting in flames.

-—◦◉ Chapter ◉◦—
Twenty-eight

BO LEADS US down four flights of steep metal steps. I anchor my arm around Melik's waist and descend slowly, focusing on moving my body and not on the horrifying images in my head. My heart beats like a caged bird. All those men. All that pain. All that blood. So far beyond what my father could ever fix. And yes, I am glad Melik was spared. But I can still hear the screams, the pleas for mercy and help. Some of those men had families. Some of them had daughters. Did they deserve this kind of end?

My fingers curl into Melik's side. Maybe they did, if they were so eager to kill him. If I had had the power, maybe I would have crushed them just as mercilessly, if it meant saving Melik. I'll never feel good about it, but if this is the cost of protecting someone I care about . . .

Melik's steps falter and I hold him tight. "You're doing well," I say to him.

He doesn't answer. He is intent on breathing and putting one foot in front of the other, and that is as it should be. Bo is impatient and agitated. He keeps turning around, watching us while he grinds his teeth. I want to snap at him, to scream at him. We wouldn't be here if he hadn't been so vicious, if he hadn't been determined to destroy the boy next to me.

We also wouldn't be here if he didn't have a conscience. If Bo were all machine, if his heart were made of cogs and springs, Melik would be dead now, strangled by the noose, and I would probably be standing on the conveyor belt, awaiting my turn to die.

I have never been so confused, and now is the time to be certain, because I have to get Melik out of this alive. His brother needs him. His people need him.

I need him too.

"Where are we going?" Melik asks me in a raspy whisper.

"My home," Bo answers.

Melik tenses. "I don't suppose there are more of those spiders down here."

"Of course there are," Bo snaps. "But they sleep until they are awakened, and we won't do that."

I bow my head so Bo cannot see my angry expression, and that's when I notice the bloody footprints he leaves with each of his steps, the streaks of wine red against the walls. He is very hurt, and no doubt in terrible pain. But he is not complaining, and so I won't either.

We make our clumsy way through a wide corridor with doors every few feet. This place reminds me of a giant catacomb, a huge hive of the dead, and I fight the feeling that the walls are closing in on me, that I will be buried here forever, that I will never see the sky again. Melik's arm is tightening around my shoulders, and at first I think he needs more support to walk, but when I look up at him, I see his bloodred gaze has sharpened. He is recovering, quickly, but still weak and torn.

The air here is dank and cold. Even in my dressing gown, I shiver as goose bumps ridge my skin. Water trickles in green black rivulets down the walls, upon which grow patches of fuzzy brown moss. The emergency lighting glints off spider bodies nestled in corners and crannies, but they remain still and silent. Every once in a while Bo tells us to step over a trip wire, or to avoid a square depression cut into a step, or to tuck our arms against our bodies and walk single file to keep from brushing the walls. He is harsh with his words, but he does not fail to help Melik when I am not strong enough.

Finally we get so deep that there are very few traps, because the only person who comes here is Bo himself. He leads us to a steel door and flicks at the fingers of his metal hand, but his other hand is fumbling and unco-ordinated, probably because of the deep wound in his forearm. He leans back against the wall and stares at the ceiling. "Wen . . ."

I step forward as Melik's arms become steel at my waist. I squeeze his hand in reassurance, then let it go. "You need help," I say to Bo.

He nods. "There's a key built into the hand, but I can't . . . I can't . . ." There is the slightest tremble in his voice. He is scared. If he loses his other arm, he will lose himself. He has already been torn apart, and he cannot afford to lose the pieces of him he has left. I take his injured forearm in my hands and gaze down at it. "I'll help fix this. All I need is needle and thread." I sound more confident than I am. "Now show me what to do."

"The ring finger. There's a catch at the base of it."

With his help I hold his hand up to the light, the metal veins, tendons, muscles, threads of brilliance, woven through this dangerous weapon, this human-shaped war machine. I flick the tiny, delicate catch like he told me, and a jagged key unfolds from the center of his metal ring finger. I guide his hand and insert the key into the lock, which comes undone with a deep, echoing click.

In front of us is Bo's bright metal world, his family of statues awash in lantern light. We walk through a gleaming archway and into the massive chamber, and Melik's eyes grow wide with fear, but also with admiration. He mutters something in Noor and then asks, "How long have you been here?"

"Seven years." Bo limps along a metal walkway and nudges a small, broom-pushing spider off the path. It falls on its side, legs scrabbling.

"You did all this in seven years," Melik says in a flat voice.

Bo turns around slowly. "I wonder what you would do if you had seven years in solitude, Noor. Would you break? Or would you build?"

Melik stares at him. "I honestly don't know."

Bo pivots on his heel and keeps walking. I shuffle past Melik and catch up with him. "I need to look at your wounds."

He shrugs me off and waves his hand back at Melik. "Look at his first. I need to check the . . ." He stumbles, and I steady him, wrapping my arms around his waist as he sags.

He bows his head, and his lips are against my ear. "I have failed you in so many ways today."

He is so close, half man, half machine, and I think about what could have been for him. All that brilliance, shredded by the harshness of the factory, warped by loneliness. Underneath he is still a boy, one who craves a touch, a smile. So I smile. "You also saved me."

In his eye there is so much emotion that it is painful to watch. He blinks away the shine of it. "Help me get to my room?"

Melik walks quietly behind us. His footsteps are steady and solid, and I know if I looked back to see him, his shoulders would be straight and his head would be high. Because that is how he is, how he should be, what is right. I duck my head and breathe my relief.

I lower Bo onto his sleeping pallet while Melik waits outside the room. Bo reassures him that nothing will kill him as long as he doesn't go snooping around. From the tension in Melik's posture I can tell he doesn't want to be here, that half his mind is with his brother and the Noor, wherever they are, but judging by the way he looks at me, I know the other half is here and unwilling to leave my side.

Bo's skin is pale, and he is shivering. He has lost too much blood. It's oozing from his wounds, the ones in his left leg and right arm. He glances down at himself and rolls his eye. "Serves me right, doesn't it? I turn them loose and they feed on me."

"You just got in their way," I say as I examine his arm. "They're only machines, right?"

He nods, and shifts his machine arm, wincing. It is strapped over his shirt, like a vest, and I want to take the whole thing off so I can see Bo, the person, not the machine. But also because he needs to rest, and lying down with all this metal attached to his body must be uncomfortable. "Can I take this off?" I ask him.

He tenses, and his eye searches mine. "You don't . . . I don't want you to. . . ."

I touch the side of his face. He looks so young right now, so scared. "Bo, you need to rest. How can you do that like this?"

He grimaces, and I know he is in pain inside and outside, facing demons I will never understand. "All right. Just . . . all right."

With careful, steady fingers I unbuckle the leather straps that hold the machine arm to his body. I tug gently at the whole thing, and there is a slight pop as the cuff pulls loose from his skin. Bo's breathing becomes rapid and shallow as I pull the arm away from his body and finally see what is left of him. Just a withered stump of flesh-covered bone, extending from his shoulder socket, all that remains of his left arm. I don't stop there. I don't ask permission this time, I simply act. I find the thread-thin strap that holds the metal mask on his face, and I undo that, too.

From Bo's chest comes a whimper, like that of a child, full of pleading and fear. But I am merciless. I pull the metal mask away from his face to see what he hides behind the beautiful steel skin, the dead black eye.

He is a living skeleton, a living scar. Ruined skin taut over broken bone. He has no left eye, only a weeping, empty socket and a limp eyelid. He hasn't been glaring at me at all; he is half blind. I see *him*, the parts that are whole and the parts that are shattered. He is human, he is a boy, he is evil and good fused together. My Ghost. My rescuer. My enemy, my friend.

"It's bad, I know," he whispers.

"No, it's all of you, and I'm glad I can see it," I reply, stroking his hair.

His good eye searches me, looking for the fear, the repulsion, but he won't see it. There is a beauty in Bo that is not just in spite of his wounds, but because of them.

"I only wanted to know you, Wen. I've wanted to know you for so long. Ever since your father talked about you, I've been living on that wish, that one day you would come to me, and you would see me for what I am, and still you would not leave."

"I'm here now."

"Only part of you. Part of you is outside the door, watching over the Noor. Wanting him."

I cannot lie to him. "That's true. But part of him is elsewhere too, with the other people he loves. We cannot own each other, Bo. We can only offer what is ours to give."

"I wanted to give you everything," he says. "I wanted to build a world where you and I could play and live and where no one else would harm us, ever."

"You build amazing things, but I need the sky and the sun."

He closes his eyes. "I'm sorry for everything I did. For Mugo, for framing your red Noor."

OF METAL AND WISHES

"His name is Melik," I say gently.

"I know that. Will you forgive me if I don't want to say it out loud?"

I will.

Bo's hand, loose and uncoordinated but warm nevertheless, closes over mine. "When I saw how you screamed for him, how you fought for him, how it was killing you to lose him . . . I realized what a horrible mistake I'd made."

He would never have been rid of Melik like that. I would have carried my red Noor in my heart forever. "I'm glad you came to help us. You saved our lives."

I look around the room for anything that might help me care for Bo right now. I crawl over to the heavy jug on a table in the corner and pour him a cup of water. He needs fluids and food to rebuild his strength. He manages to sit up, but without the metal hand and with his remaining arm so weak, he needs my help getting the cup to his lips.

"There are preserved plum cakes, many of them," he tells me, pointing to a small cabinet beside the table. "You and the Noor should eat too. I'm sure you're hungry."

I get him a plum cake and take one to Melik, who tears into it with real desperation and thanks me with a full mouth.

By the time I return to Bo's room, he is leaning against the wall. He is brave now and lets me take off his shirt so I can see his wounds, old and new. The burn scarring covers his neck, his shoulder, and the left side of his ribs, and it looks like the fiery beast grabbed him in its clawed hand and left its ugly fingerprints all over his otherwise beautiful body. Bo turns away like he doesn't want to see how I'll react. He is naked for me now; everything he ever tried to hide is laid out in front of me. And . . . it doesn't seem worth concealing. I think I might have loved him if he hadn't. I can't tell him that, how I wish he had not left the world to hide down here—because really, what else could he have done if he wanted to survive? But now, now he is strong and smart and can offer the world so many things. He should want more than me, than to hide down here with a stupid girl who knows nothing of the world.

Well, he's not strong *now*. He's actually very weak. His fingers tremble as he places the paper wrapping of the plum cake at the side of his pallet. He looks down at his forearm, where the muscle and flesh are torn to the bone. "I'm not sure I have the things you need to put me back together," he says. "The other half of me, easy. Metal threading, screws, cogs, winding mechanism, activating circuitry. This half?" He chuckles. "I don't envy you."

"I can bandage it," I say.

There is a distant slamming noise, and I jump. Bo gives me a tired smile. "Your father has come to see us."

His footsteps tap down the stone staircase, and I hear Melik stand up to greet him. They talk for a few seconds in low tones, but I can hear enough to know my father is examining Melik's neck and face, which makes my heart heavy with gratitude. Then my father is in Bo's chamber, staring at Bo's hand over mine. His expression is impossible to read. "I've been trying to reach you for the last half hour," he says to Bo.

Bo points to a chair in the corner, inviting my father

to sit. "I told you I would get them, and I did. She is unharmed. The Noor . . . well, he will recover. And I . . . I got what I very much deserved."

My father gazes down at Bo's wounds with a sharp clinical eye. "You will recover too. I can easily treat these wounds. But we'll have to do that topside. We don't have time right now."

I notice the determined clutch of my father's fists. "What's wrong?"

"We need to leave," he says. "They're coming."

‑‑◦❧ Chapter ❧◦‑‑
Twenty-nine

THE TENSION ZIPS through Bo's body like lightning, and I feel it in our joined hands like an electric shock. "What are you talking about?" he asks. "I took care of them."

My father shakes his head. "They regrouped, and they've been joined by the local police. There were survivors, and some of them were able to describe you. They know who you are, Bo, and they're coming to get you."

Bo's teeth click together. "Help me up."

My father and I pull him to his feet.

"I need my arm," he says quietly, and my father helps him strap it to his body like he's done it hundreds of times before.

Bo touches the left side of his face and looks out to

where Melik and all the perfect metal statues await. "And my mask, please," he says to me.

I lift the metal half-face from the floor, smooth, sculpted and shining, fatally marred by the terrible, dead black eye. And then I look at Bo's face, his real, whole face, half hideous, half beautiful. I stand on my tiptoes and kiss his scarred cheek, lingering long enough to hear the catch in his breath. Then I fit the mask in place and fasten the thin strap, unable to look at the results. "What are you going to do?" I ask, staring at his feet.

"I'm going to see what's coming."

He turns and walks from the chamber, fighting not to limp, and my father and I follow. He stalks past Melik, toward the chamber full of pipes where he spies on the people of Gochan One. He hunches over one, his metal hand moving with machine precision to adjust the knob on the side. "They won't get far," he mutters.

"It depends on how determined they are to find you," Melik says in a hard voice.

Bo pivots around to face him. "Probably very, since I saved a Noor from swinging and destroyed the factory floor, killing dozens of men in the process. But that won't protect them from what lies in those corridors. They'll turn back."

"No, they won't," says my father. His voice sounds as hollow as the pipes. He's bent over one of them now, his eye to the hole.

Bo frowns and joins him, peeking into the pipe next to it. He curses.

I am next to him in an instant. "I want to see."

"You don't," says Bo.

SARAH FINE

I ignore him and lower my head to the opening of the pipe beside his.

And gasp.

I am looking down the hallway outside the cafeteria, the one near Bo's altar. From my skewed vantage point I see a few men with the high-powered electric cattle prods in their hands.

They are driving a cow toward the stairs.

Melik ducks his head and peers into the adjacent pipe. His hisses something in Noor and turns to me. "They're trying to drive the cattle through the corridors. To trigger the traps."

I watch the men jab at the cow's bony backside. They are relentless, and slowly, slowly, the beast inches forward. "Can cows even walk down stairs?"

"They can," my father says grimly, "if what's behind them is frightening enough." He points to a pipe. "There are already several in the hallways below the killing floor."

My heart hurts for these creatures that are already condemned to slaughter but will now be killed in a way no soul should have to suffer. Bo is cursing nonstop under his breath, skipping from pipe to pipe as he watches the cows plow through his trip wires and bump against the walls, triggering his arachnid soldiers to fight and kill. I step back from the pipes; I don't want to see it. I can already picture it, because I witnessed what happened to Ugur.

Melik turns to Bo. "You have to get Wen out of here," he says in a low voice. "If they make it all the way down here, she needs to be far away."

Bo stands up and looks Melik in the eye. "I know that."

Somewhere above us there is a deep, percussive boom,

304

and my father moves over to a pipe on the far left side of the array and peers in. "The cows triggered an explosion on the fourth sublevel." His eyes are bright with fear as he straightens up. "It won't be long before the mob comes through those tunnels."

"Come on," Bo says. "Time to go."

He limps out of the pipe room and leads us all the way to the back, past the hulking factory machines, past the dead-eyed metal Melik who is poised on the edge of the walkway. When the flesh-and-blood Melik walks by it, he pulls up short. He is reaching out to touch its face when there is a crash above us, followed by the faint lowing of cows.

"They're in the metal hallway," my father says to me. "They've probably triggered the spiders."

Bo reaches the elevator and yanks open its sliding metal door. "This will take you to the roof, and you can get out through Gochan Two. Guiren, you know the way."

I stare at Bo. "What are you doing?"

He bows his head. "I'm not going."

"Yes, you are," I say, taking his hand. "We can all go, now. We can escape!"

He rewards me with a sad smile. "What is there for me outside this factory?"

"Seems to me you can do almost anything you want," Melik says, laying a protective hand on my shoulder. "Do what she asks. Come with us."

Bo chuckles as his eyes light on Melik's fingers on my body. "You obviously believe me to be a better man than I am." His gaze travels to Melik's face. "Keep her safe."

Above us I hear men yelling and crashing. They

are pounding on the door to Bo's fortress. They are almost here.

"They'll hurt you," I say in a choked voice, tugging Bo toward the elevator. My father steps inside and waits, and he seems to be riveted by his own shoes. He won't look at me.

"And if I run, they'll chase me." The lanterns overhead glint off his metal face. When he speaks again, his voice is almost a snarl. "They're invading my *home*, Wen."

I will not let this happen. I whip the metal syringe out of my dressing gown pocket, but he is too fast. My arm is caught in his machine grip before I know it, those skeletal steel fingers wrapping around my wrist. I gasp, expecting pain, but it doesn't come. He merely holds me there, and he doesn't take his eyes off me as he gently pulls the syringe from my grasp and hands it to my father.

I look over my shoulder at Melik. "Help me."

He and Bo exchange looks, and Melik shakes his head. "I won't try to force him." He reaches for me. "We have to go, Wen, please. They can't find us here."

Bo releases my wrist and fishes inside his pocket, pulling out a small object. He opens my fingers and places the object on my palm.

"I would like to make a wish," he says quietly. "This is my offering."

My fingers close over the white seashell. Tears burn my eyes. The crashing is louder now, rhythmic booms as they assault the door. Any second now they will break through. "What is your wish?"

"One kiss," he whispers.

My heart is caving in. There is only one reason he feels

bold enough to ask this of me. He thinks he's about to die. I don't look at Melik. I don't look at my father, either. The only one I look at is Bo. I focus on his deep brown eye, the one full of secrets I will never learn, the one that belongs to a boy who built an entire world where we could play together, where neither of us would ever be lonely. I raise my head and tilt my chin, and he spends a few seconds looking stunned that I'm actually going to grant his wish. But then he lays his hand on my cheek and bows his head, lowering his lips to mine. His kiss is brief and so full of sweetness it forces the tears from my eyes. They roll down my face as he pulls away. "Thank you," he says to me.

He herds me onto the elevator, where my father and Melik wrap their arms around me. Bo looks at my father. "Guiren, thank you for these years."

My father nods, and when I look closer, I see he is crying too. But then his head jerks up at a resounding crash, and his eyes widen as the first men descend the steps. Bo steps back from the elevator and turns to face his attackers, who are armed with cattle prods and knives and guns.

Slowly, like a gesture of defiance, he raises his metal arm and presses a button on his wrist. Current hums through the arm, ending in a sharp popping spark between two of his steel fingers.

The whirring of gears is louder than any I've heard before.

Every single statue in the room raises its head at the same time.

My father makes a frightened noise and lunges for the

elevator's red button. He punches it as the metal statues stand up or turn around, whatever programmed movement is required for them to face Bo's attackers. They all step forward at once—Mugo, Jipu, Melik, even Minny's tiny little boy. Bo turns his head to look at me. He smiles.

The last thing I hear before the elevator whisks us up is the screams of the mob as the metal army attacks.

Chapter Thirty

MELIK CRUSHES ME against his chest and bows his head over mine as the elevator accelerates, carrying us past floor after floor. The metal cage shakes me to my bones. I don't know what's louder: Melik's heartbeat or my own sobs. I barely notice as the elevator stops and my father slides the door open, as I am half dragged and half carried along a path littered with broken glass and bird droppings.

We have just reached the catwalk when a tremor shakes the entire building, making the remaining glass around us clank and rattle in its panes. Suddenly I feel dizzy, and I stumble against the wall. My father does the same.

Only Melik keeps his balance. "The building. Could he destroy the building?"

My father shoves off the wall and puts his arm around

my waist. "I am not surprised at anything Bo can do. Hurry."

Another tremor sends my father careening into a wall. "It's going to come down," he says, his voice rising to a panicked squeak.

Melik grabs my hand and pulls me to the catwalk, then pushes me ahead of him. He's muttering under his breath, something like "Go, go, go"—suddenly we're thrown forward and I land hard on my stomach. My tiny white seashell falls through the grate and plummets to the ground four stories below. Melik is on top of me, crushing my face into the metal, but then he's up and so am I. We scramble as the entire Gochan One factory shifts and cracks, enough to loosen the catwalk where it's fastened to the brick. It's going to be sheared off, and we're going to fall.

I throw myself toward the hatch in the ceiling of the Gochan Two warehouse as the catwalk drops away below my feet. I heave myself through the opening, with Melik's large hands on either side of mine. "My father!" I scream.

"He's holding my legs," Melik grunts. "Help me." He's grasping for anything that will give him leverage, and all there is . . . is me. I wrap my arms around his shoulders and tug, and he grits his teeth and drags himself through the hatch. Slowly we pull my father through as well, in time to watch Gochan One disappear in a roaring cloud of dust.

We sit there for what feels like days but is probably only a few minutes. My father says he should go attend to the wounded, and I know that is where I belong as well, even though I am wearing only a dressing gown and sticky, crimson woolen shoes. Father leads us down a side stairwell of Gochan Two, and it is clear to me he has been here before. "Did you help him put together the arm?" I ask.

He nods. "Bo drew up the design when he was only fourteen. As soon as he recovered from the injuries, he was coming over here to learn. I got him the parts, but once he had that arm, he never needed me again, not really."

He sounds so sad. He has lost a son today. I link my arm with his as we get to the factory's side exit, one that opens onto a small plaza between Gochan One and Two. My father stops Melik before we open the door. "We have to do something about your hair."

Melik nods toward the door. "The dust will be my disguise."

We pull the fabric of our clothes over our faces and walk into the brown fog, and the world is full of the cries of injured men, panicked men, frightened men. Layered under sirens and over the pops and crackles of fire, buried in black smoke. I follow the dim outline of my father. Tears stream from my eyes, from both grief and the sting of grit. It is a slow journey, as we must climb over piles of rubble, all that remains of Gochan One. My hands are torn and bleeding by the time we make it.

The compound square is chaos, with the dead and dying laid out in a tangle while the living search the rubble. The firefighters spray their hoses on the flames. Some of our cafeteria workers and office girls are tending to the wounded. I look over my shoulder to tell Melik I should be helping.

He's disappeared.

I turn in place. I should be able to spot him; he's taller

than most, and I'd recognize the way he carries himself. But he has melted into the dust. Without saying good-bye.

Too many losses for this one day. Too many. I sink to the ground and cover my head with my arms, blocking out the noise, the sights, the pain. People touch me, move me out of the way, try to talk to me, but I have nothing left for them. My heart has been crushed. I am as empty as the tiny white seashell now lost in the rubble, shattered into jagged pieces.

Someone smacks me lightly on the shoulder. "I need your help," my father says. "Put aside what's happened and work." His face is streaked with grime; his shoulders are dotted with blood; his eyes are shining with grief. But he has not crumbled or snapped.

And so I stand up and get to work.

I don't stop for the next six days.

On the seventh day after the collapse I tell my father I want to go back to my mother's cottage. I'm going to sell the last of my dresses to give us enough to have some choices about what we want to do next.

The autumn sun glows bright above me as I make the walk past rubble to massive factory to genteel mansions clinging to the side of the Hill. I tilt my face to the light, thankful that I am here and alive and able to see the sky. I unlock the door to my mother's cottage and inhale what is left of her scent, lotus and apple blossoms. I pull the jade green silk dress from my closet. It is the last thing I have from her, the last dress she ever made for me. The sleeves, waist, hem, and neckline are intricately embroidered, the work of an artist.

I run my fingertips over each bud and leaf and swirl

of thread, remembering her voice, her smile, her songs. Before I realize what I'm doing, I am wearing this dress, humming the song about the girl and boy in the field of citron. The warped mirror on my dresser shows me a girl with shoulder-length black hair too short to braid. Her face is heart-shaped but less full than it used to be, less childlike. This dress fits her perfectly because her mother made it so.

The time for this dress is over, though. I change back into the new brown work dress given to me by the factory store matron so that I didn't have to spend the past week wearing a torn and bloody nightgown. I wander out into the overgrown walled garden, where I sit on the stone bench and stare out at the Western Hills. No more do I wonder what is on the other side. I know. I *ache* with knowing.

"I was wondering when you would come," he says, stepping out from behind my mother's gardening shed.

I stifle my cry of surprise and jump up, my mouth opening and closing like a fish without water. "You were gone," I say stupidly.

Melik has wound a makeshift bandage around his neck, and his eyes are still red. But the bruises have faded and his face is beautiful again. He bites his lip and looks at his boots. "I had to find Sinan."

"Is he well?"

He nods toward the hills. "He's waiting for me, along with the others. He curses me every day that I lost my head over a girl."

I stare at him. "You disappeared without saying good-bye."

He runs a hand over his head, and his rust red hair sticks up. "I stand out. Right now people think I'm dead. But if I were to hang around the Ring . . ." He shrugs apologetically. "Do people assume we're gone? Have you heard rumors?"

I let out a raspy breath. "Those are rampant these days, but not many are about the Noor. Many are fixated on how the Ghost got his revenge and took over a hundred men with him. But mostly things are being blamed on the unsafe factory conditions and the unstable building. It's quite a scandal." I tuck my short hair behind my ear.

Melik gives me a concerned look. "How are you?"

I'll fall apart if I answer him honestly. "We've been using the company store as a clinic. Lots of broken bones and burns. Many people have been helping us, though." Both Vie and Onya have been by my side, bandaging and splinting the survivors, horrified at what happened to all our good Itanyai boys and men. "There's always work to do," I say in a thin voice.

"Wen always has medicine," he says softly, his words snatched by the breeze. "And your father?"

"I shouldn't be happy about this, but the collapse of the factory might be a wonderful thing for him. For all the surviving workers, actually."

He tilts his head.

"All the records of their debts were destroyed," I explain. "The company's trying to figure out who owes what, but everything's in chaos. I'm hoping that everyone's slates will be wiped clean."

Melik gives me a weary smile. "That might be too much to hope for."

I feel so hollowed out that his voice echoes inside me. "I know you're right." I clear my throat. "And without the factory, there's no meat—not in this area, anyway. Many people are blaming the government, and others are blaming the companies that run the factories. Things are very tense in the Ring."

His smile fades. "Things are tense everywhere."

Yes, they are. Including right here. I've been thinking of Melik every moment of every day, no matter how hard I try to stop, but seeing him hurts so badly I can barely catch my breath. I clench my teeth and will my eyes to stay dry.

"Wen, please look at me." He waits until I do. "I'm sorry I left so suddenly that day. I didn't want to, but—"

The pain of it twists in my chest. "I wanted you to be safe. I understand." But I'm choking on my words, and now he's rushing toward me. He lets me collapse onto him, lets me hold on tight.

"I'm sorry, I'm sorry, I'm sorry," he mumbles into my hair as the grief and longing of the past seven days come gushing out of me.

He lifts my chin and kisses me, and I feel it pouring from him as well, a want as deep as the ocean, wishes as unreachable as the moon. This will never last long enough for me, but I let him hold me against him and pretend it might.

He sets his forehead on mine. "I have to go back to the west. My family needs me."

"Take me with you." There is nothing for my father and me here, nothing I love, not anymore.

Melik kisses me again and shakes his head. "The road

between here and there is too dangerous, and nothing waits for me but sorrow. Still, I have to go." He bends to kiss my neck, murmuring his words into my skin so they will seep into my heart and stay. "If you think this is the last time you will see me, you are wrong. Say you believe that."

And then he is kissing me deep, demanding the answer he wants, making promise after wordless promise. He does not object when I unbutton his shirt and slip my hand underneath to feel his chest, to slide my fingers over the scar that runs from the spot over his heart to his shoulder. At some point in the last week he has removed the stitches, and now there is only a thin red line that has already started to fade. But it reminds me of what we've already been through, and how we are standing here now, together.

"I believe that," I finally whisper.

As soon as I do, he leaves me under the autumn sun, which does nothing to warm me. Shivering and shoving my hands into the deep pockets of my dress, I watch him walk away with his shoulders straight, unbowed and unbroken, still not knowing his place. He leaves me there to pray to gods I don't believe in for his safety, to weave my wishes together tightly and hope they keep me warm, to make offerings to a ghost who no longer exists. . . .

My fingers close around the object and lift it from my pocket, into the light. I have no idea when or how it got there, and it makes my heart thump heavy and fast. It is my tiny metal girl with her Wen face and body, but she looks different now. The long, fine braid at her back has been snipped; it is now shoulder length. Knitted to her side is a boy, and his arms wind around her waist and chest, holding her against him, keeping her safe. I twist them this way and that, and cannot figure him out.

He doesn't have a face.

I raise my head and search the Western Hills, but Melik has long since vanished from sight. I turn from them and look out on the Ring, to the still-smoking gap where Gochan One used to be.

With the metal couple clenched tightly in my hand, I begin my long walk back.

Acknowledgments

Everything that has happened with this book has felt strange and wonderful, and that is due in large part to the people who have encouraged and challenged me through this journey. My very first thanks must go to Brigid Kemmerer, who read the first few chapters of this story at a moment when I was very unsure if I had the time or skill to write it properly. Her "go go go!" email set me in motion, and less than three weeks later I had completed this book. So Brigid, this is all your fault. (Thank you.)

Major gratitude, as always, goes to my agent, Kathleen Ortiz, who didn't freak out when I told her I needed to take a few weeks off working on something else so I could write this story, and who later put her foot down and said *this* was the next thing we needed to submit. Thank you, Kathleen, for keeping me sane, organized, and focused, and for managing all the behind-the-scenes details. You're amazing. Thank-yous are also due to the phenomenal team at New Leaf Literary, Joanna, Danielle, Jaida, and Pouya especially.

To my editor, Ruta Rimas: working with you is as wonderful as I thought it would be. Thank you for understanding this story, for helping me make it better, and for being its champion. This is me, putting my hand over my heart and turning my palm to you. Thank you also to the team at Margaret K. McElderry Books, who have been instrumental in making everything about this book exquisite: managing editor Bridget Madsen, copy editor Erica Stahler, proofreader Katie Grim, and especially Debra Sfetsios-Conover, for designing the cover and interior formatting, and Michael Frost, for the beautiful photography.

So many people have supported me as I've bobbed along in the current of the publishing world. Dearest Dr. Lydia Kang, there's no one else with whom I'd wish to share a case of *folie à deux*. All the shrimp toast goes to you. Jennifer, you are my first and best cheerleader. Jennifer Walkup, Jaime Loren, Justine Dell, and Stina Lindenblatt, you are astute and awesome beta-readers. Catherine, Kim, Anne-Marie, Yerissa, Chris, Casey, Heather, and the entire staff of CCBS: you are excellent, and that makes it possible for me to do both my jobs. Paul, Liz, and Leah, you are practically family—maybe we should go camping sometime. And to the bloggers and readers who were willing to take a closer look at this story just because I wrote it, I hope you know how amazing that feels and how honored I am.

To my sister and brother-in-law, Cathryn and Nicholas Yang, thank you for answering my incessant questions, for providing linguistic consultation, for reading with a critical eye, and for understanding my liberal application of creative license. Thank you to Susan Walters for providing naming inspiration.

And for the rest of my family—Mom and Dad, thank you for always sounding happy when I call at 7:30 a.m. and for making sure I know I will always have a home in your hearts no matter where I wander. Robin, thank you for inspiring me and being my sister, and please know that I'm still waiting for a picture of the singing hair stylists. Joey, thank you for being patient and making sure I have time to do this strange job. Alma, thank you for being such a powerful, mysterious, and delightful creature. And Asher, thank you for building and building and building. I am in awe, and so proud.

CIVIL WAR LOOMS AS THE NOOR WAGE
A REBELLION IN THE WEST.

CAN WEN FIGHT FOR A LOVE THAT ONCE WAS,
BUT MAY NO LONGER BE?

TURN THE PAGE AND FIND OUT IN THIS
BITTERSWEET, THRILLING SEQUEL,

of Dreams and Rust.

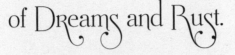

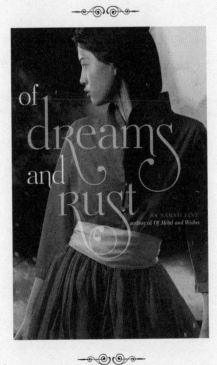

IN THE LAST year I have come to understand the traitorous nature of skin. We cannot live without this barrier between our beating hearts and the outside world, yet it is the most fragile of things, as well as the most deceptive. My own, despite its golden undertones, cannot keep me warm. The memory of Melik's, the ruddy tan of earth under sun, leaves me aching in darkness. My father's, thin and buckling under the weight of his years and all the things he's lost, hides his silent strength.

And Bo's, so broken and torn, is woven from sheer betrayal. Stretched over his bones like the work of a clumsy tailor, carelessly patched, heedlessly sewn. I have come to know it almost as well as I do my own, and I hate it for its failure, for the painful story it tells. I hate it because, despite its weakness, it is somehow powerful enough to keep him from the world.

"Stop," he snaps, wrenching his forearm from my grasp. "You're making it worse."

I quickly rub my fingertips together, the rose hip oil slick between them. "It will keep the scar from growing stiff." I gentle my tone. "I'm sorry if I was pressing too hard."

Bo's machine hand, a work of mad, relentless genius, covers the scar on his arm, shielding it from me. His human skin is the same color as mine, but his machine parts glint silver beneath the lantern dangling from the rough rock ceiling of this chamber. Despite the fact that I have seen him without his mask, Bo always wears it when I visit. I am reflected in his half-metal face, my cheekbones and chin sharp, my forehead wide and distorted, my eyes dark. They, at least, tell the truth. The weariness and sorrow within them is as deep as the canyon that leads through the Western Hills.

Bo tilts his head. "You were far away just now. Again."

I lower my gaze to my fingers. I hurt him when I am not with him, but I seem to hurt him almost as much by being here, and I can't figure out how to change that. "Shall I continue?"

Bo blinks his brown eye. His ebony hair hangs over his forehead, part steel, part flesh, yet all smooth. "I'm sure Guiren will be missing you. It is almost time for the clinic to open."

"And I am sure you have many plans for today, all of which involve the use of this arm and these fingers, as well as both legs." I glance over at his long work table, strewn with metal body parts, a bicep here, a pectoral there, circuits for blood vessels, gears and springs and bearings waiting for Bo to give them purpose, to bring them to life. Usually I love hearing about his creations and inventions. When he talks about a new idea, his whole face lights up. Sometimes I come down here just to watch him work, a few hours on a quiet afternoon spent staring at his hands moving in concert while his face cradles the tiniest of contented smiles. I have even made peace with his metal spiders, for the most part. However, when Bo began designing himself a complete steel shell, when he started to fashion a machine arm to fit over his human one, and then a set of legs, I began to realize he was the creation this time.

Now the sight of them chills me to the bone.

"I have a few minutes before I must go," I say to him. "Let's make the most of it."

"All right." He sags a bit in his chair, its legs squeaking against the patterned metal panel that covers the floor. His machine arm arcs with precise grace to hang at his side. Sometimes it seems to move on its own, walking his skeletal fingers through a dance set to electrical pulses, transmitted by wires and circuits that wind like veins within the contours of his steel muscles. My own fingertips move hesitantly over the scar on his arm, the healed wound inflicted by his own fearsome spider creations as he rescued me and Melik from a mob—a trap that Bo himself had set for the rust-haired Noor boy who had claimed my heart. Bo's own heart would not allow him to see it through, though, and he paid for that mercy with blood. Four seasons have passed, but Bo's flesh has an unfailing, unforgiving memory.

"Any interestingly gory cases yesterday?" he asks as casually as he might inquire about the weather.

I smirk. "I am probably the only girl in the country who does not find that to be a repulsive and offensive question."

"You're the only girl in the country I talk to, so I guess I'm lucky." With his playful smile, he lifts some of the weight off my shoulders. It is magnetic, drawing the corners of my mouth up to match.

"Dr. Yixa is still put off by my eagerness to suture his patients' wounds. He makes the funniest faces whenever he witnesses me washing blood from my hands." I imitate it, lowering my eyebrows and grimacing, and Bo laughs. "But at this point he knows my stitches are neater and straighter than his own."

"Then I give him credit for being observant."

I wonder if Bo realizes how his simple faith in me melts away some of my own doubts.

"He should be grateful," Bo continues. "Gochan One was dangerous, but Gochan Two is as heartlessly deadly as the war machines it creates. He needed the help."

"Father and I were fortunate he did." After the destruction of Gochan One, Father and I thought we might have to leave in search of work, but Dr. Yixa, the chief physician and surgeon for the neighboring factory, discovered us caring for victims of the catastrophe, and he offered my father a position. My father refused to accept unless I could come along as his assistant.

"I was fortunate he did, too," Bo murmurs. "I thought I'd never see either of you again, and then Guiren found me."

I think of the little steel-and-wire girl that I keep tucked under my pillow, her hair short like mine was right after a spider sliced off my braid with its fangs, her body enfolded within the arms of a faceless, unknowable boy. Given how injured Bo was at the time, it must have hurt him to create her, to sneak her into the pocket of my dress. "You had sent me a message." He was giving me the chance to return to him—or to stay away. "I was happy that it helped us find you."

Bo's smile has not faded. "Not as happy as I was."

I'm not so sure about that. This morning, like every morning now, I woke to the light of the stars and moon winking dimly through my tiny window and the faint sound of my father's snoring coming from the next room. I pulled on my work dress and crept down the darkened stairways of Gochan Two, a sprawling beast that sleeps until the sun rises over the high factory fence. I slipped around the few traps, knowing well where they are and what they hold in store for trespassers.

Within the old mining tunnels and caves beneath this weapons factory, Bo is once again building himself a world.

Unlike his skin, his mind never fails him.

I followed his instructions, long since memorized, to find the hidden door that marks the entrance to his kingdom, merely the bones of what he plans to build someday. He escaped through these tunnels when he brought the Gochan One slaughterhouse down, burying a hundred men in a tomb of metal and brick and burned meat. And though he was wounded, he immediately began to weave his steel web around him. My father and

I helped. Bo is ours, and we could not let him go. And now I look forward to every morning, because in this hour I am more myself than I can be for the rest of the day. Bo knows my secrets, and whether he likes them or not, he seems to forgive me for having them. Knowing he looks forward to our time as well makes me determined to carve it into my day, no matter how early I must rise. It is an unspoken promise. It binds us to each other, out of mutual need.

And yet, lately, I feel like I am losing him, circuit by circuit.

Bo flinches again as my thumb follows the path of his jagged scar. "Must you always press right where it hurts the most? I don't see how it helps."

"Father says that if we do this every day, you'll be able to retain the mobility in your arm." I duck my head to make sure he is looking at me. "He also said that if you wear those mechanical frames around your arm and legs for too long, if you let them do the work of your body for you, you will lose strength in these muscles." I skim my palm over his forearm, a silent apology, but draw back quickly when he shivers.

Bo presses his lips together as he glares at his imperfect flesh. "Sometimes I wish I were made entirely of steel and wire," he says. "I often wish that, in fact."

"I don't." I continue to massage the rose hip oil into his arm, over the puckered, mottled pink and white of his scar and the light brown of his unmarked skin. "I like you this way."

He sighs. "When you are here, I like myself this way too," he says quietly. He draws himself up, setting his jaw.

"But you are not here most of the time. Including when you are sitting right in front of me."

The silence between us is alive with wishes, his and mine. We want pieces of each other that we will never have. Bo wishes I would stop missing Melik—and I wish Bo wanted to be human. If one of us could move, I believe the other could as well, but because neither of us can move, our hearts are frozen in place. And yet we give each other what we can.

"I am here now," I say. "And we have time to work on your leg—if you're willing? You said it was bothering you."

He frowns. "Give me a minute." His cheeks have darkened.

I fidget with my oil and cloth as he disappears behind a partition. His arm hums and fabric whispers as he pulls off his pants. We are about to do a delicate dance, one that sways between clinical and intimate. I never know, from moment to moment, if I want it or if I want to pull away, and I think Bo feels the same.

"I'm ready," he mumbles.

I rise from my chair and move around the partition, my skirt swishing around my ankles. Bo lies on his sleep pallet, his blanket pulled over his hips and his right leg. His left, the one savaged by a metal spider a year ago, is bare and goose-bumped. Bo's face is turned to the wall. He never looks at me when I do this.

"This scar looks a little better. Faded," I say as I sink to my knees beside him.

"I don't care what it looks like. I only care whether my leg is functional."

If that were truly the case, I don't think he would be trembling, but I don't call attention to it. I am careful with him. I always have been. Not because I am afraid he will lash out; he has never hurt me, and I think he would die from the pain of it if he did. No, I am more concerned with hurting him. If I cajole, if I hold back, if I craft my words just so, it makes it easier for Bo to stay with me, to stay himself. "Of course. I only meant that it looked stronger."

He laughs, just a hiss of breath from his nose. "I see right through you."

I pour a bit of rose hip oil into my palm and rub my hands together. "How so?"

"Do you really think I am so naive, Wen? You don't have to always say what I want to hear."

"I know."

He turns his head and looks at me. "Do you?" His human hand reaches across his body and touches mine. "How can I be your friend if you are always protecting me?"

I let him take my hand. I let him stroke my fingers. It feels both comforting and dangerous. "You always protect me. Why can't I do the same?"

His grip tightens. "Because it's not the same. I would protect you from anything that threatened you. Any man, any creature, any machine. And you, you protect me from . . . you, I suppose." He lets me go and then clenches his fist so hard his knuckles go pale. His metal fingers click, startling me. "It's the last thing I want to be protected from."

"That's not fair." I lay my warm palms on his bare thigh, over the thick, ropy scar. Bo's chest stills and his eyes close. "You know me better than anyone does."

He shakes his head. "Only the parts you allow me to see."

I press down a swell of frustration and begin to massage his leg, long downward strokes toward his knee and then upward to midthigh, as my father taught me. It will keep the muscles supple, the blood flowing, the skin from growing taut and angry. I am gentle at first, cautious. I watch my hands moving over his skin. I've memorized every flaw. It makes the perfect parts that much more exquisite, but as soon as that thought surfaces, I try to drown it. It would be utterly scandalous for me to be alone with a man, touching him like this with no one to supervise, but my father trusts us both. Bo is a patient right now, nothing more.

It is impossible to think of him as nothing more. But so is thinking of him any other way.

I remind myself to be like my father, to think like my father, and my movements harden. My hands become instruments, my thoughts technical . . . but with shamefully ragged edges. Bo clutches at his blanket with both hands. His face glitters with pinpoint beads of sweat. I'm hurting him, but Father said it would hurt if I did it right. What he didn't say: how my stomach would knot, how my eyes would burn, how my precision would be worn away by the desire to smooth back Bo's damp hair and kiss his forehead.

"You could take off your mask," I tell him after a few minutes. It must be uncomfortable when he sweats like this.

"No," he says in a choked voice. "I don't want to."

"I see only the parts you allow me to see," I say, a warped echo, an accusation that I for once do not hold back.

"How can you possibly think it's the same?" he whispers. "You hide beauty from me. The only thing I hide from you is ugliness." A tear suddenly slips free from the corner of his tightly closed eye, and he swipes it away as his face twists with anger and humiliation. I bow my head because my own tears are about to betray me as well.

Bo sits up abruptly. "I've had enough."

He says it so sharply that I freeze. For a moment there is only silence and stillness, but then he tips my chin up with his callused fingertips. I wonder if my eyes are red like his, if his chest is as tight as mine. His mouth opens, but his words are locked inside him. We stare at each other. I don't understand why this happens, why we make each other fall apart, why it can't be simple and easy. But as I look into Bo's face, half handsome and half monster, the space between us fills with all the things we do not say. The things we'll probably never say.

His hand falls away from me, landing in his lap like a dead weight. "I'll be out in a moment." His voice is rough, uneven.

I move quickly, eager to give him the privacy he needs so badly right now. While he gets dressed, I set a bun on a plate for him and start a pot of water heating on a small burner he keeps on his worktable. Once the coil flares red hot, I fill a large teapot with tea leaves and set out the strainer. "Someone saw you two nights ago," I say, longing to steer our conversation toward calmer waters, to occupy Bo's mind with the now, the real, the things he can control.

"Where?" he calls from behind the partition.

"Have you been to the construction site?"

His metal fingers click together, driven by the jolts from muscles in his shoulder, and he steps into the open, fully clothed once more. "I needed some tools."

"One of the foremen was still there. He told his crew to be on the lookout for you. One of them was injured by a beam yesterday and told us the story while we were splinting his arm. Some think you were just a thief, but others believe the foreman saw the Ghost."

Bo snorts. "'Just a thief.'" He comes over to stand next to me as I prepare our tea.

"It's safer for everyone if that's what they believe," I remind him.

"I'll be more careful," he mumbles. "I didn't expect anyone to be there so late."

"They have received orders to get the slaughterhouse running earlier."

His eye bores into mine. "You know why, don't you?"

"Feasting season, of course." My heart skips.

"No, because they want to make sure they have rations for our soldiers on top of the demand for meat during the feasting season. Gochan One supplied much of the beef for the central part of Itanya, and with the need to feed an army moving west, it is indispensable."

"We are not at war." It is a silly thing to say and I know it. We have been on the cusp of war for months. The western province of Yilat is churning with rebellion and revolution, and the sentiment is slowly creeping east.

Lost in thoughts of men with guns, I reach for the pot and whimper as my fingers skim over the burner.

Bo's machine hand moves quickly, like reflex. It snatches the pot away from me. "Let me do this. I never get burned." He flashes a grin that fades instantly. His impervious metal fingers pour the water over the little pile of tea leaves, then place the lid on the ceramic teapot. "You may be worrying over nothing, Wen." He looks at me out of the corner of his eye. "He may already be dead."

My throat aches, like he's closed those metal fingers around the stalk of my neck. "Melik is alive," I whisper. Right before he walked away from me to return to the west with his younger brother, Sinan, and all the men from his village, he promised me that I had not seen him for the last time. I believed him.

Bo rolls his eye. "You can't know that. It's been a year of fighting and bombing and turmoil in Yilat. The Noor are staking their claim on the west. And this time they have united with the lower-class Itanyai in that province." He slaps two teacups down and pours the bitter brew. "They are better equipped and organized than they have ever been. They want their own autonomous region." He fumbles with the strainer as he removes it from his cup, leaving a spray of sodden tea leaves across his meticulously neat worktable. "Don't tell me you believe your red Noor would sit idly by while his brethren fought for such a ridiculous goal. He was always full of similarly romantic, unrealistic sentiments. It very well could have gotten him killed, just like it almost did when he was here."

"What nearly got him killed when he was here was

the irrational hatred of the Noor." And the fact that Bo framed him, but I don't mention that. I never mention that, or how often I've had to forgive Bo for it, because every time I think of it, it leaves me hot with anger.

It's one of the things I hide from him. I doubt he would find it beautiful.

Bo turns his back on me and carries our cups to the table, where he sits down. "He was agitating for more rights for the workers. It made him an easy target." He puts my cup in its usual place and waits for me to join him.

I use my cloth to wipe his work surface. "You didn't know him, Bo." He won't even call Melik by his name.

"I watched him like I did everyone else." He grimaces. "More, even."

I stare at the floor. "I cannot think of him dead. No more than I could think of you that way."

"Do not compare us." Now even his voice is made of steel. "I am here. He is gone. Long. Gone."

To continue this conversation would be like stepping into one of his traps. I tuck my hands into the pockets of my skirt. "I need to go help my father. I will see you tomorrow morning."

Bo is silent as I walk past my steaming teacup and out of his chamber, as I stride through the tunnel toward the stairs. But just before I reach the door that opens to the world above, I hear a low curse followed by the sharp slam of metal onto metal.

I do not go back to see if he is all right.

love this **book**?
ready for **more**?

One night to rejoin the living.
One girl who touches his heart.

And one moment that shatters
everything.

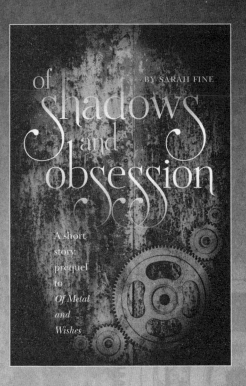

An unlikely romance.

A terrifying dream world.

One final chance for survival.

Nevermore

KELLY CREAGH